**AMANDA BRITTANY** was born in Hertfordshire. At school she was considered a dreamer, and left with few qualifications, spending the ensuing years happily working in offices, and bringing up her three children.

Being in a serious car crash ten years ago, prompted her to fulfil her dream to write. She gained a BA in Literature, and a Diploma in Literature and Creative Writing, and since then has sold almost 200 stories to women's magazines globally.

When her younger sister became ill, Amanda hoped to publish her novel with all author profits from book downloads going to Cancer Research UK. *Her Last Lie* is that book.

## Also by Amanda Brittany

*Tell the Truth*
*Traces of Her*

# Readers Love *Her Last Lie*

'Totally gripping'

'Enjoyed this read had many twists and turn'

'Gripping from the start with a twist at this end'

'It's certainly gripping and really keeps you in suspense'

'Found the book hard to put down!!'

# Her Last Lie

## AMANDA BRITTANY

ONE PLACE. MANY STORIES

HQ
An imprint of HarperCollins*Publishers* Ltd
1 London Bridge Street
London SE1 9GF

First published in Great Britain by
HQ, an imprint of HarperCollins*Publishers* Ltd 2020

ISBN: 9780008389192

**MIX**
Paper from
responsible sources
**FSC˚ C007454**

Printed by CPI Group (UK) Ltd, Croydon CR0 4YY

# Prologue

**Saturday, 23 July**

**NSW Newsroom Online**

*Serial killer Carl Jeffery convicted of triple hostel killings, granted appeal.*

Six years ago, the so-called Hostel Killer, Carl Jeffery, now thirty-one, was found guilty of the murders of Sophie Stuart, nineteen, Bronwyn Bray, eighteen, and Clare Simpson, twenty-six. He got three life sentences.

Now his younger sister, Darleen Jeffery, hopes to get him acquitted.

Mr Jeffery was accused of targeting women travelling alone in Australia. He would gain their trust, and when the women ended their relationship with Jeffery, he would tap on their window in the dead of night, wearing a green beanie hat and scarf to disguise his appearance, striking fear. He later killed them.

The main prosecuting evidence came from his intended fourth victim, Isla Johnson from the UK, who survived his attack and identified him as her assailant. She suffered physical and psychological injuries. Following Mr Jeffery's trial, she returned to England where she now lives with boyfriend Jack Green.

During his trial, Jeffery broke down when questioned about his mother, who left the family home when he was eleven, leaving him and Darleen to live with their abusive father, who died three months before the first murder.

Darleen, who penned the bestseller *My Brother is Innocent*, has campaigned for her sibling's release for almost six years. She claims her brother's DNA was found on Bronwyn Bray's body because they had been in a relationship, and that this wasn't taken into account fully at the trial. She also insists the court should re-examine Isla's statements of what happened the night of her brother's arrest, suggesting there is no proof that he started the 'bloodbath' that unfolded that night.

Canberra's High Court granted permission today for an appeal, agreeing there are sufficient grounds for further consideration of the case. The hearing will take place on 30 September.

Leaving court today, Darleen, wearing a two-piece royal-blue skirt suit, told reporters, 'I'm over the moon. I believe we have a sound case, and I can't wait for my brother to be released.'

We contacted Isla Johnson in her hometown of Letchworth Garden City, England. She told us she wouldn't be attending the hearing. 'They have my original statements, and I've no more to offer,' she said.

# PART 1

# Chapter 1

**Tuesday, 26 July**

It was hot.

Not the kind of heat you bask in on a Majorcan beach. No tickle of a warm breeze caressing your cheek. This was clammy, and had crept out of nowhere mid-afternoon, long after Isla had travelled into London in long sleeves and leggings, her camera over her shoulder, her notepad in hand.

Now Isla was crushed against a bosomy woman reading a freebie newspaper, on a packed, motionless train waiting to leave King's Cross. The air was heavy with stale body odour and – what was that? – fish? She looked towards the door. Should she wait for the next train?

She took two long, deep breaths in an attempt to relieve the fuzzy feeling in her chest. She rarely let her angst out of its box any more – proud of how far she'd come. But there were times when the buried-alive anxiety banged on the lid of that box, desperate to be freed. It had been worse since she'd received the letter about the appeal. Carl Jeffery had crawled back under her skin.

She'd hid the letter, knowing if she told Jack and her family they would worry about her. She didn't want that. She'd spent too much time as a victim. The one everyone worried about. She was stronger now. The woman she'd once been was in touching distance. She couldn't let the appeal ruin that.

She ran a finger over the rubber band on her wrist, and pinged it three times. Snap. Snap. Snap. It helped her focus – a weapon against unease.

'Hey, sit,' said a lad in his teens, leaping to his feet and smiling. Had he picked up on her breathing technique – those restless, twitching feelings?

*I'm twenty-nine, not ninety*, she almost said. But the truth was she was relieved. She had been on her feet all day taking pictures around Tower Bridge for an article she was working on, and that horrid heat was basting the backs of her knees, the curves of her elbows, making them sweat.

'Thanks,' she said, and thumped down in the vacated seat, realising instantly why the bloke had moved. A fish sandwich muncher was sitting right next to her.

Her phone rang in her canvas bag, and she pulled it out to see Jack's face beaming from the screen.

'Hey, you,' she said, pinning the phone to her ear.

'You OK?'

'Yeah, just delayed. Train's rammed.' It jolted forward and headed on its way. 'Ooh, we're moving, thank the Lord. Should be home in about an hour.'

'Great. I'm cooking teriyaki chicken. Mary Berry style.'

She laughed, scooping her hair behind her ears. 'Lovely. I'll pick up wine.'

The line went dead as the train rumbled through a tunnel, and Isla slipped her phone in her bag, and took out her camera. She flicked through her photos. She would add one or two to Facebook later, and mention her long day in London.

*Your life is so perfect*, Millie had written on Isla's status a few months back, when she'd updated that she and Jack were back from France and she was closer to finishing her book. It had been an odd thing for Millie to say. Her sister knew Isla's history better than anyone. How could she think Isla's life was perfect, when she'd seen her at her most desperate? Felt the cruel slap of Isla's anger?

Eyes closed, Isla drifted into thoughts of Canada. She was going for a month. Alone. Canada. The place she would have gone to after Australia if life hadn't forced a sharp change of direction. Going abroad without Jack wouldn't be easy. But then he couldn't keep carrying her. She had to face it alone. And it would be the perfect escape from the pending appeal.

With a squeal of brakes, the train pulled in to Finsbury Park, and fish-sandwich man grunted, far too close to Isla's ear, that it was his stop. She moved so he could pass, and shuffled into the window seat.

Through the glass, overheated people poured onto the platform, and her eyes drifted from a woman with a crying, red-faced toddler, to a teenage boy slathering sun cream onto his bare shoulders.

'Isla?' Someone had sat down next to her, his aftershave too strong.

She turned, her chest tightening, squeezing as though it might crush her heart. 'Trevor,' she stuttered, suddenly desperate to get up and rush through the door before it hissed shut. But it did just that – sucking closed in front of her eyes, suffocating her, preventing any escape from her past.

'I thought it was you,' he said, as the train pulled away. He was still handsome and athletic. Gone were his blond curls, replaced by cropped hair that suited him. He was wearing an expensive-looking suit, a tie loose in the neck, his tanned face glowing in the heat.

Her heartbeat quickened. It always did when anything out of the ordinary happened, and seeing Trevor for the first time in years made her feel off-kilter. The man she'd hurt at university was sitting right next to her, his face creased into a pleasant smile, as though he'd forgotten how things had ended between them.

'You haven't changed,' he said. 'Still as beautiful as ever.' He threw her a playful wink, before his blue eyes latched on to hers. 'I can't believe it's been eight years. How are you?' She'd forgotten how soft his voice was, the slight hint of Scotland in his accent. He'd always been good to talk to. Always had time for everyone at university. But the chemistry had never been there – for her anyway – and they'd wanted different things from their lives.

'I'm good – you?' she said, as her heart slowed to an even beat.

He nodded, and a difficult silence fell between them. This was more like it. This was how things had been left – awkward and embarrassing. An urge to apologise took over. But it was far too late to say sorry for how she'd treated him. Wasn't it?

'I've often thought about you,' he said, and she tugged her eyes away from his. 'You know, wondering what you're up to. I heard what happened in Australia.'

'I prefer not to talk about it.' It came out sharp and defensive.

'Well, no, I can see why you wouldn't want to. Must have been awful for you. I'm so sorry.'

Quickly, Isla changed the subject, and they found themselves bouncing back and forth memories of university days, avoiding how it had ended.

'You're truly remarkable,' Trevor said eventually. 'You know, coming back from what you went through.'

After another silence, where she stared at her hands, she said, 'It was hard for a time . . . a really long time, in fact.' She hadn't spoken about it for so long, and could hear her voice cracking.

'But you're OK now?' He sounded so genuine, his eyes searching her face.

She shrugged. 'His sister . . .'

*Would it be OK to talk to Trevor about the appeal? Tell him about Darleen Jeffery? Ask him what kind of woman fights their brother's innocence, when it's so obvious he's a monster?* There was a huge part of Isla that desperately needed to talk. Say the words she couldn't say to Jack or her family for fear they would think she was taking a step back. Vocalise the fears that hovered under the surface. The desire to tell someone about the Facebook message she'd received from Darleen Jeffery several months ago was overwhelming. *'I need to discuss the truth, Isla,'* it had said.

'His sister fought for an appeal and won,' she went on, wishing immediately that she'd said nothing.

'Jesus.' He looked so concerned, his eyes wide and fully on her. 'When is it?'

'The end of September.' The words caught in her throat.

'Are you going?'

She shook her head. She'd contacted the Director of Public Prosecutions. Told them she wouldn't be attending, that she didn't want to know the outcome. Being in a courtroom with *him* again would be like resting her head on a block, Carl Jeffery controlling the blade.

'I can't face it,' she said, her voice a whisper.

'I don't blame you.' He shook his head. 'It's sickening that he killed three women. Unbelievable.'

She thought of lovely Jack, knowing how hurt he would be if he knew she was keeping the appeal – and the way it was affecting her – from him. He would be hurt if he knew that within a few minutes of meeting her ex, she was confiding in him – letting it all out. But there was something oddly comforting in the detached feeling of talking to an almost-stranger on a train – because that's what he was now. Someone she probably wouldn't see again for another eight years.

'I'll be in Canada when it takes place. I can forget it's even happening. And I've told them I don't want to know the outcome.' She pinged the band on her wrist, before turning and fixing her eyes hard on the window, a surge of tears waiting to fall. She needed to change the subject. 'So what are you up to now?'

'I'm a chemist,' he said, his tone upbeat.

'Not a forensic scientist, then?' That had been his dream.

'Never happened, sadly,' he said. 'I'm working on a trial drug at the moment.'

'Sounds interesting.' Her eyes were back on him.

He shrugged. 'Not really. Not as interesting as travel writing.'

She stared, narrowing her eyes. 'You know I'm a travel writer?'

He smiled. 'I guessed.' He nodded at her camera. 'You wanted to be the next Martha Gellhorn.'

'You remember that?'

He nodded, entwining his fingers on his lap, eyes darting over her face. 'You haven't changed,' he said again.

She knew she had. Her blonde hair came out of a bottle these days, and there was no doubting she was different on the inside. She looked away again, through the window where fields were blurs of green.

As seconds became minutes he said, 'Maybe we could catch up some time. Now we've found each other again.'

Words bounced around her head, as a prickle of sweat settled on her forehead. She didn't want to be unkind, but she was with Jack, and even if she wasn't, there was nothing there – not even a spark.

She turned to see his cheeks glowing red, and an urge to say sorry for hurting him all those years ago rose once more. 'I'm with someone,' she said instead.

'That's cool. Me too,' he said, with what seemed like a genuine smile. 'I meant as friends, that's all.' He pulled out his phone, the yellow Nokia he'd had at university. 'We could exchange numbers.' His shoulders rose in a shrug, making him look helpless. 'It would be good to meet up some time.'

* * *

Triple-glazed windows sealed against the noise of heavy traffic rattling along the road outside, and a whirring fan that was having little effect, meant the apartment felt even hotter than outside. Isla hated that she couldn't fling open the windows to let the fresh air in. Sometimes she would grab her camera, jump into her car, and head to the nearby fields to snap photographs of the countryside: birds and butterflies, wild flowers, sheep, horses, whatever she could find – pictures she would often put on Facebook or Instagram.

'Can you open that, please?' She plonked the chilled bottle of wine she'd picked up from the off-licence in front of Jack on the worktop. 'I desperately need a shower.'

He looked up from chopping vegetables. 'Well hello there, Jack, how was your day?'

'Sorry,' she said, tickling their cat, Luna, under the chin before stroking her sleek, grey body. 'I'm so, so hot. Sorry, sorry, sorry.' She disappeared into the bedroom, stripping off her clothes, and dropping them as she went.

Fifteen minutes later she was back, in shorts and a T-shirt, damp hair scooped into a messy bun. She picked up the glass of wine that Jack had poured. 'God, that's better,' she said, taking a swig. She smiled and touched Jack's clean-shaven cheek. 'Well, hello there, Jack, how was your day?'

He laughed and plonked a kiss on her nose. 'Well, Tuesday's done. I'll be glad when I'm over hump Wednesday.'

'Wednesday's the new Thursday, and Thursday's the new Friday.'

'Must be the weekend then.' He raised his glass. 'Cheers.'

She pulled herself onto a stool. 'I saw an old boyfriend on the train home. Trevor Cooper.' The guilt of talking about the appeal made her want to tell Jack.

'The bloke you went out with at uni?'

'Aha.'

'Should I be jealous?' he teased.

'God no.' She took another gulp of wine, before adding, 'He was suggesting I meet with him some time.'

Jack's eyebrows rose and a playful smile dimpled his cheeks. 'Do you fancy him?'

She shook her head. 'Of course not.'

He laughed as he put chicken onto plates. 'Well, go ahead then; you have my blessing.'

'I'd go without it, if I wanted to,' she said, with a laugh. They'd been together two years. He should be able to trust her. 'To be honest,' she continued, 'I'm not sure I want to meet up with him. I'll think of an excuse if he texts. Maybe come down with something contagious.'

Jack smiled and shoved a plate of delicious-looking food in front of her. She picked up a fork and began tucking in, making appreciative noises. 'I probably shouldn't have given him my number.'

'And you did, because?'

She shrugged, remembering. 'I suppose I didn't want to hurt his feelings *again*.'

There was a clatter, and Luna, green eyes flashing, jumped off the worktop with a huge piece of French bread in her mouth.

'Luna, you little sod,' Jack yelled, diving from his stool. 'Has that "how to train a cat" book arrived yet?'

Isla didn't respond, deep in thought.

'If you don't want to meet him, Isla,' he said, long legs leaping after Luna, 'just ignore him if he texts.' He grabbed the cat, wrestled free the bread, and chucked it in the bin. 'Simple.'

'Maybe,' she said.

Later, Isla sat on her mobile phone watching cute cats on YouTube, as Jack watched a documentary about Jack the Ripper.

Her phone buzzed. Trevor had sent her a friend request on Facebook, and a message saying how great it had been to see her again. She stared at the screen for some moments, and then looked at Jack sprawled full length on the sofa. Trevor was just being friendly, and anyway, her conscience wouldn't allow her to ignore him. She had loads of friends she barely knew any more on Facebook. What harm could another person do?

She added him as a friend.

# Chapter 2

***Three months later***

***Tuesday, 25 October***

Isla dashed towards Heathrow Airport's luggage claim conveyors, and eased her tired body between a heavy man in his fifties with a mobile pinned to his ear, and a family with two teenage daughters staring at phone screens. She sighed. Just a solitary red case was going round and round and round. The cases hadn't been released yet.

Heavy-man turned and flashed her a smile. He'd sat next to her on the plane, taking up part of her seat as well as his own, his sickly aftershave making her head throb.

'Hold this,' one of the girls said, handing her sister an energy drink and stomping away, eyes still on her phone. 'I need the loo.'

Isla closed her eyes. Her head ached worse than it had on the plane. Drinking several small bottles of wine hadn't been a good idea. Her mouth was dry, as though someone had installed a dehumidifier on her tongue.

Thirty-six hours ago she'd been snapping incredible photographs from a train window. The ice-capped peaks and remarkable alpine lakes of the Canadian Rockies had been just two of the many things that had made the leap of faith to jump on a plane alone worth it.

'I landed about an hour ago, Sean, mate.' Heavy-man's tone jarred. 'Should be at yours by ten if the traffic isn't shit.'

A trolley bumped her ankle.

'Fuck,' she muttered under her breath, turning to give the culprit her best cross look. But the man was elderly with white hair and wire glasses, reminding her of her granddad. She would let him off, but still needed to free herself from the people-coffin she'd found herself in. The eight-hour flight from Canada had been bad enough, but *this*, when she was tired and hungry, was too much. She rubbed her cheeks and neck. She wanted to be at home in her shower, letting water flow over her, and then to fall into bed next to Jack and enjoy a long uninterrupted sleep.

At first she'd missed having Jack by her side, like a child deprived of her security blanket. Taking off on the trip alone hadn't been anywhere near as easy as it had been eight years before, when she'd raced into the unknown after university for what was meant to be a gap year, but had drifted into two. Back then, she'd travelled alone, clueless about where her next bed would be, or what job she might pick up along the way, all without fear. She longed to be that person again: the girl with her life ahead of her, before Carl Jeffery took a metaphorical sledgehammer and wrecked the mechanics of her mind.

She pinged the rubber band on her wrist and, taking a long, deep breath, tucked her hair behind her ears, and moved away from the crowd, clinging to how perfect Canada had been.

She pulled her phone from her carry-on bag and turned it on. She'd avoided the Internet and social media while away, worried she might find out something about the appeal. But now a month had passed. Whatever the outcome, it would be old news. And being off the Internet meant she'd immersed herself in her Canadian adventure, and also worked on her book.

Her phone adjusted to the London time zone, and picked up her network, bleeping, pinging, buzzing, as she was sucked once more into the frenzy of social media. Within moments she was blocking newsfeeds on Facebook and Twitter, muting notifications, hiding friends who continually shared news articles. She didn't expect there to be any news about the appeal – it had been a month, after all – but she was taking no chances.

On WhatsApp, Millie had added her to a chat about a six-part murder mystery on Netflix. Isla hadn't seen it, but her sister had given away so many spoilers, adding emoticons, that it probably wasn't worth watching it now. Julian had added a comment: *You're totally useless, Millie.*

Isla sighed. Why did her sister stay with him?

On Instagram, Roxanne had put on a stream of photographs of struggling refugees – another cause for her best friend's overcrowded, want-to-help-everyone head.

Millie had put on twenty-or-so photographs of her new puppy, Larry, who looked good enough to eat. And Isla's mum, who didn't understand Instagram, and was pretty rubbish with anything to do with social media, had added a photograph of a chicken casserole for no apparent reason.

Twitter was dominated by Roxanne's pleas to save foxes and badgers, and there was a string of Tweets by a magazine Isla regularly wrote for, and several updates from UK Butterflies.

Facebook was crowded by engagements and late holidays to the Mediterranean all jostling for attention. There was a wedding of an online friend Isla had forgotten she had, and another friend's mother had passed away – *Expected, she was 91, but still gutted – feeling sad.*

There was a rare update by Trevor Cooper – *Really must get on here more, and stop being an Internet dinosaur.* Nobody had liked it, but then he didn't have many friends. When he'd failed to get in contact again three months ago, after their chance meeting on the train, Isla hadn't thought any more about him, pushing him far from her thoughts. Maybe she could unfriend him now.

As she scrolled, she realised she could whittle her eight hundred or so friends, mainly picked up from university and her travels, down to a hundred, and still not recognise some of them in the street. She wasn't sure she even liked Facebook. In fact, sometimes she'd go on there and feel exposed.

'Isla, nobody's looking at you, lovely lady,' Roxanne had said, when Isla had tried to explain her feelings. 'And I mean that in the nicest way. They're just having fun sharing what they've been up to.'

There was a thump behind her, and she turned to see a black case rumble down the conveyor. Heavy-man barged forward, grabbed it, and once it was on the floor in front of him he yanked out the handle as though gutting a fish. He pushed past the teenage girls and the elderly man, veins in his forehead pulsing as he marched towards Isla.

'Facebook,' he said, nodding towards Isla's open screen as he walked by. 'Dangerous place, the Internet. You heard it here first.'

She watched him rush through Nothing to Declare.

*Not if you use it right, surely.*

Sidling up behind the elderly man, she waited for her case to appear, her eyes back on her phone world. She began typing:

**WhatsApp:** *Hi, Jack, I'm back. Hope you're OK. I'm SO tired, and probably won't be home until gone midnight. Don't wait up, as you need your beauty sleep. Not that you're not beautiful, of course. Love you, Isla XX*

**Text:** *Hi, Mum, back safe. I hope you and Dad are OK. I'll call you soon. Love you, Isla XX*

**Facebook:** *Landed in the UK – Canada was a-ma-zing. I'll upload some photos here on the train home. Feeling exhausted, but still have to tackle the underground. AHHHHH!*

She was about to close the Facebook app, when she noticed Trevor had liked her status, and that Julian had left a comment.

*Does this mean you've FINALLY finished your book?*

Before either could properly sink in, her phone pinged.

**WhatsApp:** *Welcome back, gorgeous lady. I'm not at home, won't be back until tomorrow. My mum was taken ill so had to go down to Dorset. Will fill you in more in the morning. Should be home around ten. Luna's with your mum. I'll pick her up on my way home. Hope you had a great time. Love you, Jack x*

# Chapter 3

www.travellinggirlblog.com
*0 followers*
*Tuesday, 25 October 11.30 p.m.*
**CANADA**

So here I am, travelling home on the train after my wonderful trip, and uploading the photographs I promised to post here before I left. Hope you like them. Canada was a-ma-zing.

I've so enjoyed posting photos and news about my travels over the last few months, but, the truth is, I need somewhere to free my mind or I'll explode into teeny tiny pieces. Nobody in my real world knows about my blog, and they certainly wouldn't understand what I'm about to say.

God, I'm having doubts whether I should write it here. But then I don't get many hits. Those who do visit are one-off visitors, searching images to look at my photos, rather than read my incessant travel ramblings. So I guess then it's OK. It could be therapeutic for me to offload into the abyss.

So here goes. I met someone in Canada. His name's Andy, and quite simply I'm in love with him. There, I've said it. It's out there now. I know I'm with Jack, and I feel bad about that. But Andy's different. He's from Toronto, and has the most amazing accent, but, of course, that's not all I love about him.

I'm smiling now, and the woman sitting opposite me, about sixty, attractive, dressed trendy, is giving me a funny look. She can't see inside my head. That I'm thinking of the quirky way Andy flicks his gorgeous auburn hair from his brown eyes. How giddy I felt when he was close to me. The way my skin tingled when he touched me – kissed me.

I sound ridiculous. Like a pathetic heroine in a novel, all loved up and besotted. But it's true. I never thought I'd feel this way about anyone. Not after what happened in Australia.

And I suppose I've always thought women who said that the urge to cheat is uncontrollable were foolish. That nothing would make me do anything to hurt sweet, kind Jack. But when something like this happens the draw is too strong. It's painful. There are no choices.

It's hard because I'm still with Jack, and I know he loves me. He's always been so good to me – would do anything for me.

'Mind if I join you?' Andy had said when he approached me in a café in Toronto, where I'd taken to going each afternoon. *Mind if I join you?* A line right out of a 1950s film. Up there with: *Is this seat taken?*

He was standing so close I could smell his aftershave, and he was holding a cappuccino in his hand, a swirl of steam rising from it. His smile was seductive, and his eyes locked me into a stare. He pulled his scarf free from his neck, as though I'd already said yes to him sitting with me, as though he had everything planned.

Without a second's delay – not even the nagging memory of six years ago made me pause for thought – I took my jacket and bag from the chair next to me, and said, 'No, no it's free. It'll be great to have the company.'

We started talking. And as though we'd known each other for ever, I spilled my life. Told him what happened in Sydney. How it had made me feel. *How it still makes me feel.* I'd talked about it all before, but somehow Andy made me feel safer than I ever felt possible.

We drank wine, and I told him where I was staying. He was travelling on business and renting a place nearby.

That night we made love. And the next.

Oh God, the guilt is bubbling up now, making me uneasy, faint and unsteady. My fingers are trembling on the keyboard. Should I have slept with Andy without talking things through with Jack first? Did I have a choice? Does anyone have a choice when the passion is so strong?

Andy cancelled his business meeting, and over the next few days he was right there by my side, the smell of him making me delirious, his dark eyes melting me.

He told me how he'd grown up in Toronto, an only child of two university professors. He loved the summer there, he said, but the winters were so cold, day and night, sometimes dropping to minus twenty-five. He took me to places I might never have found alone. Graffiti Alley, just south of Chinatown, was the most remarkable. The vibrant colours and stunning pictures of the murals painted by street artists on the walls of connecting alleyways were incredible. I got carried away and took far more pictures than I will ever need. As we walked, Andy nodded down a narrow alley, closed off by a fence.

'That was once the site of the secret swing,' he told me. 'I remember it.' He'd paused, clearly thinking back. 'The swing had a kind of cold, haunted feel about it, hanging there between the walls. I can see it clearly, even though it's not there any more.' He'd slipped his arm around my waist, and I was glad I wasn't alone. That I was with him.

The following day we travelled to Niagara Falls, and shared a hotel room. Our passion grew stronger, which I never dreamt possible.

We screamed with laughter when we took a boat trip, and the cascading waterfall sprayed our bodies.

For a month he travelled with me – the train journey through the Rockies was the best experience of my life.

At the airport, just before I headed for home, I felt as though I was about to leave part of myself behind. I felt bilious and delirious at the same time.

He's texted me already to check I landed safely, and my heart ached as I read his words. He said he can't go another moment without seeing me. That he's desperate to come over and will jump on the next plane.

I must tell Jack about Andy.

I know that.

God, I'm crying. The woman opposite is rummaging in her bag – bringing out a pack of tissues, handing me one. She's probably wondering about the weird woman tapping away on her laptop.

I dab my cheek with the tissue. The self-hatred bouncing against the ecstasy is impossible. But I have no choice. It's such a mess.

But surely you should be with the person you love. Life is too short. We're a long time dead, as my mother once said.

Andy is my drug – my cocaine – and I need to hold on to this feeling. I refuse to let it go at any cost. Surely, I deserve happiness after everything I've been through.

I know I'm supposed to be on my blog to tell you about Canada, because that's what it's set up for – to talk about my travels. But I'm tired, and my head feels fuzzy. So, for now, I'll point out the stunning shots of Graffiti Alley, and my favourite photograph of Niagara Falls. Those cascading waters took my breath away. They're to die for – like Andy.

*Comments*                                                              *disabled.*

20

# Chapter 4

***Tuesday, 25 October***

Isla emerged from Letchworth Garden City Station just before midnight, dragging her case behind her. Her carry-on bag, laptop and camera inside, was draped over her shoulder. If only her apartment was closer. She was exhausted.

A taxi was parked next to the entrance, and as she headed towards it, the driver got out, took her case from her and put it into the boot.

'Where to, love?' he said with a smile, slamming the boot closed, and walking round to the driver's side.

'Oakley Court. It's an apartment block in—'

'I know it,' he cut in, as she climbed into the back seat. 'My daughter lives near there.'

Once in the taxi, the driver accelerated away. The journey would only take five minutes, but the thought of being sealed in with a man – even a pleasant-faced man in his fifties wearing a turban – prodded at Isla's anxiety. It was probably because she was tired. When she craved sleep, thoughts she could normally control encroached. *Was it really safe to get into a car parked outside a railway station with a man she didn't know?*

'You been on holiday?' the driver asked.

21

Oh God, he was going to be a talker. She could do without a talker right now.

'Yes,' she said, cursing the fact she'd been brought up to be polite. Never wanted to offend.

He indicated and pulled onto the main road. 'Somewhere nice?'

*Please stop talking.* 'Canada,' she said.

'Very nice indeed.' He nodded, approvingly. 'I've always wanted to go. Did you see Niagara Falls?'

'I did, yes.'

'I read on the Internet that five thousand people have committed suicide there.'

*Why would anyone say that?* 'Yes I know, it's awful.'

He shrugged. 'Sorry, not a very cheerful subject.'

*No, no it's not.*

His brown eyes met hers in the rear-view mirror, and even though his tone was light and friendly, her neck tingled, and anxiety bubbles rose in her chest. She ran her finger over the band on her wrist and averted her eyes.

'And there was that woman who went over the waterfall in a barrel and survived. I saw a documentary on the telly-box.' He paused. 'Not that I watch documentaries very often. I like gardening programmes. Alan Titchmarsh is my favourite. Do you like Alan Titchmarsh?'

'I don't mind him.'

'It's my wife who's the documentary addict. If there's been a documentary about it, she has watched the documentary. Ooh, I seem to have said documentary rather too much.' He laughed, as he indicated and turned a corner. 'We saw that documentary on Netflix about the chap who got charged with murder and went down for years. He didn't do it, so they got him out again. Then he got banged up again for another murder, would you believe? And now they're trying to get him off again. He must feel like he's doing the murder hokey-cokey – in, out, in, out, shake it all about. You seen it?'

Thoughts of Carl Jeffery pushed into her head. Would it be better if she knew the outcome of his appeal? She shook away the thought. If he was out – free to kill again – the knowledge would break her.

'Santa's beard,' the driver said. 'Who's this pillocky person behind me?'

'Sorry?'

'Some ruddy moron's gating my tail.'

Isla glanced over her shoulder and squinted. The back window was filled with the full beam of a car's headlights, far too close.

The taxi driver slowed, and whoever was behind heeded, putting some distance between them.

'Sports car,' the taxi driver said with a grumble. 'Some idiot going through a midlife crisis, I shouldn't wonder. Probably bought a guitar too and wants to be the next Bryan Adams.'

He pulled into the car park at Oakley Court, which had once been the sweeping drive of a now-converted Victorian house.

'Thanks,' Isla said, opening the door, relieved the journey was over.

He jumped out, opened the boot and pulled out her case.

'Thanks,' she said again, paying him.

He drove away, and she began stabbing the passcode into the keypad on the front door, before glancing over her shoulder. The sports car that had tailgated the taxi was parked across the road, lights on. Someone was sitting at the steering wheel, but it was impossible to see who it was – no more than a silhouette.

Unnerved, she fumbled the rest of the code into the keypad and pushed open the door. She heaved her case up the flight of stairs, and put her key into her front door and turned it. As she pushed against the door, something prevented her from opening it fully. Her heartbeat cranked up a notch, but she realised quickly that a newspaper and a pile of letters were blocking the door. She reached her hand round and pushed them aside.

Inside, once the door was closed behind her, she stood in the darkness and took a long, deep breath, frustrated that her anxiety had risen to what she called silly levels. She'd been fine in Canada. Things had gone so well.

The apartment was quiet without Jack and Luna to greet her, and she missed the comfort of their presence.

Jack rarely went to Dorset. His mum must be very ill.

She flicked the hall light switch, but the inky darkness remained. The bulb had blown.

As she wheeled her case through the blackness, she noted the air was musty and heavy with a faint mingling aroma of Jack's aftershave and the slight waft of bacon.

The floorboards in the lounge creaked as she padded towards the window and looked out. The sports car was still in the lay-by opposite, lights off. She yanked the curtains closed.

In the kitchen, she turned on the tap and streamed water into a glass. She swallowed half of it, her dry throat thanking her, and poured the rest onto the dry soil of a sad-looking plant that Jack had forgotten to water. She took off her coat and slipped off her shoes. She knew she should shower to eradicate the journey, but instead made her way into the bedroom and fell onto the bed fully clothed. Closing her eyes, she drifted into a doze.

Five minutes later, the intercom buzzed. Her eyes sprang open. Could it be Jack home early? He often forgot his key. She rose and headed from the bedroom, her heart pounding as she took in how still and silent the apartment was. She approached the front door, fighting back memories of six years ago, frustrated by her fear. She didn't do this any more, she told herself. She wasn't afraid any more.

She pressed the talk button on the intercom. 'Hello. Jack, is that you?' There was no reply. Maybe the intercom hadn't buzzed. Perhaps it had been part of a dream. It wouldn't have been the first time her dreams seemed real. When she'd been taking tablets, she would often have vivid nightmares that felt far too real. But that was a long time ago. 'Jack?' she said again, noting the wobble in her voice.

She released the button, headed into the lounge, and crept towards the window. She peered through the gap in the curtains. Someone, hood up, was crossing the road, jogging away from the apartment block. The sports car's lights flashed, and whoever it was flung open the door, jumped inside, and sped away with a screech of tyres.

Isla hurried back to bed and dived under the duvet, where she cradled her knees. Tears filled her eyes, as memories of Carl Jeffery swooped into her head.

## Six years ago

He stood at the bar, pretending to look lost. 'You're so pretty, I've forgotten what I was going to ask for.'

She'd known immediately it was Carl Jeffery. Bronwyn, a girl who was staying at the same hostel as Isla, had told her about him. 'He's fucking gorgeous,' she'd said. And there was no doubting that he was. Rugged good looks, dark hair curling into the collar of his checked shirt. The kind of Aussie she could imagine living in the outback in a shack, boiling water in a tin kettle on an open fire, undeterred by huntsman spiders and venomous snakes.

But Carl's flattery was transparent.

'It can't be that hard to remember what you want,' Isla said, folding her arms and rolling her eyes. 'It's a bar, for Christ's sake. Now what can I get you?'

Charmers had never taken Isla in. In fact, she wasn't interested in men at all at that time. Her breakup with Trevor still rattled around her head even then. How he'd wanted her to settle down. How he didn't want her to travel. It had all got so messy. The last thing she wanted was another relationship.

'So, what's your name, pretty lady?' Carl's smirk was lopsided, his eyes deep set.

She thrust her hands on her hips. 'Seriously? That's your best line?'

He laughed. 'Oh come on, give a guy a break.'

'You're really not my type.' She smiled. 'Don't waste your time.'

'You're gay?'

'So I have to be gay not to fancy you?' She knocked the lid off a bottled lager and handed it to a worse-for-wear customer who was leaning on the bar holding out a five-dollar note.

'So what will it be?' she said, eyes back on Carl.

'Lager,' he said, pulling himself onto a stool.

'Coming right up.' She bent to get one from the fridge.

'So when did you arrive?' he asked, as she handed him the cool bottle. 'I haven't seen you around.'

'Two weeks ago,' she said, watching as he parted his lips and took a long gulp.

'Staying at the Bristol?'

She nodded.

'You like it there?'

'Yeah, it's cool.' She moved away. She really wasn't interested. And anyway, Bronwyn fancied him.

During the evening, women gravitated towards him, and he ended up at a table with an attractive blonde who seemed to fuel his ego and kept him topped up with drinks. His laugh was loud and confident, and Isla found herself watching him, despite an inner instinct not to. She watched the way he leant forward to listen, attentive as the woman spoke, the way he rested his tanned hand over hers, so it became invisible.

'There's a fucking dancing possum in here,' yelled the drunken bloke at the bar, snapping Isla out of her dream world, as he fell off his stool. 'Did you see it? Did you see it? It's wearing clogs and a pink hat.'

'Oh, Ernie, you're imagining things again. You need to give up the amber nectar,' she said, coming out from behind the bar. Despite her small size, she pulled him to his feet. 'You've had enough, mate,' she continued, escorting him across the bar, and out through the door. 'Now go home to Mrs Ernie.'

'Chucking out the drunks again?' said Bronwyn, appearing through the night, and following Isla back into the bar. 'So how's it going?' she continued, her friendly Irish lilt just one of the things that made her so likeable.

'Yeah, I'm good; be glad when I've finished,' Isla said, hurrying back behind the bar.

'I'll have a wine, please,' Bronwyn said, tipping coins from a tatty zip-up purse onto the bar. She sat down and dragged her fingers through her red, layered hair. She was eighteen and travelling alone, but seemed to have an aura that said 'don't mess with me'.

'Good to see you, my little Irish beauty.' It was Carl approaching, after leaving the blonde woman alone. 'I'm loving the cut-off shorts.' He ogled her thighs, and then lifted his eyes to meet Isla's, holding her gaze. Isla looked away, annoyed with herself for getting drawn in by his game playing.

'I'll have another lager,' he said to her. And once she'd handed it to him, he lifted Bronwyn from the stool, and carried her, her legs gripping his body, her lips on his, to a table in the corner. Her giggles were almost childlike.

\* \* \*

'He asked me out,' Bronwyn told Isla later, as they walked back to the hostel. 'Says we should have some fun together.'

'Did you say yes?'

'Yep, I like fun. My mums have told me since I was a little girl that I should get as much out of life as possible. And he is pretty gorgeous, don't you think?' She skipped ahead, and turned to face Isla, continuing to skip backwards, her skinny body being swallowed by the darkness.

'Bron,' Isla called after her, when she'd fully gone from view. 'Wait up.'

'I've told him I'm not sticking around here for too long,' Bronwyn called out.

'And he's OK with that?' Isla called back.

'Why wouldn't he be?'

The darkness was suddenly total, the silence only punctuated by Bronwyn's distant footfalls, and the intermittent sound of an owl hooting. 'Bronwyn, please wait up,' Isla called, picking up speed. 'Bron? I'm knackered. I can't be arsed to run.'

'Ahhh!'

'Bron!' Isla called out, grabbing her torch from her rucksack and searching the darkness. 'Bronwyn, are you OK?'

'Over here,' Bronwyn called out, laughing. The beam of Isla's torched picked her out among the trees. She was sitting on the gravelled earth, brushing down her knees. 'Lost my balance,' she said, her face spreading into a wide, intoxicated smile. 'Should have been looking where I was going.'

## Now

'Get out of my head,' Isla cried, burying her head in her hands, tears burning. The appeal had got to her more than she realised. 'You can't hurt me any more, you bastard.'

But she knew she wouldn't sleep. She couldn't even close her eyes.

# Chapter 5

*Wednesday, 26 October*

Water streamed from the shower over Isla's hair, and soapy bubbles slid down her back. She could have stayed there for hours, washing away her tiredness, the harshness of the journey home and the awful unease of the night before.

She turned off the water, reached out for a fluffy towel to wrap around her, and stepped onto the mat in the steamy bathroom, determined she wasn't going to let Carl Jeffery ruin everything. In fact, the smoothness of the water had already worn away the sharp edges, perspective almost restored. The person in the sports car could have been anyone visiting the apartment block, she told herself, and she wasn't even sure the buzzer had been activated.

The door nudged open, and she looked up from rubbing moisture from her hair with a hand towel. 'Luna.' The cat ran towards her, meowing, and Isla crouched and tickled her ears. 'I've missed you so much, my little angel.'

'I hope you missed me too.' It was Jack, outside the door.

'Hey, you,' Isla called.

She smiled as a head of wayward dark hair appeared, along with a familiar smile. He crossed the bathroom and took her in his arms. 'So all went OK in Canada?'

She nodded. 'It did, yes.'

'You should feel pretty pleased with yourself.' He touched her hair and leant in to kiss her lips. Luna mewed and made a quick exit, as he began trailing kisses down Isla's neck. He went to unhook her towel, but she flinched and pulled away.

'What's up?' he said, his eyes wide and hurt.

'Nothing. Sorry.'

He went to reach out to her once more, but she stepped away. 'Have you been smoking?' she said.

He narrowed his eyes. 'Just the one. It was bloody stressful with my mother.'

'Oh God, yes, sorry.' A pang of guilt. 'Is she OK?'

'Heart attack.'

'Jack, that's awful.'

He shrugged and screwed up his nose. 'It was mild. If she listens to the doctors, which she probably won't, she'll be OK.' He reached out his hand and touched the St Christopher necklace hanging around her neck. 'Is that new?'

She placed her hand over it. 'Sort of,' she said with a shrug.

'I didn't think you were into the saints.'

'No, no I'm not, not really. It was a gift.'

'A gift?'

'Jeez, Jack, what is this, the third degree? Roxanne bought it for me, if you must know. Before I left for Canada.'

'Easy, Isla. Don't bite my head off. I'll put some coffee on, shall I?' he said, turning his back and leaving her alone.

Isla dried herself, and pulled on a pair of leggings and a crumpled Fat Face top she'd retrieved from her case. She grabbed the rubber band she'd discarded to take a shower, pulled it back onto her wrist, and pinged it three times.

In the kitchen, she plonked three magnets on the fridge – Toronto, the Canadian Rockies and Niagara Falls – as Jack took two ready-made rolls from a paper bag and placed them on plates.

'Cheese and pickle OK?' he asked, as she headed towards him. 'I picked them up on the way home. Thought you might be hungry. There's nothing in the fridge.'

'Sounds great,' Isla said, reaching him and pulling him into a hug. 'Listen, sorry about earlier . . .' She nodded towards the bathroom. 'It's just . . .'

'You hate me smoking. I know.'

'No, well I had thought you'd given up, but it's more that I didn't sleep too well, that's all.' She bit her lip. If she told him about the car, the buzzer, he would think she was taking a step back.

She released him and pulled herself onto a stool at the breakfast bar.

'I have given up, by the way,' he said, as his phone screamed out the *Spider-Man* theme tune. He picked it up, looked at the screen, and cancelled the call.

'Who was that?'

'My mother – she can wait.' His eyes were on Isla. 'I've had one cigarette in three months.'

'You sure about that?' she said with a smile.

'OK, two, maybe three, tops. But that's pretty good.'

Isla tucked her damp hair behind her ears. 'Yes, you're right. Sorry.' She bit into the roll, crumbs sprinkling the breakfast bar, and chewed slowly. 'So you don't think your mum will listen to the doctors?'

He shook his head, a crease forming between his eyebrows. He looked pale, his eyes shadowed, as though he'd had little sleep in Dorset. 'I don't know,' he said. 'I only went out of duty, and I'm not sure I even owe her that.' He sounded cold, so unlike Jack, and Isla felt lost for the right words. His relationship with his mother had always been rocky. She'd been a drinker when he was a kid and neglected him, especially after his dad left.

Luna jumped onto the breakfast bar and attempted to sniff Isla's roll. 'You're so naughty,' she said, lifting her from the worktop and putting her on the floor where she gave a little mew. 'Was she good at my mum's, do you know?'

'Good as gold, apparently,' Jack said, a smile breaking through. 'Christ, we sound like we're talking about a baby.'

Isla didn't catch his eye. She knew he wanted kids one day. She took another bite of her roll and glanced at her phone on the worktop, noticing a Facebook notification.

'And my mum and dad are OK?' she asked, picking up her mobile and looking at the screen.

'Yeah, great, happier now you're back in the UK, of course.'

'God, when will they stop worrying about me?' she said, opening up Facebook. 'I just wish they'd see I'm fine now.'

'So tell me all about your trip.' He sat down opposite her. 'Have you taken lots of photos? The ones you put online are fantastic.'

'Yes . . .' she said, but she was distracted by an event invitation. 'Good God, I was only thinking about him yesterday.'

'Who?'

'Trevor Cooper.'

'The old boyfriend who you don't fancy?'

She laughed, eyes glued to the screen. 'That's the one. He's invited me to a university reunion.'

'I thought he didn't get in touch after you saw him on the train.'

'He didn't, and I hadn't noticed him on Facebook either, well not until yesterday, oddly enough.'

'Maybe he came on to sort out the reunion.'

'Yeah, probably.' She glanced up. 'I like your beard, by the way,' she said, touching his face. 'Suits you.'

'What, this ol' thing?' He smiled. 'It's just something me and Ryan Gosling are trying out.'

'Well, you're much cuter,' she said, but her eyes had drifted back to her phone screen.

'Coffee?' Jack asked, and Isla startled. 'Bloody hell, you're a bit edgy,' he continued, getting up after a bite of his roll. 'You OK?'

'Yes, yes I'm fine. And yes please. Love one. Thanks.'

Jack headed for the coffee machine, as she tapped the phone screen to open the event.

The cover photo was Wetherspoon's in Cambridge.

**Event Invitation:**
University Reunion, Wetherspoon's, Cambridge. Friday, 28
October 7.30 p.m.
INVITED: 6
COMING: 3
NOT COMING: 2

*I'm trying to get together a few old uni friends for a reunion.
I thought it was about time. It's been years! Do you guys fancy
it? Trevor*

Isla looked to see who'd been invited. Roxanne wasn't there, but
then she'd fallen out with Trevor. Sara Pembroke, who had studied
chemistry with him, had already accepted. Isla hadn't had much to
do with her at university, but recalled she was tall and overweight,
with short dark hair. An insular girl, if she remembered rightly.
Super-intelligent.

She clicked on Sara's profile to try to find out what she was like
now, but there was a hedgehog for her profile picture, and a field of
poppies as her cover photo. Her friends list and settings were private.

The declines were Stephen Grant and Jenny Dawson. They'd
been the dream couple at university and were getting married on
28 October. The other acceptances were Veronica Beesley and Ben
Martin. Their profiles were set to private too, their friends lists
hidden, but Isla recognised them, even though they'd matured over
the years. They'd unfriended Isla on Facebook a long time ago, at a
time when they were clearing out old university friends and moving
on. She was amazed they'd agreed to meet up with Trevor. But then
Trevor had been popular at university.

She read the comments on the event page:

Veronica Beesley: *Sounds like fun. I'm in! x*
Reply: Trevor Cooper: *Great. Looking forward to it! What are
you up to now?*

Reply: Veronica Beesley: *Fashion design. I'll bore you about the last eight years when I see you. Can't wait!*

Isla's eyes widened as she took in the words. She could hear Jack talking in a cute voice to Luna as he made some coffee, but she was fully locked in cyber-world.

She did a quick search for Veronica's company and clicked on her website. She sold her own designs, with a quirky vibe about them. They were the kind of things Isla loved to wear, but were way out of her price range.

She clicked back to Facebook.

Ben Martin: *I'll be there if it kills me, Trev, mate.*
Reply: Trevor Cooper: *Great news. Be good to catch up. Are you still in publishing?*
Reply: Ben Martin: *I am indeed. See you Friday!*

'What's up? You look as if you've seen a ghost,' Jack said, sitting back down and placing two freshly poured mugs of coffee in front of them.

'I think I have,' she said in a whisper. 'Well, a haunting of ghosts, actually.'

'A haunting of ghosts?'

'Like a gaggle of geese, but ghosts,' she said, with a smile.

'Pretty sure you just made that up.'

She hadn't really looked at Trevor's Facebook profile when he'd added her in July. She'd just registered at the time that his profile picture was a wolf howling on a mountain and his cover photo a generic beach somewhere. But she looked at it now. He had a dozen friends, including those he'd invited to the reunion.

'Isla?'

'What?' She glanced up and met Jack's enquiring eyes. 'Sorry. Sorry.'

Jack placed his hand over hers. 'I was thinking, do you fancy

34

taking off on Saturday? Maybe have a picnic by the sea? I know it's October but . . .'

'Yes, yes, why not? Sounds great,' she said, barely hearing his words.

'So when is this reunion?' He removed his hand from hers and nodded at her phone.

She sucked in a breath. 'Friday night.'

'Where?'

'Spoons in Cambridge.'

'Will you go?' He swallowed a gulp of coffee.

She shrugged. 'I don't know.'

'Could be fun meeting up with old friends. And I've got a backlog of *Game of Thrones* to watch, so I need you out of the house.' He laughed.

'Yeah, maybe I will.' She looked at the phone once more. 'Ben Martin is going. He's in publishing.'

Jack's eyes widened. 'That could be good, right? He might publish your book.'

She smiled at his naivety. 'I'm not sure he'd be best pleased if I started bombarding him with questions, but you never know.'

'You should go, Isla,' Jack said, his voice serious. 'You'll have a great time.'

She returned her eyes to the screen, clicked *yes* before she could think too much, and put down her phone. 'Done,' she said, leaning over the breakfast bar and pressing her lips on Jack's, kissing him long and hard.

'That's more like it,' he said, slipping down from the stool. Taking her hand, he led her to the bedroom.

\* \* \*

Later, Isla spotted a butterfly on the work surface next to the kettle. Her stomach leapt, as she reached out to touch it, expecting it to spring into life and flutter around the kitchen, but it didn't. She stared at the bright turquoise triangles on its wings, the deep black around the edges, recalling the photos she'd taken of the species when she was in Sydney.

Carl had called her Butterfly Girl because she took so many pictures. He'd teased her, saying the Blue Triangle was common out there – nothing special. 'You need to search out a Richmond Birdwing,' he'd said, his smile seeming so genuine. She'd thought he loved her. Perhaps he had in his warped way – that's what Roxanne had said in a bumbled attempt to heal her.

'The Richmond's wings stretch almost sixteen centimetres,' Carl had gone on. 'Saw one once when I was a kid.' Now the thought of his smile – and the way he'd later morphed into a monster – sent a shudder down her spine.

'How did it get in?' she said, her words barely audible, as she glanced around at the sealed apartment windows.

Jack looked up from shoving clothes from his holdall into the washing machine. 'Sorry?'

'A butterfly.' She felt strangely helpless. 'Where did it come from?'

'Ah.' Jack rose and slammed the washing machine door closed. 'I found it by our front door yesterday. Forgot to say. I know you like butterflies, and —'

'On our doormat?'

'Yeah. But I'm pretty sure the poor thing's dead.'

She gently touched its wing once more. 'It's not dead, Jack. I don't think it's real. It's made of silk or something. What the hell was it doing on our doorstep?'

He shrugged. 'No idea. I just brought it in. Thought it might get a new lease of life.'

'It's silk, Jack. I just told you that.'

'Yeah, well I didn't know that at the time.'

She held it in her palm, a slight tremor in her hand. 'What was it doing out there?'

'I guess somebody must have dropped it. The bloke upstairs likes weird and whacky things. Maybe it's his.'

'What bloke?'

36

'Some professor type, moved in while you were away.' He stepped towards her, and she flinched, dropping the butterfly, and it floated to the ground. 'It's just a butterfly, Isla.'

'No, it's not just a butterfly, Jack.' She was close to tears. 'It's the Blue Triangle, found in Australia.'

He looked at her for a long moment. 'Isla, I don't get what the problem is. Is this something to do with Carl . . .?'

'No. No, of course not,' Isla cut in. 'Ignore me, I'm just a bit jet-lagged, that's all.' She pushed the heels of her hands into her eyes to stop the tears.

'You sure you're OK?' he said, and she looked up to see him studying her face.

She couldn't tell him that Carl had burrowed his way into her head. That she was worried he could be out, but was too afraid to find out. He'd be upset she hadn't told him about the appeal and then he would worry about her – she couldn't have that.

Jack stepped closer and pulled her gently into his arms, where she leant against his chest. A tear burned the corner of her eye, before rolling down her face.

# Chapter 6

*Two years ago*

'It closed in 1994,' Jack said, coming up behind Isla as she photographed Aldwych Station in London.

She turned into the bright sunshine, squinting as her eyes met his. Taking in that he was tall and slim, and wearing a faded Captain America T-shirt and a cap over dark hair. His hands were rammed into the pockets of knee-length shorts.

'Sorry?' she said.

'The underground station.' He nodded towards the building she was photographing. 'It opened in 1907, closed in 1994.'

'Yes, I know.' She turned away from him. She'd already researched the building ready for an article on the London Underground she'd been commissioned to write. 'And before Aldwych, it was Strand Station.'

'Yeah, but the sign gives that away.'

She glanced at the 'Strand Station' sign on the red-brick wall above the closed metal gate.

'So that's kind of cheating,' he said.

A smile flickered on her lips, as she aimed her camera.

'Did you know it's been used in films?' he said.

'Aha.' She kept her eyes focused. '*Atonement.*'

'*Superman.*'

'*28 Weeks Later.*'

'*V for Vendetta.*'

'*The Krays.*'

He smiled through a brief silence, where they locked eyes, before saying, 'So are you a professional photographer, or . . .?' He stopped talking and took off his cap, glancing down as he brushed hair from his forehead with the back of his hand.

A feeling she hadn't felt for a long time absorbed her body. A good feeling – a feeling she thought had died four years before.

'Sorry,' he said, turning and stepping away. 'Being nosey . . . ignore me.'

Her instinct was to shove her camera into her rucksack and disappear into the London crowds. She was having good days now. More good than bad, since she'd accepted she would never be quite the same person she'd once been, and found ways of dealing with that. But she still avoided strangers – especially men. There was something about Jack though. Something about his innocent boyishness that she liked.

'I'm a freelance writer and photographer,' she said, pushing her camera into her bag, and he turned back. 'Photography is my passion. It's amazing how many fascinating and beautiful places there are in Britain.' *And the world,* she wanted to add, but she felt her days of travelling abroad were over.

He smiled. 'Yeah, I grew up in Dorset,' he said. 'Some stunning places down that way. Have you ever walked along Chesil Beach?'

'Yes, I went last year.' She'd done a series of pieces on the area for a travel magazine. 'An amazing part of the country.'

He moved closer. Not so close that he invaded her space. 'So, can I see your photographs anywhere?'

She shrugged. 'I've had articles published in magazines and Sunday supplements,' she said. 'But they've come and gone. Ooh, and I wrote a small guidebook on York that you can probably still get in . . . well, York.'

'Cool.' He stuck out his hand. 'I'm Jack Green, data analyst by day, London film location tour guide by weekend.' He paused, a smile dancing around his lips. 'I'm guessing by your face you didn't realise that was your cue to be impressed.'

She laughed again, taking his outstretched hand. 'Isla,' she said and, for the first time in four years, her guard lowered.

Within a month they were seeing each other every moment. He even gave up his tour guide job, so they could spend weekends together. The passion was great, but it was more than that.

'These are amazing, Isla,' he said the night she showed him the photographs she'd taken before everything went so wrong. Pictures of the Taj Mahal, Humayun's Tomb, and the warren of back streets in India, and those she'd taken in Australia and New Zealand too. He read her words about her early travels, as she looked on, cross-legged on the floor, cradling a glass of wine, and finding herself wondering what their children might look like, whether they would have his amazing eyes. 'You're so talented,' he went on. 'You should put this together. It would make a great book.'

She laughed, embarrassed, but pleased. There was nowhere near enough for a book, and she wasn't convinced her words and pictures were good enough. But still his excitement and enthusiasm washed over her, and the idea of her book took hold.

That's when their adventure began.

Later, they travelled to America and Africa and many parts of Europe, Isla making notes and snapping pictures.

Something she thought would never happen.

# Chapter 7

'Who's Andy?' Jack said, barely looking up, as Isla headed across the kitchen. He'd arrived home from work about an hour ago and plonked himself at the breakfast bar with a bottle of lager. He was watching film previews on his laptop, while Isla finished writing up an article that needed submitting. They would grab a takeaway later.

She stopped and stared at Jack, who finally looked up and smiled. 'Andy?' she said, moving on towards the fridge, and grabbing a bottle of wine.

'Andy Fisher?'

She looked over his shoulder to see he had Facebook open. He only used it for pages on his favourite films and TV programmes, and only had Isla and a couple of mates as friends.

'He's commented on your last update.'

'Has he?' She sloshed wine into a glass. 'You want some?'

'No, thanks.' He pointed at his half-drunk lager. 'He's put, "Miss you already. Had such a brilliant time with you."'

'Has he?'

'Did you meet him in Canada?' His tone was upbeat.

'I met quite a few people in Canada, Jack,' she said, putting the

41

bottle back in the fridge, and slamming the door shut. 'Most added me on Facebook. I can't remember half of them, and I can't remember him, if I'm honest.' She paused. 'Let me see.'

'No point,' he said. 'His profile picture is a maple leaf. There's nothing to see from my profile. You've loved his comment.'

'Have I? Well you know me, I "love" everyone's comments.' She took several gulps of wine. 'You're not jealous, are you?' she added with a half-laugh.

'Of course not.' He looked horrified. 'If I was jealous, I wouldn't let you go to that reunion.'

'Let me?' Her eyes widened with a mixture of playfulness and annoyance.

'Oh, come on, you know what I mean. I'm just saying I'm not jealous. I trust you.'

She thought for a moment, not meeting his eyes. 'Actually, I'm pretty sure Andy was one of a group of oldies at a hotel I was staying at. They knew how to have fun and joined me in. Made a fuss of me because I was young and on my own. That's all.'

'So Andy's a fun-loving OAP?'

She laughed, scooping her hair behind her ears. 'Yep, something like that. They're the best kind.'

She smiled and sat down next to him, opening her laptop and keying in a website address she'd found earlier for a lodge in Sweden.

'Where's that? It looks beautiful,' he said, looking over at the snowy scene.

'Abisko,' she said. 'It's in the Arctic Circle.'

'Bloody cold then.'

'Yes, well at the moment it is. I was thinking of going. It will be so peaceful, less than a hundred people live there. I thought it might be a great place to include in my book.' She clicked through some pictures on the site. 'It's a fascinating place. For three months in the summer the sun never goes down, and in winter it doesn't come up.'

'You want to go somewhere where it's dark all the time?' He looked bewildered.

She smiled. 'There's about five hours of daylight at the moment, which will be plenty to take lots of photos,' she said. 'It's not until December and January that the sun doesn't come up.' She paused, searching his face, unsure if he minded her going. 'I don't have to go. I have just been away.'

'When were you thinking of taking off?'

'Well, I'd like to try and finish my book by the end of the year, and Scandinavia would be the perfect final chapter, don't you think?'

'It would, yes.' His tone was even.

'I was thinking maybe the second week in November. Perhaps you could come with me.' But her words were empty, and she felt mean even saying them. She knew he couldn't get time off work at short notice.

He shrugged and shook his head. 'I can try to get it off, but I doubt I will,' he said, confirming her thoughts. 'Plus the cold freaks me out.' He broke into a smile. 'There's my recurring freezer dream to consider.'

She smiled too, but knew there was more to it than that. He'd told her how as a six-year-old he'd climbed into the chest freezer to get an iced lolly, and the lid had fallen down on him and locked.

'Mum had fallen asleep,' he'd told Isla a while back. 'Pissed, I realised later. I was always left to my own devices. If Dad hadn't come back, I'd have died.' The trauma had stayed with him. He hated the cold.

'Did you know that it only takes seventy seconds to freeze your little finger,' he said, holding his finger close to his face. 'Must depend on the size of your finger, I guess.'

'Good God, Jack, please don't tell me you've tested out that theory.'

'No, of course not – I read it on the Internet.'

'Must be true then,' she said, with an air of sarcasm.

'Yeah it is, some physiologist experimented on himself. I wonder if your finger becomes brittle, like ice?'

'Please stop talking.'

He laughed and looked into her eyes. 'Go to Sweden, Isla,' he said, putting his arm around her shoulders. 'It's time to finish your book.'

# Chapter 8

www.travellinggirlblog.com
*0 followers*
*Friday, 28 October, 2 a.m.*

So here are a few more photos of Canada. I hope you like them. My next adventure will be Sweden in November, so watch this space for more news on that.

Andy called. Said he hasn't been able to come to the UK because something's come up. He wouldn't say what. It was so good to hear his voice, but not those words. I told him I'm going to Abisko, and he said maybe we could meet there, if he doesn't get over to the UK.

*If he doesn't get to the UK.*

I desperately need to see him now. I miss him so much it hurts. I told him that, and he said I wasn't to worry, that he loves me, that he will be with me soon.

I'm so close to telling Jack. But it's hard. Maybe once Andy is here I'll be able to come right out and tell him. I feel wretched that I'm not being fair on Jack. Am I a horrible person? God, how I want to give way to the tears.

I'm not sure I want to go out tomorrow night to this ridiculous reunion. Do I really want to see Trevor again? Do I need that complication in my life right now?

But then what if Ben can help me with my book? I'd be a fool to miss a chance like that.

*Comments*                                                    *disabled.*

# Chapter 9

'So you're going on another holiday, you lucky thing. Where's Abisko?'

'Sweden, but it's not exactly a holiday, Millie.' Isla tugged the kinks from her hair with her straighteners, catching her sister's eye in the black-framed mirror above the fireplace. 'It's work.'

'OK, if you say so.' Millie smiled from the sofa, where Luna was purring on her knee. Her hair was scraped back in a haphazard ponytail, and she'd gained weight, despite her dieting efforts. Isla thought curvy suited her, but Millie had never been happy with her appearance. And now her acne was playing up again, a cluster of angry spots on her chin, cruel at almost forty.

'It really is work,' Isla insisted. 'I'm paying for the trip with a couple of commissions, and hoping to finish my book while I'm there.'

'So, have you got a publisher yet?'

Isla shook her head, eyes still on her sister. 'No, although I admit I haven't really tried,' she said, sighing as she bent to turn off the fake-flicker fire. It was burning her legs. Making them red. She glanced over her shoulder. 'I feel bad that you've come over when I'm going out.'

'It's OK, I just felt like popping in and surprising you.' Millie

46

smiled again. 'You look lovely by the way.' She bit into a biscuit, crumbs sprinkling her tracksuit bottoms. 'You always look lovely.'

'What? No, I don't.' Isla turned back to the mirror and screwed up her face, never seeing herself as attractive.

'Actually, I should get back soon to cook dinner,' Millie said. 'Did I tell you Abigail's gone vegan? I'm trying a cashew and mushroom korma tonight.'

'Bless her. How is my lovely niece?'

'Fine, although sometimes things seemed easier when she was younger. But I guess that's true for all parents of teens.' *Especially those with a child with Asperger's.* 'She seems so grown up at times. She likes a boy she met at the chess club she goes to, but, on the other hand, she's still obsessed with dinosaurs.' She paused for a moment before adding, 'She still loves the stegosaurus you and Jack bought her for her birthday.'

Jack had bought the large plastic figure. Isla had only remembered her niece's birthday at the last minute.

'You're an absolute genius,' she'd said, when he walked through the door with it, making silly dinosaur noises and waving the thing about.

'She loves the puppy too, of course,' Millie continued, glancing at her watch. 'Another reason I should get back. Larry's taken to chewing everything in his path. He's already ruined the ballet pumps Abigail got from Lindy Bop.'

'Oh that's a shame.'

'I know. She just stared at them for ages, as though they would miraculously mend in front of her eyes. I've had to order another pair quick.' She smiled. 'Why didn't someone tell me puppies are harder than babies?' She dragged Luna to her face and plonked a kiss on her black nose. 'I should have got a cat. So much easier.'

'Sometimes,' Isla said. 'Although Luna is super naughty, and has been known to poop in my trainers.'

Millie laughed, and Isla paused from straightening her hair, her eyes on her older sister once more.

Millie worked almost as many hours as Julian, as a teaching

assistant at a village school just outside Letchworth, and Abigail, at fifteen, still needed as much help as she always had done. Isla felt it wasn't right that everything fell on Millie's shoulders all the time, while Julian snuck into the garage each evening and weekend to play with his ever-growing model train set.

'Julian should help more,' Isla said, glancing over her shoulder.

'He wouldn't know where to start.' Millie crunched on another biscuit, and Isla couldn't work out if her sister actually liked the idea that they couldn't survive without her.

'But it's not the 1950s,' Isla continued, before she could warn her mouth not to open.

Millie's face wrinkled into a frown, and she prodded a spot on her chin.

'And don't touch that – you'll make it sore,' Isla said.

Millie whipped her hand away from her chin. 'And there's me thinking my spots weren't noticeable.' She pulled a fake sad face.

'They're not, not really.' Isla shook her head, regretting her words.

'It's OK. I know I look like a fifteen-year-old boy, at times.'

'No, you don't. It's just . . . maybe you could get something from the GP to clear them up.'

Millie shrugged. 'Yes, maybe I could, although there never seems time, somehow.' She paused again. 'And let's face it, nobody looks at me anyway.' She laughed, but Isla could tell she meant it.

'Are you OK?' she said softly. She wanted to be there for Millie. 'You know if you ever need anything . . . to talk . . . you know I'm here.'

'Blimey, Isla, where's this come from?' Millie sounded way too upbeat. 'I'm absolutely fine. Always am.' She turned from Isla's gaze. 'So are you going to tell me where you're off to tonight?'

'Spoons in Cambridge.' She turned, eyes back on her reflection, and once more dragged her hair straight. 'A university reunion.'

'Bit of a trek, isn't it?'

'Not really. I'll get the train and a taxi.'

'You hate taxis.'

'Used to hate taxis,' Isla said. She refused to let on that the enclosed feeling of a taxi had triggered her anxiety only a few days ago. 'I'm OK now. If I can go to Canada alone, I'm sure I can get in a taxi.' She wondered if she sounded smug, although she felt far from it.

Millie had never travelled. Married at twenty-three with Abigail on the way had meant they'd struggled at first. And later Millie hadn't seemed to want to go far. Although lately, Julian had taken off to European countries alone, claiming to need space. 'Abigail wouldn't cope,' was all Millie said, when Isla suggested she should go too. 'I could take care of her,' she'd offered, but Millie had declined.

Not that her sister had ever given Isla reason to think she wasn't happy with her life. Bringing up a child with Asperger's syndrome had been difficult at times, of course it had, but Millie had never complained.

'I think you were amazing doing the journey to Canada on your own,' Millie said. 'Really, really brave, after what you went through in Sydney.'

Isla felt a prickle behind her eyes. Millie had always had a knack of barging in with mentions of Carl Jeffery over the years. Oblivious, it seemed, to how wretched it made Isla feel.

'Can we not talk about that?' Isla said. 'You know I try to put it out of my head.' She turned and slammed her straighteners down on the coffee table, and padded across the room.

'Sorry,' Millie said. 'I didn't think. Sorry.'

'It's fine, don't worry.' Isla tugged her make-up bag from her handbag and glanced out of the window at the star-free night sky. She lowered her gaze to the road crammed with traffic: vehicles slowing as they approached the roundabout. About to close the curtains, she noticed someone standing on the other side of the road, silhouetted against the trees that edged the park. The bright light behind her made it hard to see, so she moved closer to the glass, narrowing her eyes. Someone was watching her.

'What are you looking at?' Millie asked, and Isla glanced over her shoulder to see her sister pick up the mug of coffee she'd made her fifteen minutes ago and take a sip. 'Jesus, this is cold,' she said, banging it back on the table, startling Isla. 'It's your fault, Luna, darling,' Millie went on, tickling the cat's head, 'demanding so much attention.'

Isla returned her eyes to the figure, tingles biting at her neck.

'Are you OK, Isla?'

'Yes, fine,' she said, running her hand over her rubber band. Whoever it was wore dark clothes and a scarf and hat, their face barely visible. She snatched the curtains closed and stepped back from the window.

Millie rose and headed over. 'Did you see something?' she asked, cracking open the curtains and looking out.

Isla stood behind her. 'It's just . . . well . . . I thought I saw someone, that's all . . . someone staring up at the apartment.' Her voice was soft and uncertain. She pinged the band three times, snap, snap, snap.

'Well, there's nobody there now,' Millie said, turning and touching her sister's arm gently.

Isla peered over her sister's shoulder. Whoever had been there was gone.

'Perhaps you were mistaken,' Millie said.

'Yes, yes, I must have been.' She yanked the curtains closed once more, scooped her hair behind her ears, and moved back to the mirror.

Millie followed her, and looked into Isla's eyes through their reflection, in a way she had after Carl Jeffery. It was her *I'm worried about you* look.

'I'm fine,' Isla insisted.

Millie touched Isla's arm again – the protective older sister. 'Are you sure?'

'Yes, yes of course I am. Honestly.' But she wasn't sure she was.

Eventually, Millie returned to the sofa, picked up the last biscuit from the packet Isla had put on the table earlier and bit into it.

Isla stared at her own reflection, breathing deeply, before unzipping her make-up bag and pulling out her mascara.

'So you're meeting up with old uni mates?' Millie said, clearly trying for a change of subject, and putting on a bright voice.

'Yes ... sort of.' She was distracted. Certain someone *had* been looking up at her. Someone in the shadows, watching like Carl Jeffery had. Was he free? She pinged the rubber band again, making her wrist sting. Maybe she shouldn't go to Cambridge. But then if she didn't, she would be letting him win. She was being ridiculous. Whoever it was was probably waiting for someone, and just happened to glance up at the moment Isla looked out. Or maybe they were searching for someone in another apartment, like the person in the sports car. After all, there were six flats in the converted house.

'Isla?' Millie snapped her from her thoughts.

'What?' She pulled the mascara brush from the tube, leant towards the mirror, and flicked the brush over her fair lashes.

'Tell me about these uni friends you're meeting,' Millie said, as the cat leapt back onto her lap and curled up.

'Oh, OK, yes, well, Ben and Veronica studied English lit with me, and Sara studied chemistry. Just people I once knew. I wasn't that close with any of them, well, apart from Trevor Cooper.'

'Trevor Cooper? The bloke you went out with?'

'God, do you remember that?'

'Of course. You were with him for ages. Didn't he get a bit clingy?'

Isla shrugged. 'I suppose so, but it was mainly that I wasn't ready for a serious relationship. I wanted to travel.'

'Didn't he turn a bit weird when you dumped him?' Her eyes were wide.

Isla pushed her mascara brush back in its tube. 'He was upset that's all.'

'But he followed you home, didn't he?'

'God, what is this, the Trevor Cooper Inquisition?' She sighed. 'He was a mess, Millie. The way I broke up with him was unkind. I regret that.'

'Oh God, that's right – you got Roxanne to dump him for you.'

'I couldn't face it. I gave him enough hints, but he didn't listen.' She rubbed her temples, a headache coming on. 'And later he wanted to talk it through, but I didn't have the bottle. I feel guilty even now.'

'No, Isla, you were young, and didn't know how to deal with it.'

'Do we ever know how to handle breakups?' She sighed deeply.

'Perhaps you shouldn't go tonight.'

Isla shrugged. She was beginning to doubt whether she should. She pulled out her blusher brush, and flicked it across each cheek in turn, before pulling out her lip gloss.

'Is Jack going?' Millie asked.

Isla shook her head. There'd been no talk of partners on the event invitation. 'He wouldn't enjoy it,' she said. 'It doesn't involve sci-fi or fantasy.'

Millie laughed. 'It's about time you got engaged, isn't it? You're almost thirty. Your body clock is ticking.'

The front door swung open, as Millie added, 'Jack's such a great bloke. You could do a hell of a lot worse.'

'Did I hear my name?' Jack said, as the cat jumped from Millie's lap, and raced towards him, twirling her body round his jean-clad legs. He put a brown paper bag on the breakfast bar, and the waft of Chinese food filled the air. He bent to pick the cat up and lifted her to his face. She looked tiny in his arms.

'I was only saying good things about you, Jack,' Millie said, getting up, and brushing biscuit crumbs from her lap. She looked at Isla. 'You should tell Jack what you saw . . .'

'Saw?' Jack said.

'It was nothing.' Her mind whirred, as they stared her way. 'Just a cute cat earlier, which looked a bit like Luna.'

'Well there's only one Luna,' he said, with a smile, plonking a kiss on the cat's head.

Millie looked at Isla, but Isla couldn't read her expression. 'I'd better get back,' she said mildly. 'Or they'll send out a search party.'

# Chapter 10

Millie left, and Isla finished getting ready.

'Are you sure you don't want some Chinese?' Jack said, sitting at the breakfast bar and spooning chow mein from a foil container onto a plate. He'd texted her earlier to ask if she fancied her favourite chicken in black bean sauce, but she'd declined, far too nervous to eat.

'I'm not really hungry,' she said. 'But thanks.'

'Do you want a lift to the station? It looks like rain.'

Isla glanced through the window. 'I'll be fine. It's only a ten-minute walk, and I need the air.' She pulled on her boots then leant across the worktop to kiss him. 'I feel a bit weird actually, meeting up with people I haven't seen for years.'

'I'm sure you'll have a great time.' He smiled. 'Go wow them, and call me if you need picking up.'

'Yes, thanks, I will.' She'd barely got the words out when his phone rang. 'Can't you change that daft ringtone?'

'*Spider-Man* is not daft,' he said, fake indignant, grabbing the phone and looking at the screen. He rejected the call.

'Your mum?'

He nodded. 'You look great, by the way,' he said, biting into a prawn cracker.

'Thanks,' she said, but felt he was just being kind. She knew she

53

looked as if she was about to go for a job interview. She'd dug out a brown skirt suit from the back of her wardrobe that she'd only ever worn once, hoping, for some bizarre reason, that a professional look might make a good impression on Ben Martin.

'Right, I'm off,' she said, kissing Jack, and grabbing her coat and bag. 'See you later,' she called before closing the door behind her.

Isla had forgotten her high-heeled boots rubbed. She rarely wore them, preferring flats. By the time she got to the station, although the rain had held off, her ankles throbbed, and she wished she'd taken Jack up on his offer of a lift.

The train appeared within moments, and she headed down the almost empty carriage. Just a woman wearing earphones, her head down, engrossed in her laptop, at the far end. Mizzling rain splattered the window, as the train rattled along the track, and as though the movement had loosened her memories, thoughts of Carl Jeffery invaded.

*Six years ago*

'I'm taking off,' Bronwyn said.

Isla smiled and turned from where she'd just snapped a photo of a kookaburra perched high in a tree near the hostel.

'Now?' she said, greeted by her friend's freckled face beaming at her from under a cap, the midday sun burning down on her from a clear blue sky. Bronwyn was wearing denim shorts and a T-shirt with the peace sign that matched the small tattoo on her arm, and her thin but sturdy legs led down to battered walking boots.

'Uh-huh.' Bronwyn hitched up her backpack, which was almost as big as she was. 'Got that wanderlust feeling again. Need to carry on.'

'I'll miss you, Bron,' Isla said, a pang of sadness rising. This was what she hated about travelling. You got so close to people, and then they'd leave, morphing into a profile picture on Facebook or MySpace. Or, if you were lucky, you'd receive a text every so often. Despite only knowing Bronwyn for a short while, Isla would miss her. In fact, home had crept into her thoughts more than ever lately. After Canada she would head back to the UK. 'So what's your plan?'

'I'll probably hitch into Sydney,' Bronwyn said, grabbing a bottle of water from the side of her backpack, and taking a gulp. 'Then get a flight to New Zealand.'

'You'll love it there,' Isla said, memories of her own visit fresh in her mind. 'North or South?'

'Both, I hope. I'm desperate to see where they filmed *Lord of the Rings*.'

Isla pulled her into a hug. 'We've had some laughs, haven't we?'

'Sure have. I'll never forget being chased by those kangaroos, or that bloody great spider in the loo.'

Isla laughed. 'So, have you told Carl?' They'd been seeing each other for around six weeks, although *It's only a bit of fun* was still Bronwyn's stock phrase.

'Yep, told him a couple of days ago.'

'Was he OK with it? He's pretty besotted.'

'To be honest, he acted a bit weird at first. But I told it like it is. Said he was a being an eejit, and it was never meant to be anything serious. He has to be cool with it.'

'He'll be fine.' Isla took her friend's hand. 'Don't forget me, will you?'

'Of course I won't.' Bronwyn squeezed Isla's hand, and looked back at the hostel, her eyes narrowing as she stared at the two-storey, red-brick building. 'Do you like it here?' she said, screwing up her nose.

'Pretty much, yeah.' But Isla had picked up on Bronwyn's unease. 'Why?'

'Oh, nothing – my imagination probably – it's nothing. Ignore me.'

'Oh God, you can't say that and leave me hanging.' She wasn't one for worrying, but if there was something about the place, she needed to know, and move on.

Bronwyn met Isla's eye. 'It's just I'm sure someone knocked on my window last night.' She shrugged and took a deep breath.

'And?'

'Nothing. That's it really. Ignore me.'

'Did you look out?'

'Yeah, yeah I did.' She studied her feet, scuffing her trainers on the dry earth.

'And?'

She looked up and squinted into the sun, before arching her palm over her dark eyes. 'I got a bit freaked,' she said. 'Might have been my imagination, but I'm pretty sure someone was out there. Watching me.'

## Now

Isla's phone rang, jolting her back to the moment. She rummaged in her bag for it and saw Roxanne's picture on the screen.

'Hi, you,' she said brightly into the phone.

'Hey, Isla, I can't believe you've been back since Tuesday, and we haven't had a catch-up.'

'I know,' Isla said, pleased to hear her friend's voice. She'd missed her. 'It's been far too long.'

'So how was Canada? I saw your fab pics on Facebook.'

'Truly amazing,' she said, as a surge of emotion at how wonderful it had been came and went.

'Cool. I so want to hear all about it. You free tonight? We could try the new tapas bar.'

'I can't, sorry. I'm on my way to a uni reunion, would you believe?'

There was silence on the other end. A kind of 'why wasn't I invited?' silence.

'I didn't organise it, Roxanne,' Isla said, guilt rising. 'If I had I would have invited you.'

'Yeah, 'course. No worries. I wouldn't have gone anyway.' A pause. 'So where you heading?'

'Spoon's in Cambridge,' Isla said, sensing the chill on the other end of the line.

'Who's going?'

'Veronica Beesley.'

'Good God, Verony Beeswax.' Roxanne laughed, and the tension between them lifted. 'That girl was so up herself, I'm surprised she could walk properly. I bet she's a millionaire or something.'

Isla laughed. 'Well, she owns her own company.'

'There you go. It doesn't surprise me. Remember when she slept with Mr Jenkins?'

'Broke up his marriage.'

'Yeah, and he wasn't the only lecturer she shagged.' Another pause. 'Who else is going?'

'Umm . . . Sara Pembroke.'

'Know the name. Can't bring her to mind.'

'I don't remember her that well either. She was really quiet, head in a book all the time. Nice enough, I think. Oh, and Ben Martin's going.'

'Ooh, nice. Now you're talking.'

Isla sucked in a breath. Roxanne would think she was crazy. 'And Trevor Cooper,' she said, as though she'd lit a touchpaper and was about to witness an explosion.

'What the . . .? Turn back now! Save yourself! Why would you go near him after Trevor-gate?'

Isla laughed. Her friend was a strong character, tough at times, which Roxanne had always claimed was down to her no-nonsense father. At university, Roxanne had a reputation for being a bit badass, modelling herself on Scary Spice for a while, calling Isla Baby Spice, although Isla was far from a baby. Roxanne had toned it down over the years, honed her personality, and focused her abundance of energy on trying to save the world.

'Are you in your right mind, Isla?' she said, the comedy gone from her voice.

'Roxanne, I saw Trevor back in July, and he was perfectly pleasant.'

'Perfectly pleasant, aye? Well, it's your funeral,' she said, and Isla shivered.

'So what have you been up to while I've been away?' Isla asked.

57

'Work's busy, busy, busy, and I'm volunteering at an animal shelter on Sundays.'

'Aw, that's lovely.'

'I know. The dogs are so cute. I want to take them all home.'

'Hey, what about the cats?'

'Them too.' Roxanne paused. 'So are you free Tuesday?'

'Definitely. What time shall we meet?'

'Say, seven-thirty at the tapas bar?'

'Sounds great.'

'OK, gotta run – see you then, Isla. Have fun tonight. Don't do anything I wouldn't do.'

The train continued to roar through the blackness of the evening, picking up and spewing out passengers as it went. Isla gazed at her reflection in the window, and a train thundering by in the other direction made her jump. She was more on edge than she'd realised.

A youth with a lip and nose ring, and a sweatshirt with the word 'Evil' splashed across it, had joined the train, and now sat opposite her. He paused from jabbing his phone screen and leered. She tugged at the hemline of her skirt, cringing with embarrassment, her neck tingling. Thankfully, before she crumbled completely, the train arrived at Cambridge Station.

Incessant rain hammered down from the night sky as the taxi she'd jumped into pulled up outside The Regal, a building that still resembled an old cinema. Isla paid the driver, and with a sigh of relief got out of the back seat. Avoiding puddles, she dashed across the pavement and through the doors of Wetherspoon's.

'A large Sauvignon Blanc, please,' she said as she reached the bar, her hand trembling slightly as she rummaged in her bag for her purse. What had possessed her to come?

She scanned the bar as she paid, looking for the almost-strangers she was about to spend the evening with. But as she drifted away from the bar, sipping wine in the hope it would relax her, she grew more anxious. Half of the tables were filled with people eating – enjoying Friday night out – and her head began to throb with the noise of chatter and laughter. Men's voices grew louder as they tried to make themselves heard: 'Shall we order a bottle of red?', 'I don't fancy yours much', 'Did you see the match?' and snippets of women's conversations jabbed Isla's ears: 'Oh my God, really?', 'Fuck, what a bitch', 'When are we going to eat? I'm starving.'

Isla pulled out her mobile phone. It was gone seven-thirty. Surely one of the uni crowd should have been there by now.

In fact, why wasn't Trevor there to greet her? It didn't make sense.

# Chapter 11

Isla brought up Trevor's Facebook profile on her phone. He'd added a picture of himself standing by a TR6, his fair hair longer than it had been on the train and beginning to curl. But otherwise he looked the same.

She scanned the bar once more. A few men resembled Trevor, one with a goatee beard who winked at her, another with his arm around a bloke. But he wasn't there. Well not that she could see.

She sat down at an empty table, planning to give her old friends until eight o'clock, and then leave. As she took another gulp of wine, her phone trilled and her mother's face appeared on the screen. Isla had taken the photo last Christmas, when her mum had a ring of red tinsel round her dark hair and her cheeks were rosy from cooking. She pressed answer and pinned the phone to her ear.

'Hi, Mum,' she said, keeping her voice low.

'I can hardly hear you, Isla, darling.' A bash of crockery in the background meant she was either filling the dishwasher or cooking. 'Where are you?'

'In a pub in Cambridge, about to meet up with old uni mates.'

'That's nice. Is Jack with you?'

'No, no I'm on my own.'

A pause. 'Well, don't leave your drink unattended.'

Isla opened her mouth and closed it again.

'I'm just ringing to see how your trip went,' her mum continued.

'Good, yes. Canada was beautiful.' It already seemed like a lifetime ago. 'Niagara Falls is stunning.'

'I did worry about you while you were away. You know that. It was a big step going to Canada alone.'

Before Sydney, her mum had been super-chilled about Isla travelling the world. She'd helped her sort out flights and accommodation, getting discounts because of her job as a travel agent. She'd understood it was Isla's life to do with what she wanted. But things had changed after Carl Jeffery. She'd become far too overprotective. Which was part of the reason Isla never confided in her about the appeal.

'You always worry, Mum,' Isla said. 'It's your job.'

She laughed, relief in her voice. 'I was also calling to see if you and Jack are free on Sunday to come for dinner.'

'Yes, I think so . . .' Isla glanced up towards the entrance, noticing a woman with red hair who looked like Veronica. But as the woman got closer she knew it wasn't her.

'You think so?'

'Sorry. Yes. I know so.' She looped her hair behind her ear. 'Sounds lovely – I'll look forward to it.'

'You can tell us about your trip. Bring along lots of photos, won't you?'

'They're all on Facebook.'

'You know I rarely go on there. Not since my cock-up.' She'd had her privacy settings wrong back in the summer and discovered that everyone could see her phone number and email address. She'd felt vulnerable. Despite Isla putting it right, she'd stayed away.

'OK, fine,' Isla said. 'I'll bring my laptop.'

'Lovely. I thought we might have turkey with all the trimmings.'

'Great.' Isla shifted on her seat, turning away from a couple who appeared to be listening to her conversation. Although her chat with her mother was more fifty shades of boring than *Fifty Shades of Grey*, so hardly eavesdrop-worthy.

'I realise we have turkey at Christmas,' her mum continued, as though confirming her thoughts. 'But I thought I might blow tradition this year, go crazy and have beef on Christmas Day.'

'That's very daring of you.'

'Mmm, I might change my mind before then.' She gave a small laugh. 'I really must pick up a nut-loaf for Sunday for Abigail. This whole turning vegan thing is making my head spin. It's all very admirable, but between you and me I'm not sure she even understands what vegan means.' A gushing sound – probably the dishwasher – reverberated down the phone. 'Can vegans eat cranberries?'

Isla smiled. 'Of course they can.'

'Well, it's not easy. They can't have anything dairy, apparently. So that's my vegetarian lasagne out the window.'

'But there's no dairy in cranberries.'

'No, no of course there isn't. And while we're on the subject of Christmas . . .'

'Were we?'

'Will you come on Christmas Day this year? Gran and Granddad are coming up from Devon. I know how much you like to see them.'

'Listen, can I let you know nearer the time? I'm not sure . . .'

'It's almost November, Isla.'

'I know.'

'Well, I like to get things sorted in my head. Particularly as I wasn't sure we'd see you this year.'

'Why wouldn't you see me?'

'Well, you might take off to Dorset to see Jack's mum. Jack said she's been quite poorly.'

Isla's neck tingled. She felt sure Jack wouldn't want to go to Dorset. 'Listen, I'd better go. My uni friends have arrived.' It was a lie; there was still no sign of them.

'Oh, OK, darling, enjoy your evening. Love you.'

'Love you too, Mum.'

Isla ended the call, pressed the Facebook icon on her phone screen, and updated her status.

*In Wetherspoon's, Cambridge, waiting to meet up with old uni friends.*

She added a fingernail-biting emoticon, to reflect her nervousness, regretting it instantly, imagining Trevor seeing it.

Should she delete it? But it had already attracted two likes. A silent scream echoed in her head. She longed to leave, craved fresh air. Too hot in her stupid skirt suit, to the point where perspiration trickled between her boobs. She rolled her finger over the rubber band on her wrist, before pinging it three times. But it didn't help her rising anxiety levels, and neither did a long sip of her wine.

Clutches of youngsters; a man with a walking stick; three blokes tapping on their phones; a couple who needed to get a room; and a stream of giggling women dressed in pink boas and high heels all gushed in, as though blown off the street.

A man in his sixties, passing Isla on his way to the gents', smiled. 'Been stood up, love?'

Isla ignored him and looked down at her phone again. There were now four likes on her status and a comment by Trevor Cooper.

*Can't wait to see you again, Isla! I've missed you. x*

He'd missed her?

Her skin prickled, as a flash of memory crept in. Trevor, eight years ago, sitting in his car opposite the house where she'd rented a room, crying and thudding the steering wheel; and the stream of text messages he'd sent, begging her to talk to him, that she'd ignored.

She drained her glass and went to the bar for another wine. She took a long gulp as she headed back to the table. She was being silly. Trevor couldn't have been nicer on the train. But then what if Jack read his comment? What would he think? Should she delete it?

Back at the table she knocked back the wine in ten minutes, before rising to her feet. She'd made a mistake coming. She didn't need this kind of hassle in her life.

'Isla?'

She turned to see a slim, stunning woman, with blonde wavy hair to her shoulders. For a moment Isla thought it was Veronica. But it couldn't be. This woman was taller, and Veronica was a redhead now if her latest profile picture was anything to go by.

'Yes,' Isla said, her voice small and cautious. She picked up her bag, ready to make a swift exit. There was an eight-thirty train. If she was quick, she could make it.

'It's me, Sara.' The woman giggled, showing a row of perfect white teeth, her blue eyes bright. 'Sara Pembroke from university, remember?' She flung her palms in the air like jazz hands, and wiggled. 'Ta da!'

'Wow, Sara, you look amazing.' Shocked didn't cover it. It was bizarre – no, surreal – to think this woman in front of her had once been the dark-haired, chubby girl who always had her head in a book.

'You look great yourself, Isla. Just the same as you did at university,' Sara said, moving forward and air-kissing each side of Isla's face, her subtle yet distinctive perfume wafting like a sea breeze. 'I can't believe we're all meeting up. It's totally amaze-balls,' she squealed, grinning widely.

'Yes, yes it is.' Isla lowered herself back onto the edge of her seat. She couldn't dash for the next train now. However much she wanted to.

'Can I get you a drink?' Sara asked. She was well spoken, with a hint of Judi Dench, and Isla realised Sara had barely talked at university. Or, if she had, she couldn't remember.

'OK, yes, thanks. A white wine please,' Isla said, noticing her empty glass.

'Large?'

'Please.' She definitely needed a large one.

Sara removed a short, figure-hugging jacket, to reveal attractive toned forearms, and slipped it over the back of the chair.

As she floated away, men's heads turned at the sight of her

sashaying towards the bar in her flared-at-the-waist Fifties-style dress. Isla was transfixed, amazed by the transformation. She would have to stay now. Her curiosity wouldn't let her leave.

# Chapter 12

'So what are you up to these days?' Sara placed a mineral water for herself and a glass of wine for Isla on the table and sat down, smoothing her dress over crossed legs.

'I'm a freelance writer and photographer.'

'Really? Wow, that's utterly amazing. What sort of writing?'

'Travel.' Isla shrugged. 'I'm a photographer primarily, but I write too.'

Sara reached forward and pressed a hand on Isla's arm. 'You know I reckon I've got a novel in me,' she said, removing her hand, and leaning back in her chair. 'They say everyone has, don't they? Have you?'

Isla shook her head. 'God, no, I couldn't write fiction. I'm not very imaginative.' She paused for a moment. 'Although I dream that my travel journal will be published one day.'

'How exciting. Tell me more.' Sara sipped her water, her eyes on Isla.

'Well, OK then, but stop me if I bore you.'

'Yep, promise I will.'

'Well, it's about travel, obviously.'

'Obviously.' Sara smiled.

'And it's a blend of the quirky and traditional places I've been to.'

'Intriguing.'

'I hope so. I loved researching and photographing unusual places, which hopefully contrast with those everyone wants to see. Like I adored the Colosseum in Rome, but was equally thrilled by the Torre Argentina.'

'Never heard of it.' Sara's gaze was fully focused on Isla, her elbows now on the table, hands propping up her chin.

'Well, it's an excavation that includes the Theatre of Pompey, where Caesar was killed.' She felt a tingle of excitement as she talked about what she loved. 'But, for me, the best part was that it's home for over two hundred of Rome's stray cats.'

'That's incredible.'

'I know. They're all cared for there. It's amazing. I took loads of photographs.' Her voice brightened further as she spoke, and memories of her trip with Jack woke her endorphins. This was her passion. She glanced towards the entrance. 'I had hoped to meet Ben Martin. I think he's in publishing.'

Sara nodded, and leant back once more. 'I heard that along the grapevine too. He owns his own publishing company, apparently.' She looked towards the entrance too. 'Fingers crossed he comes and signs you on the spot.'

Isla laughed. 'Unlikely, but maybe he could point me in the right direction. Give me a bit of advice, perhaps.' She paused to take a sip of her drink. 'Anyway, that's enough about me. What about you? What have you been up to all these years?'

Sara straightened her shoulders. 'Well, I'm a chemist. No surprise there. I work for Tomlins Pharmaceuticals in London, and I have a tiny apartment near Finsbury Park, although I'm not living there at the moment.'

'Sounds like a great job.' Isla smiled, as she took in Sara's perfect face once more. 'I still can't get over how different you look,' she said.

A grin sliced across Sara's face. 'It's down to a good diet, a personal trainer and a great hairdresser.' She touched her hair and gave a confident laugh.

Isla found herself staring. *Surely there's more to it than that.* She must have had work done – perfect nose, lips with just the right amount of plumpness, amazing breasts. But then how hard had she really looked at Sara Pembroke at university? In fact, she could barely bring her to mind.

'So do you see any of the old uni lot?' Sara asked. She was looking down at her hands, seeming to admire her manicured fingernails.

Isla shook her head. 'Not really. Although I see Roxanne. Do you remember her?'

'God, yes.' Sara looked up and snagged her into a stare. 'If I'm honest, I never did like her.' She leant closer. 'I can't believe you still see her.' There was a hint of concern in her voice. 'I'm surprised you still trust her after—'

'She's still my best friend,' Isla cut in, before Sara could go on. She picked up her wine and took a long sip. 'We see a lot of each other.'

Sara put up her hands, as though waving white flags. 'Sorry,' she said. 'Ignore me.' She looked at her watch. 'You know, I have the feeling we've been stood up.' She glanced towards the entrance again. 'Odd that none of them have arrived yet, don't you think?'

Isla let Sara's comment go. The last thing she wanted was to bicker with a woman she barely knew. 'Mmm,' she said, screwing up her nose. 'Especially as Trevor left a comment on my Facebook status earlier, saying he was looking forward to seeing me again.'

'Did he? Oh dear, I hope he's OK.' Sara's perfectly made-up eyes widened. 'You don't think something awful has happened to him, do you? Maybe he's been in an accident.'

Isla cheeks burned. It hadn't occurred to her to worry about him.

'Tell you what, I'll send him a private message.' Sara pulled out her phone, and within seconds her fingers danced across the screen. 'I haven't seen him since uni, have you?' She looked up.

'Once, briefly, a few months back.'

'You went out with him, didn't you?'

Isla nodded. 'For a while.'

'He was in most of my classes.' Sara put her phone on the table.

'We studied for the same degree and got on well. It's a shame we lost contact. I was looking forward to seeing him again.'

'Are you married?' Isla asked. She'd spotted the ring on Sara's wedding finger when she first walked in, but it had taken more wine to loosen her tongue enough to ask her.

'Oh, this.' Sara touched the ring and, with a faraway look in her eyes, shook her head. 'I get a lot of come-ons when I go out – the downside of looking like this.' She laughed and turned the ring around her finger several times. 'Not that it puts some men off – they still think they can try it on.' She paused. 'This was my mother's ring. She died a while back.'

'I'm sorry.' Isla could only imagine how awful it would be to lose her own mum.

'It was over a year ago,' Sara said. 'We weren't that close, if I'm honest. I was more upset for Dad. They were a perfect couple, so in love. He depends on me now. We're really close.'

A vague memory of Sara arriving at university with her mother, an upright, stern-looking woman, drifted in. But it vanished as quickly as it came.

'Still, it couldn't have been easy for you.' Unsure what else to say, Isla took another gulp of her drink and swallowed.

'Life can be hard at times.'

Isla looked into Sara's eyes wondering if she had read about what happened to her in Australia. It was in all the papers at the time – on the news. But then she wasn't about to bring it up.

Sara looked about her. 'I wonder where Veronica and Ben are. Weird, if they don't come, after agreeing to.' She shrugged. 'Although in some ways, I'm not surprised they haven't turned up. Veronica was utterly self-absorbed at uni. Do you remember? I can't imagine her wanting to see me again.' She picked up her phone. 'Still no reply from Trevor. He hasn't even read my message. Has he contacted you?'

Isla felt a shiver run through her body. It was becoming awkward. She didn't care any more whether they turned up or not, and the bar had filled up with diners and drinkers. It was far too noisy.

She tugged out her phone and shook her head. 'No nothing,' she said, looking at Sara, who was fiddling with her phone.

'Hey, you should take a selfie of us, and put it on Facebook,' Sara said, her blue eyes brightening once more. 'We can smile, as though we're enjoying ourselves.'

*As though we're enjoying ourselves?* So Sara wasn't having fun either, despite her perky expression.

'It will make them jealous when they see it,' she continued, excitement in her voice. 'They'll wish they'd come. Come on, let's do it.' She nudged her chair closer, her perfume tickling Isla's senses, and she flicked her hair forward over her shoulders.

'OK,' Isla said, feeling she had no choice. She fumbled with her phone, before leaning in, and raised her mobile in the air in front of them. Their heads touched, as the camera flashed.

Together they looked at the picture. 'Ooh, don't we look good?' Sara said, with a laugh, watching as Isla added it to her timeline.

*Great fun in Cambridge with old uni friend, Sara Pembroke. Good to catch up.*

It sounded ridiculous. But maybe Sara was right. If the others saw it, they might regret not coming. Except Ben and Veronica weren't even her friends on social media. And frankly she didn't care if they were jealous or not. It all felt rather silly.

'Add me on Facebook,' Sara said, as her phone bleeped. 'It's a text from my dad,' she said, looking at the screen, and losing her smile. Her eyes moistened, and the bright happy image she'd been portraying seemed to dissolve in front of Isla's eyes. 'Sorry,' she said. 'Do you mind if I reply to this? He'll only worry if I don't. He's so dependent on me.'

'Not at all,' Isla said, draining her glass of wine and deliberating whether to go to the bar for another. She stopped herself. Once Sara had finished texting, Isla would suggest they called it a night. She'd already had three glasses of wine on an empty stomach, and needed to head home. It was almost ten.

Isla opened Facebook once more. Several people had liked the photo of her and Sara, and there were a couple of comments.

Jack Green: *Hope you're having a great time. You two could be sisters! XXX*
Roxanne Furaha: *Say hi to Sara from me XXX*

Isla smiled, but it didn't last. A private message had appeared in her inbox. It was from Trevor.

*Hi, Isla, I got as far as the door and saw you sitting there in your brown skirt suit, but couldn't find the courage to come over. But I want to see you again. Maybe another time. Trevor X*

'Are you OK, Isla?' Sara was saying. Her lips moved but her words sounded far away, quiet under the thud of Isla's heartbeat and the noise of the bar.

'I'm not sure.' Isla's eyes flitted around the bar, zooming in on faces, focusing for a moment, and then moving on, over and over. Had Trevor been in the bar? Had he been watching from a distance? Her skin prickled and she snapped the band on her wrist. Why had he mentioned what she was wearing?

She put her phone away, hand shaking, and looked at Sara. Should she tell her what Trevor had said in his message? That he'd been there.

'I should probably head for home,' she said, deciding against it. She barely knew her after all. She rubbed the tips of her fingers over the rubber band on her wrist once more, resisting the urge to ping it. 'I need to get to the station.'

'Oh, OK, no worries.' Sara pulled her jacket from the back of her chair and slipped it on. It was clear she'd had enough too. She was putting up no resistance. 'Maybe we could share a taxi to the station. I've got to go that way too.'

'Yes.' Isla paused, still feeling stunned, her body trembling.

'My stop is Newmarket. I've been staying there with my father for the past six months. He's been so low since Mum died. But he says me being there for him helps.' She sighed. 'I do what I can.'

'It must be so hard.' Isla wished her words didn't feel so hollow. She was trying to be a good person and fought to keep focus on Sara. But Trevor's message was set on repeat inside her head, making her dizzy. Was she over-reacting? He'd been perfectly nice on the train.

'Yes, it's hard at times,' Sara was saying.

'I'm so sorry.'

'Thanks. I suppose I thought if I went to stay with him for a bit, I could help, but I can't stay much longer. The commute into London is so tiring.' She sucked in a sigh.

'I'm so sorry,' Isla repeated. It sounded generic, but she couldn't think what else to say. She could hardly pull her into a hug.

'*Anyway* . . . as Chandler says in *Friends*.' Sara threw Isla what felt like a fake smile. 'Where are you heading?'

'Letchworth. It's just a few stops, not far.'

At the station, Sara air-kissed Isla's cheeks. 'We must keep in touch,' she said, pulling out her phone. 'Shall we swap numbers?'

'OK,' Isla said, trying to disguise the reluctance in her voice. She was relieved as her train approached, and time had run out. She'd dodged the exchange. But Sara was so insistent – looked so keen – that she found herself rummaging in her bag for one of her cards. She'd had them made in the hope it would give her a more professional image, but rarely used them. 'Text or email me,' she said, handing it to her, as she stepped onto the train.

There were lots of '*We must do this agains*' and '*It's been fantastic*' as the doors closed. But, when the train pulled away, and Sara waving became a memory, Isla felt relieved to be going home.

She would never do it again. It had all been a terrible mistake. The past was better left in the past.

# Chapter 13

www.travellinggirlblog.com
*0 followers*
*Saturday, 29 October, 6 a.m.*

This is no longer a travel blog.

It is a place for thoughts that whir around my head, keeping me awake at night. I've changed my settings to private. I need this tiny piece of cyberspace – my place – to spill my inner thoughts. Nobody has a right to see inside my head.

The reunion was a disaster. Only two of us turned up. Sara Pembroke and me. It was uncomfortable, yes, that's what I'd call it, but the thing that unsettled me most, although I keep trying to rationalise it, was the strange message I received from Trevor. He'd organised the reunion, but didn't turn up. Said he'd been watching me in the bar. Even described what I was wearing. I go over and over his words. It's unnerved me, reminded me of what an awful person I was back then, when I asked Roxanne to dump him for me. Refused to talk to him. I was a terrible person. Still am.

And it's not only that, I keep worrying Carl Jeffery is free and in England. I'm sure he was there, opposite my apartment. What if he's coming for me? What if he's been released?

And, as if that wasn't enough, Andy texted to say he still can't get over to see me. He won't talk to me on the phone any more. Says we can only talk by text for now. I don't understand.

I've added a photo of Andy and me sitting together at the lovely café in Canada where we first met. I like to look at it, but it makes me cry.

I'm going to be with him, if it kills me.

*Comments*                                                            *disabled.*

# Chapter 14

Isla lifted her throbbing head from the pillow, and squinted at the digital clock on her bedside table, trying to bring the numbers into focus. Finally, they de-blurred: 10.15 a.m.

'Shit,' she whimpered, thudding back onto the pillow. She'd hoped to get up at nine to work on her book.

The half-open curtains let in a beam of sunlight that reached across the bedroom and highlighted dust particles raining down. She squinted again, eyes now on the window. Heavy grey clouds had gathered in the sky, like demons determined to overpower the sun.

She'd got up earlier, desperate for the loo and a drink of water to quench her thirst, but eventually she'd returned to bed and taken hold of Jack's hand as he slept. She hadn't called him the night before when she reached Letchworth Station, deciding a walk in the mizzling rain might unclutter her mind. It hadn't.

At home, the blisters on her heels throbbing, she'd found Jack in bed asleep. His phone was on the cabinet beside him, telling her he would have been there, had she needed him. He hadn't woken then, or when she got up earlier, but now he was gone. Just a crumpled sheet and the familiar smell of him remained.

She pulled herself to a sitting position, dragged her legs round, and slipped her feet into her slippers. She hadn't slept well, her mind too full of everything that had happened over the last few days. She sighed, eyes falling on her screwed-up skirt suit on the floor. She would never wear it again. Why the heck did she think it would impress Ben Martin? What had she been thinking? Publishers are interested in words and pictures, not bloody brown skirt suits, and certainly not her. She shook her head, cross at how unbelievably naive she'd been, and a wave of confusion, sadness and embarrassment filled her senses. How could she have been so stupid?

And why hadn't Trevor Cooper come over? He'd been friendly on the train.

The door creaked open, and Luna jumped onto the bed next to her, meeting her eye to eye, her stance and lack of a purr saying, *Thank God I didn't rely on you for my breakfast.* Isla stroked her, comforted by soft fur under her hand. 'Oh, Luna,' she whispered. 'I'm a first-class idiot.'

The cat turned, giving Isla a view of her bum, twitching the tip of her tail.

'I deserve that, I suppose,' she said, grabbing her robe and pulling it on over her pyjamas.

She stumbled across the bedroom and into the bathroom, where she scrubbed off last night's make-up and cleaned her teeth. 'Jesus,' she said, and quickly turned her back on her reflection, hating the pale, dark-eyed monster staring back at her.

She padded towards the kitchen, passing the photographic prints she'd taken over the last two years that hung on the walls of the hallway. Black and white studies of her and Jack in each other's arms, looking so happy.

She opened the kitchen door, the aroma of toast and coffee hitting her.

'Hey, gorgeous,' Jack called from the lounge, where he was sprawled on the sofa, watching a catch-up of a sci-fi programme she'd never been interested in. 'How was it?'

'How was what?' she said, moving towards the coffee machine, craving caffeine.

'Last night, the big reunion.' He aimed the remote control at the TV and froze the screen on a weird-looking alien. 'I saw the photo on Facebook.'

'It was OK,' she said, filling a mug with coffee, and splashing in skimmed milk. She grabbed some paracetamols from the cupboard and popped two from the foil casing.

Jack got up and walked over. 'You don't sound convinced,' he said. 'Did they all turn up?'

'Barely anyone came.' She sighed, wishing she hadn't gone. 'Just two of us in the end – Sara Pembroke, who seemed OK, and me.' She pulled herself onto a stool, rolling her head from side to side, in an attempt to ease the tension in her neck, before swallowing the tablets with her coffee. 'No idea what happened to the others.' She paused, unsure whether to tell Jack about the message from Trevor.

'You OK?' He sat down opposite her, concern in his eyes.

'I'm fine,' she said, deciding to put Trevor out of her mind. 'Jaded, that's all. I haven't even attempted to type up my travel notes, and on top of that I've given myself a bit of a hangover. Remind me next time that three large wines on an empty stomach isn't a good idea. I can't take the pace any more.'

He smiled. 'I said you should have had some Chinese.'

'Yeah, I know. What can I say? I'm a numpty.' She took another sip of coffee. 'Hopefully a boost of caffeine will inject life back into me,' she said. 'Then I'll crack on with typing up my notes.' Her tone was reluctant. 'I need to get it done.'

'OK, I'll leave you to get on.' He sounded disappointed.

'Is that all right? You don't mind, do you?'

'No worries. I have loads of things to watch on Netflix.' He smiled again, but there was something in his eyes.

'Oh, no . . . we were supposed to be going out, weren't we?' she said, spotting a picnic basket. 'I forgot. I'm so sorry.'

'No worries, it's nothing that won't keep for another day.' He glanced out of the window. The sun had gone. The grey clouds had won. 'Anyway it's too cold for the seaside.'

'And it looks like rain.'

'Yeah, we can go some other time.' He shrugged, got down from the stool, and threw himself back on the sofa.

A pang of guilt radiated through her. 'Although we have umbrellas,' she said.

He turned back, face brightening. 'I could even break out my cagoule.'

She laughed. The thought of the sea air was tempting. She could do with getting as far away from home as possible. 'OK, why not?' she said, taking another gulp of coffee. She stood up, yawning, and stretching her arms above her head. 'Although don't get any ideas about staying over – my mum's invited us round tomorrow for one of her famous Sunday dinners, and I haven't seen her since Canada. If we don't turn up she'll go into meltdown.'

'No problem. I'd never say no to one of your mum's roasts,' he said, with a smile. 'Her Yorkshire puds are to die for.'

'Well, I'd better get dressed then. It's already ten-thirty,' she said, her brain untangling by the moment. 'I'll grab a shower and then we can head off.'

**Facebook:** *Hunstanton for the day with Jack Green. Umbrellas and cagoules at the ready. Haven't been there since I was a kid. Feeling excited.*

\* \* \*

Jack appeared from the joke shop, and, pretend-sulky, headed towards the bench where Isla had been sitting for the last ten minutes huddled in her coat, looking out to sea.

She'd been ravenous since she got there, first tucking into the picnic, and now she was finishing off a bag of chips. 'It must be the sea air,' she'd said earlier, dashing into the fish and chip shop. But it was more that she'd barely eaten anything the day before.

The rain had kept off, and a strip of pale blue sky, sandwiched between grey clouds and the sea, seemed determined to break through.

Jack dropped down next to her on the bench, as she wiped her hands clean on a serviette.

'I've bought a Spider-Man costume for Millie's party,' he said.

'Brilliant,' she said with a smile, screwing up the chip wrappings. 'Spider-Man's cool.' She laughed. Truth was, Isla could take or leave Marvel and DC, but Jack bordered on obsessed. Their spare room shelves were brimming with collectable action figures and Pop Vinyls, although she'd drawn the line at an Avengers duvet cover he'd hinted he wanted.

He pulled a cloth Spider-Man mask from the bag and dragged it over his head. 'What do you think?' he said, voice muffled by the cloth, and a little boy with wide blue eyes and curly blond hair stopped and stared, hands on his hips.

'Jacob,' his mother called.

'But, Mummy, look, it's Spider-Man,' the boy said, as she grabbed his hand and whisked him away with a smile.

Isla laughed, took out her phone, snapped a photograph of Jack, and put it on Facebook.

*Jack's mask for Millie's 40th #Spider-Man. Thought I'd put it on the Web. Ho Ho! Sorry!*

'Well? What do you think?' Jack repeated, as she put her phone away. 'Be honest. I can take it.'

'Whatever turns you on, I suppose,' she said, giggling, and tossing the screwed-up chip paper into a nearby bin.

'But does it turn *you* on?' he said, pulling the mask free, so his hair stood on end with static electricity. He leant forward and kissed her gently on the lips. 'That's all I care about.'

Isla laughed again and flattened down his hair with her hand. 'So, what do you want to do now?'

'Arcade? I have coins.'

'How old are you? Five?'

'I was deprived as a child,' he said, rising and shoving the mask in the plastic bag with the rest of the costume.

He took hold of her hand as they walked down the hill towards the amusement arcade near the beach, passing gift shops and a café where people sat outside, despite the cold.

'Wait,' she said, dashing into one of the gift shops. 'I need a Hunstanton fridge magnet for my collection.' Moments later she reappeared, shoving a paper bag into her coat pocket.

Jack smiled and took her hand once more. 'You're so easily pleased,' he said.

They crossed the road on a zebra crossing, and dived inside the arcade, like a couple of kids.

'Did you come to the seaside as a child?' she said later, as Jack tried his luck catching a cuddly toy at the metal claw machine.

'Sometimes,' he said, looking at her from the corner of his eyes, as the claw caught hold of a Minion. He twisted round to look at her, and the Minion dropped from the claw's grasp. 'My dad, before he left, would take me to Chesil Beach, and we'd search for dinosaur fossils, that kind of thing.' He looked into her face, a hint of sadness in his eyes. 'But then he left, and Mum and I moved, and we lost touch.'

'I'm sorry,' she said, not for the first time.

'Yeah well, it's in the past now.' He shrugged. 'Ancient history.'

The incessant bleeping, the robotic voices of arcade games, and money crashing into metal trays jarred with his sad tone. He moved away from the grabber machine. 'Talking of walks along the coastline,' he said. 'We were, weren't we?'

She smiled.

'Do you fancy going down on the beach?'

They left the noise of the arcade and climbed down concrete steps

80

onto the sand. A seagull squawked overhead, its wings spread wide. Isla pulled out her camera and snapped a picture as it flew down and settled on a wooden post. It looked sure of itself as it continued to squawk. 'I'm convinced seagulls get bigger every year,' she said.

'Yep, pretty sure they're going to take over the world,' Jack said, with a grin. 'The invasion of the seagulls.'

'Sounds like a Hitchcock film.'

They walked for a while before Isla said, 'I came here as a child sometimes. Mum and Dad would race Millie and me along this very beach, and somehow I always won, even though I had the littlest legs. Millie would scoop me up and swing me round as she ran through the finish line.' She smiled at the thought of her sister. 'She used to tickle my cheek with butterfly kisses,' she said.

Jack smiled too. 'It's funny how when we are young we always win. Dad used to let me win at chess.'

'Chess?' she said, eyebrows rising. 'You've never told me you played chess as a kid.'

'Isla, you keep forgetting I was a geek back then.'

'Back then?' she said, with a cheeky tone.

He tickled her waist, and she laughed and ran off in front of him, her coat flapping in the breeze. When she was some distance away, she turned and began walking backwards, snapping photographs of him. 'I'm afraid you're still a geek, Mr Green,' she said.

'OK, fine. But I'll have you know, geek is the new orange.'

'What? I don't even know what that means.'

'Nope, me neither.'

They walked on in silence for some time, Isla's feet sinking in the soft sand, her trainers heavy. The sounds of the town faded into the distance. It felt good to get away for the day. Good to clear her head a bit.

'You know I love you, right?' Jack said, stopping, as the clouds separated and a watery sun beamed down on them. 'That I'd do anything for you.' He fumbled in his pocket and dropped down onto one knee.

81

'Oh God, Jack, what are you doing?' The crash of the waves against the sand sounded loud in her ears.

'Isla Jane Johnson, will you marry me?'

Isla's heart thumped as she met his eyes, noting his cheeks reddening. She knew her silence was worrying him, but time seemed to slow, the seagulls circling above making her dizzy. Getting married was the last thing on her mind. She wanted to turn away – run along the beach until she reached a silent cove, where she could sit and think and think and think.

'Isla?'

'I'm sorry.'

'Sorry?' He stood up, his wide, green eyes searching her face. 'I don't understand.' His voice was so quiet. 'I thought you loved me.'

'I do, Jack.'

'We talked about getting married one day, didn't we? I just thought . . .'

She looked again at the ring, noting the slight tremor in his hand, and then back into his sad face. 'I'm so sorry,' she said, tears filling her eyes.

'Don't be sorry, Isla. Just say yes. Please. You're killing me here.' He began to pace back and forth, his trainers scuffing the sand. 'I thought you loved me. I thought we were solid.'

She bit down on her lip, watching his eyes grow watery. Lovely, sweet Jack deserved so much more. She couldn't bear that she was hurting him. 'OK, let's get married,' she said, on impulse, wanting to bite back the words as they entered the sea air and became fact. This was the wrong time.

He stopped pacing. 'Are you sure?'

'Of course.' But she was far from it. She wasn't sure about anything any more.

He took her hand and slipped the solitaire diamond ring onto her finger, and her heart continued to race for all the wrong reasons.

On the way back, she pulled out her phone, and opened

Facebook. The place where she could pretend Carl Jeffery hadn't set up home in her head. A place where she could make believe everything was OK.

*Got engaged to Jack Green. Feeling wonderful.*

Within moments the 'likes' and 'loves' appeared, and people began commenting. With a jolt, she realised Trevor was one of them.

*So pleased for you both. I hope you've made the right decision.*

# Chapter 15

www.travellinggirlblog.com
*0 followers*
*Sunday, 30 October, 6 a.m.*

I've lost count of the number of times I've tried calling Andy. Texting isn't enough. I know he said not to ring any more, but I need to hear his voice. Tell him about Jack – that my engagement means nothing, that I'm not even sure why I said yes. That it was a stupid, stupid mistake.

'Pick up, pick up, pick up,' I cry each time, over and over, but he never has. I think he's ignoring me.

I can't think straight any more. My brain feels like fog, as I attempt to work everything out. I thought he would come to England. He said he would. Yes, he said he would.

*I'm going to try to come to Sweden, Isla*, his last text said. Try? It all feels so vague, and not what I'd hoped for at all. Not the happy ending I'd dreamed of. Why is he doing this to me?

*Comments*                                                    *disabled.*

# Chapter 16

**Sunday, 30 October**

The early morning walk was helping. It was dark and miserable, threatening rain, but it didn't matter. Isla needed the space and fresh air more than anything right now – somewhere mentally freeing, to attempt to sort out her thoughts.

She'd parked up in the pretty nearby village of Willian, before heading into the countryside on the Greenway route, the wind blowing her hair into a tangled, unruly mess. She'd already taken a stunning photo of a late migrating swallow perched on a wooden sign.

'Good luck on your journey, little chap,' she'd said, watching the straggler take off. She didn't know much about swallows, except that their flight to South Africa was hazardous. She admired how the tiny bird went on its journey, heading for its destination without fear.

Now Isla crouched to snap a photo of a Red Admiral butterfly, happy that the turmoil inside her head had lost its voice – for now. But the calm was cut short by the sound of footsteps. She rose and looked around her, her body stiffening. A gust of wind blew a shower of crispy red leaves across the path she'd taken, startling her. The field to her left spread for miles, meeting with low grey clouds that looked as though they might burst. The trees and bushes to her right were dense. She couldn't be sure whether someone might be lurking there.

Twigs snapped under what sounded like more footfalls.

'*Isla.*'

She swallowed painfully. Had someone called her name? No, it must have been the wind disturbing the bushes, or perhaps the wildlife. Still she shoved her camera in its holdall, pulled out her phone in case she needed it, and hurried away. Speed walking turned into a run, as she glanced over her shoulder every few seconds, but nobody appeared. It must have been an animal or a bird, she told herself, as she slowed to catch her breath. Or maybe she *was* losing it.

There was no doubting the thought of Carl Jeffery being freed was getting to her. *Could they have let him out? Could he really be in England, stalking her, scaring her, waiting in the wings to finish what he'd started?* She picked up speed again, her legs weak and jelly-like as she ran.

Five minutes away from her car, a heavy raindrop hit her cheek, and within moments rain hammered down. She shoved her camera holdall inside her hoodie and kept on running. By the time she reached her car, her hair was plastered to her head, and her clothes were soaked through. She opened the door, dived inside and grabbed some tissues from a box on the dashboard. As she dabbed her face, gasping for breath, a painful stitch in her side, she noticed a piece of paper under the windscreen wiper blades, saturated under the pressure of the thrashing rain.

She leapt from the car and grabbed it, her eyes scanning the pictures of Australian butterflies.

'Oh God,' she whispered, dropping it as though it had burned her skin. She looked about the silent street, pulled out her phone and thumbed the screen.

'Jack,' she yelled when he picked up.

'Hey, Isla? You OK?'

'I'm in Willian, and, oh God, Jack.' She was shaking, her voice far too high-pitched, and breathless.

'What's happened?'

She took a deep breath and looked down at the piece of paper floating in a puddle at her feet.

'Isla?'

'I'm OK,' she said, realising it was a flyer for a nearby butterfly sanctuary. Her heartbeat slowed, as she stared at it, aware of the rain bouncing inches off the ground, and the sound of it hitting the car roof like marbles. 'I'm being a numpty,' she went on, trying for a calm even tone. 'Just some wally on the road cut me up in the car, unnerved me a bit, that's all,' she lied.

'Dick.'

'I am not,' she said, trying for a laugh, and he laughed too. 'I'm OK. Just over-reacting. Ignore me.' She dashed her sleeve across her cheek in an attempt to dry the rain.

'You sure you're all right?'

'Yes. I'll be home soon. I'm looking forward to seeing Mum later. Probably wobbly from missing her, that's all.'

'OK, well I'll see you soon, yeah?'

'Yep, won't be long,' she said, ending the call.

She bent down to pick up the flyer, which disintegrated in her hands, and was now barely legible. She looked about her once more. There were no other flyers on the cars parked along the roadside, and a thought hit her.

The butterfly sanctuary had closed its doors two years ago.

\* \* \*

**Facebook:** *Yummy Sunday lunch at my parents' – Sally Johnson and Gary Johnson's house – with Jack Green, Millie Bailey, Abigail Bailey, Julian Bailey.*

'So when's the big day?' Mum asked, as they sat around the dining room table, a roast potato suspended on her fork. 'Please put your dinosaurs away, Abigail – they'll get covered in gravy.'

'I need them here, Gran,' Abigail said, straightening them into a line, in height order. One fell to the floor, and the puppy raced over to sniff it. 'Not yours, Larry,' she cried, diving down to pick it up, her dark hair falling about her face. Bobbing up quickly, she put it back in her neat row.

'We haven't set a date,' Isla said, swallowing down a carrot, and glancing at Jack from the corner of her eye. He didn't appear to be listening, his eyes fixed on his phone screen. She felt a surge of guilt. She'd changed the subject on the way home the night before, talking about Millie's pending party and Abisko instead. They'd even chatted about the latest Marvel film – anything but what they should be addressing.

He finally glanced up. 'Isla's got one more trip soon, Sally,' he said, looking at Isla's mum, his voice giving away nothing. 'I'm sure once the book's complete, we'll set a date.' He moved his gaze to Isla, before resting his eyes back on his phone and picking up his fork.

'Put your phone down, Jack,' Abigail said. 'It's rude to have it at the table.'

Jack smiled and put it in his pocket. 'Sorry, Abigail, you're right. Where are my manners?'

'You must have lost them, Jack,' Abigail said, with a serious face.

'Have you named your book yet, Isla?' Sally said, crunching down on the crispy potato. 'I know you couldn't make up your mind.'

Isla nodded. 'I'm calling it *Isla's Journey*.'

'Lovely. It's an amazing achievement, darling. I'm so proud of you. You've done so well, after what happened.' She bit down on her lip. 'Imagine, I may have a famous daughter one day.'

'Well, it won't be the first time she's been famous, will it?' Julian said, cutting into his turkey. He was forty-five, small and thin, with mousy-brown hair scooped back from his forehead with too much gel, and oval wire-rimmed glasses. Even though he'd been in her life for years, Isla still didn't feel she knew him. The truth was she didn't like him very much, and had made that obvious in her teens, but now she pretended everything was OK, for Millie.

A brief silence fell on the room, before Julian added, 'Although, I suppose being splattered across the front pages of newspapers as an *almost* victim of a serial killer is hardly the same thing.'

Isla picked up the bottle of red wine, which she'd almost drunk alone, and drained it into her glass. She picked up the glass and peered around the table, looking at her family's faces in turn, her skull prickling.

'I told Julian you thought you saw someone, Isla,' Millie said, chewing her lip, and glancing at her husband. 'I hope that's OK.'

Jack turned, meeting Isla's eye. 'Saw someone?'

'Isla?' her mum said. 'What's this about?'

'She thought she saw someone staring up at your apartment window, Jack,' Millie went on. 'Didn't you, Isla?'

'Why didn't you tell me?' Jack's eyes fixed on Isla, who took a gulp of wine, and glared at her sister. Why was she bringing it up? Isla's fingers tensed around the stem of the glass. 'It wasn't Carl Jeffery,' she blurted.

'Whoever said it was, Isla?' Julian chirped in, searching her face as though looking for cracks.

'It was nobody,' she said, her voice small. 'I made a mistake, that's all.' There was a snap as the stem broke, cutting her hand. 'Oh God,' she said, gripping her hand, as the glass crashed onto the table, and wine splattered the tablecloth like blood at a crime scene.

'Oh my goodness.' Sally grabbed her daughter's hand and pressed a napkin against the cut, absorbing the blood.

'I'm fine.' Isla pulled away and tucked the napkin round her hand. 'It's only a flesh wound.'

'Larry's thrown up in your slippers, Gran,' Abigail said. She eyed the fluffy, pink mules, bending to inspect them. 'I can see peas, and I don't think he liked the nut-loaf I gave him.' She sat up straight again, eyes on her plate, and with an outstretched finger she prodded the three slices of nut-loaf laid out parallel. 'I'm not sure I do either, actually. Can I have some turkey please?'

'But you're a vegan now, Abigail,' Millie said. 'Remember?'

'I don't want to be a vegan.'

Sally jumped up, grabbed the slippers and the broken glass, and took them into the kitchen. The puppy trotted after her, wagging his tail. There was a clatter, as it sounded like it all ended up in the bin.

Abigail pushed her plate away and began rearranging her dinosaurs across the table, avoiding the splashes of wine. 'I like dinosaurs,' she said.

Back in her chair, Sally took a deep breath and, seeming to metaphorically brush the last few minutes under the carpet and out of sight, said, 'I'm guessing there'll be lots to think about with the wedding.'

Isla nodded, still clutching the napkin. 'Yes, these things take a lot of planning,' she said, her voice quiet, as she tried to get her befuddled head in order. 'Could be quite a while, so don't go buying your hat yet.' She looked at Jack, who didn't catch her eye. 'I've heard decent venues get booked up ages in advance, and then there'll be a band or a disco or something, the flowers, the cake.' She was rambling, overcompensating, the thought of a big wedding sending shockwaves through her body. 'Or we could have a quiet ceremony, just a handful of guests, perhaps.'

'Don't you dare deprive me of a decent wedding,' Sally said, and Isla glanced at Millie, who smiled and shrugged. Isla had only been thirteen at the time, but she knew her sister's wedding had been rushed, done on the cheap.

'I want all the family to be there,' Sally went on. 'And I want to put lots of fancy photographs on Facebook.'

Isla bit down the urge to say, *But you don't like Facebook*. 'We'll need to give it some thought,' she said instead, trying to catch Jack's attention, but when he didn't notice, her gaze drifted to her dad who smiled and winked at her.

'I hope you won't make me wear anything too fancy-pants,' he said. He'd been brought up in the East End of London and had never lost his cockney accent.

'You'll wear what you're told to wear, Gary,' Sally said, spooning far too much cranberry jelly over her turkey. 'Isla will be in charge. And you, Jack, of course.'

'Well, as long as we can have superhero table centres, I'll be happy,' he said with the briefest hint of a smile.

'What?' Sally's eyes widened.

'He's joking, Mum,' Isla said.

'Am I?' Jack picked up one of Abigail's dinosaurs and whizzed it through the air. 'Is it a bird? Is it a plane?'

Abigail giggled. 'No, Jack. It's a triceratops.' She reached across the table and took back the plastic model.

'So, Isla, I hear you're off to Sweden,' Julian said, pushing his glasses up the bridge of his nose.

He was the last person she wanted to talk to about it. She glanced at her sister, knowing she had to keep the peace. 'Yes, I've booked a trip to Abisko.'

'Yes, I saw your Facebook update. Although you put so many on there, it's hard to keep up. It will be jolly freezing over there,' he said, his shoulders hunching. 'The cold will get into your bones. You'd better stock up on thermal underwear.'

Millie glared at him.

'Are you going with her this time, Jack?' Sally asked, hope in her voice. 'Protect her from those wild Scandinavian bears?'

'Jack's not coming, Mum,' Isla said. 'And before you say anything, I was fine on my own in Canada. You must stop worrying about me.' Isla's urge to jump up and throw open the French doors, to let some fresh air in, was overwhelming.

'You will be here for my party, won't you, Isla?' Millie asked, chewing as she spoke.

Julian rolled his eyes at her. 'Swallow before you talk, Millie. You look like a camel.' He gave a derisive snort.

'You won't make me wear a ruddy top hat and tails, will you, Isla?' Her dad was talking through a mouth full of mashed swede, his eyes on Julian as though deliberately making a point, always fiercely protective of his daughters.

'Christ's sake, so many questions.' Isla put down her knife and fork, her head and hand throbbing. But it wasn't the questions. It was Carl Jeffery filling her head. His thick dark hair, the rugged good looks that belied who he really was, and the way he'd dressed that day: the green beanie hat, the scarf wrapped around his face, despite the scalding temperatures in Australia.

'Eat up.' Sally wiggled her knife at Isla's half-eaten dinner. 'I've gone to a lot of trouble.'

'Carrots make your hair white and your teeth curly,' Gary said, clearly trying to lighten the moment.

'You can't have curly teeth, Granddad,' Abigail said. 'That's just silly.'

'I will eat it, Mum. It's lovely.' Isla sighed. 'And in answer to your questions: Yes, Millie, of course I'll be at your party. It's the Saturday before I leave.' She picked up her cutlery once more and jabbed a parsnip with her fork. 'And you can wear what you like at the wedding, Dad,' she added, pushing the parsnip into her mouth, and wondering how soon she could leave.

*　*　*

Jack was quiet. In fact, he hadn't spoken since her parents waved them goodbye from their drive, Sally on tiptoe, hand stretched towards the sky, until they'd turned the corner at the end of their road.

'You OK?' Isla said, finally. 'Did you have a good time?'

'I always enjoy your mum's roasts,' he said, his tone flat.

'That's not what I asked.'

'Julian's a dick.'

She smiled. 'Yeah, well we all know that. God knows how Millie puts up with him.'

'Because she's a saint?'

'Or stupid.' She stared across at Jack, but his eyes stayed fully focused on the road ahead. 'Are you OK?' she said again, when they were almost home.

'I don't know, Isla. I feel a bit numb to be honest.' He paused.

'You didn't tell me you thought you saw someone.'

'It was nothing, Jack. Honestly.'

'And not only that, I could see how awkward you were over dinner talking about the wedding. I'm beginning to wonder why you said yes.'

'Don't be silly, Jack.'

'But you didn't talk about it last night either.'

'Don't do this, please.'

'What?'

'You're pushing me, Jack. I said yes, didn't I? Just give me time.'

He pulled up with a squeal of tyres, parking haphazardly outside their apartment block, and tugged on the handbrake. 'Pushing you?' He paused. 'Jeez, Isla, I only asked you to fucking marry me. If you don't want to, put me out of my misery, like an injured dog.' A tear zigzagged down his cheek, and he dashed it away.

'Jack, you know I love you,' she said, taking his hand, but somehow it came across patronising.

'Do you? Do you really?' He didn't sound convinced.

'Yes. It's just my head's a mess at the moment. I can't seem to think straight any more.'

'Why not? What's the problem, Isla? You seem preoccupied since you came back from Canada.'

'It's just the book.' She bit down on her lip. 'I just want to finish it, that's all. I just need some time and space before we start making plans.'

'You've just been to bloody Canada for a month. How much time and space do you need, for fuck's sake?'

'I'm so sorry, Jack.' She squeezed his hand, and then added softly, 'When I come back from Sweden, we'll sort it all out.'

'The wedding?'

'Everything,' she said, leaning over and kissing his cheek, but he pulled away

93

# Chapter 17

**Email:**
From: SARA Pembroke saraapembroke@windlemail.com
To: ISLA Johnson islajjohnson@windlemail.com

*Hi Isla*
*How are you? I just wanted to whiz over an email to say what*
*a fantastic evening I had with you on Friday. It's a shame the*
*others didn't turn up, although definitely their loss. We really*
*must get together again some time, if you could bear it. I've sent*
*you a friend request on Facebook, as I'd love to see the photo you*
*took of us together. Hope you add me soon.*
*Looking forward to hearing from you.*
*Lots of love*
*Sara xxx*

Isla threw her phone into her bag without responding, grabbed her
parka, and rushed from her apartment into the beginnings of a rain
shower. Needing to get her head out of her writing and do some

shopping, she dived into her car and turned the key in the ignition. The engine whirred pathetically.

'No,' she cried, banging the steering wheel three times. 'Please start.' She tried the key again, but it gave out the same pitiful response.

She sighed. She'd get drenched if she looked under the bonnet, and her AA cover had lapsed months ago. She tried the key a third time. It continued to whir, so she got out, slammed the door, and kicked a tyre for good measure. Would another takeaway be so bad? And maybe she could grab some milk from the local shop. She fought down the desire to go back inside, pulled up her hood against the now hammering rain, and headed down the road towards the bus stop.

As she walked, she typed a text to Jack saying how sorry she was for the night before. They'd gone to bed in silence, and when she got up he was gone. She'd hoped their argument would be forgotten. Jack rarely hung on to their disagreements. Not that they'd had that many. But then they'd never rowed about anything quite so serious before.

*Oh, and you'll never guess, my bloody car battery is flat,* she added with a row of kisses, as a car pulled up beside her, and the window slid down.

'Isla.'

She glanced up from her mobile and turned to see Julian leaning across the passenger seat of his Mondeo. 'Hop in,' he said, with a smile. 'You're getting drenched. I'll give you a lift. Where are you heading?'

Isla shook her head. 'It's fine. I'll catch the bus,' she said, heading onwards. She didn't want to be indebted to him, even for something as small as lift.

Julian drove his car in time with her footfalls. 'It's no trouble,' he called. 'Get in. It's pouring down out there.'

Isla eased to a stop, and Julian braked. She was getting soaked on the puddling pavement, and the rain spilling down her collar made her shudder. The thought of cramming on the number twelve with a huddle of wet bodies was far from appealing.

He flung the door open, and Isla bent and peered into the car.

She swallowed hard, before climbing in and fastening the seatbelt. She glanced at Julian. His complexion was waxy, and there were a few broken blood vessels around his nose she'd never noticed before. But then she'd never really looked at him. Not close up.

'So where are you off to?' he said, sounding chirpy as he put the car into gear, and looked in the wing mirror at the stream of oncoming traffic.

'Just the supermarket,' she said, tucking her damp hair behind her ears.

He indicated and pulled into the slow flow of traffic when another car flashed him, and Isla realised this was the first time she'd been alone with him. She'd been twelve when her sister started going out with him. He'd looked different back then. Still small and thin, but his hair had been thicker, gelled into frosted peaks, and he hadn't worn glasses. He used to tweak her cheek. Tease her about boys. But she hadn't minded that – not really. What she'd minded then, and still did, was how he treated Millie. The way he hammered down how incapable her sister was, destroying her confidence.

'They say it will clear up later,' he said, speeding up the windscreen wipers so they clonked rhythmically, killing raindrops.

'Let's hope so.' She didn't want to talk, but felt she had to. 'So, have you got a day off work?' she asked.

He nodded. 'I'm on my way into town to pick up a new train.' He smiled. 'Flying Scotsman. A1 Class.'

He pulled up at a red light, and she turned away. Out of the window, she saw a mother dragged a crying boy wearing a duffel coat, a Batman rucksack on his back, through the relentless rain. They were drenched, and the mother's face was red with . . . what was that? Anger? Her mind drifted to Jack. He hadn't spoken to his mother since he got back from Dorset, as far as she knew.

The lights turned green, and Julian released the handbrake and stepped on the throttle once more.

'Millie's worried about you, Isla,' he said.

'Well, she shouldn't be. I'm totally fine.'

'But you thought you saw Carl Jeffery. Why would you think that?'

'No, no I didn't think that, Julian. It was nothing.'

A heavy silence filled the car. The heating was on way too high, and the smell of air freshener was making her feel woozy.

'I remember you when you were in your teens,' Julian said, his way of talking making him sound older than he was. 'You were such a spunky young thing.'

'Was I?' She'd never thought of herself as spunky. In fact, it was an awful choice of word, and the mere sound of it made her shudder.

'Do you remember that day, you must have been about sixteen, when you told me to . . . now what were your exact words?' He paused, staring her way for a few moments too long. '*Stop fucking with my sister's head.*'

'I don't remember that,' she said, but she did. And she remembered too how cross Millie had been. *Don't interfere, Isla. This is my life.*

'But that killer took it all away, didn't he?'

'I don't know what you mean.'

'Carl Jeffery stole your spunk.' He turned away, eyes back on the road.

'I suppose so, for a time anyway.' She sighed. 'Listen, Julian, can we talk about something else? I've put all that crap behind me now.'

'Have you? You seemed pretty jittery at your mum's. How is your hand, by the way?'

'Look out!' she cried, and Julian slammed on the brakes, just missing a woman who'd stepped onto a zebra crossing. The woman raised her middle finger and carried on walking.

'I think I'll walk from here. It's not far.' She opened the door before he could start moving again. 'Thanks for the lift.' She got out and hurried away through the rain.

His window whirred down. 'Isla, I was only trying to help. Millie's worried about you,' he called. But Isla's walk had turned into a run.

She was soaked by the time she reached the supermarket. And the sight of staff dressed up in Halloween costumes only added to her unease. She headed for the café, and ordered a large coffee.

Once at the table, she tried to push thoughts of Julian from her mind and pulled out her phone. She'd seen Sara's friend request the day before, but had been reluctant to add her. But now that Sara had emailed, she felt she had no choice but to accept. After all, Sara had seemed friendly in Cambridge, even spilled her heart out about her parents. There had been a sadness about her. Maybe she needed a friend.

She bit down hard on her lip before accepting it, and then noticed a message from Trevor. She hovered her finger over the delete button. He'd acted so odd – not coming to the reunion. But the temptation to read it was too much. She opened the message.

*Hi Isla,*

*I loved you at university, and I keep going over and over how you let me down back then. I've never forgotten that. Never really got over it. Never really got over you. On the train that day everything came flooding back, and I know you're engaged – I understand that you're with Jack – but if you could just meet me, talk to me. I know from your Facebook update you're heading for Sweden soon, but we could perhaps meet before that. Just let me know when you are free. I hope you are OK and managing to deal with the appeal – I know how much it was worrying you.*

*Love you always, Trevor xxx*

'Jesus,' she whispered and, with a shaky hand and barely a moment's thought, she clicked her way into her settings and blocked his Facebook profile. What the hell was he thinking? Why was he behaving so weirdly?

Oh God, had blocking him been an over-reaction?

She sat for some time sipping her drink and pinging the band on her wrist, her mind eventually drifting to Ben Martin. Although she knew she should forget the reunion, he still nudged at her. She searched for him on Facebook. There were several Ben Martins, and she found the profile picture of him that she'd seen on the event invitation. His friends list wasn't visible, like before, and there was no way of sending him a private message. If she wanted to get in touch she would have to send him a friend request. She hovered her finger over the symbol, before pressing it.

She finished her coffee, and left the café, trying to keep at bay her conversation with Julian, and the message from Trevor. As she headed through the toy section, a woman barged into her, almost knocking her to the floor. There was a scuffle as a member of security grabbed the woman's bag.

'I'm being victimised,' the woman yelled. 'I haven't even left the shop, you idiots.'

Isla moved away, her anxiety levels way too high. She needed to go home. Come back tomorrow.

She was hurrying past an array of half-priced pumpkins, and a group of children taking part in a 'Frightening Pumpkin' carving workshop near the door, when something caught her eye.

On the pavement outside the window, standing statue still, someone wearing a green beanie hat, with a matching scarf wrapped around their face, was staring right at her.

Panic shot through her. She thrust her face into her hands. 'Oh my God,' she cried. 'Oh God, no.'

'What is it?' a member of staff said, racing towards her and placing her arm around her shoulders. 'Whatever's wrong, love?'

'Carl Jeffery,' Isla whispered, her chest rising and falling in silent sobs. She moved her hands from her face, made her way slowly towards the window, and pressed her palms against the glass. Her body shook, as she forced herself to look out.

There was nobody there but shoppers.

\* \* \*

'Thanks,' Isla said, as the same member of the supermarket staff, a pleasant woman wearing devil horns and a red jumpsuit, pulled up outside her apartment block and yanked on the handbrake.

'Are you sure you're OK, love?' the woman said.

'Yes, honestly, I'm fine, thank you,' Isla said, getting out, and waving the woman off.

It had felt odd being driven home by a woman in Halloween costume. They'd got some strange looks on the way. But nothing was as disturbing as Isla's conviction that she'd seen Carl Jeffery. Could it really have been him? Had his sister won her appeal for his release? Had he come to England to torment her?

Jack was in the apartment-block car park. He'd attached jump leads to her car battery. She approached with a hesitant smile, unsure what response she'd get. To her relief, he looked up from under the bonnet and smiled.

'We'll have takeaway tonight. Is that OK?'

He smiled. 'Oh, OK. Just for a change then.'

'And we need milk.' She couldn't mention Carl Jeffery, could she? If she did, she'd have to tell him about the appeal, and he would be upset that she'd kept it from him. And worse, he might think she was crazy. She was beginning to think she was. 'What are you doing home?' she said, stepping closer and kissing his cheek.

'Half day, I booked it ages ago,' he said with a sniff. 'Matt's got a PlayStation VR and we were going to have a virtual afternoon, play a bit of *Rush of Blood*, but he bailed on me.'

'You lost me at "Matt's got",' she said, forcing a smile.

'I thought I told you I was off this afternoon,' he said, screwing up his nose.

She shook her head. He could have, and her mind hadn't absorbed it. She was becoming less focused lately.

'Anyway, I thought I'd try to fix your car, because I'm wonderful.'

'You are.' She laughed weakly. 'But you don't know the first thing about cars, do you?'

'Now, that's where you're wrong.' He rubbed the back of his hand across his forehead, covering it with oil. 'My dad taught me how to jumpstart a car when I was ten.' A fleeting smile crossed his face.

'OK, but don't you need two people?'

'Do you?' He looked puzzled, eyes back on the engine.

'Yes, one to turn over the engine and work the clutch and throttle, the other to push the car, especially if you're not on a hill, which you're not.' She smiled. 'My dad taught me when I was eight.' She touched his cheek. 'You have oil all over your face, by the way.'

'Does it make me look manly?'

'Almost,' she said, trying hard again to smile. She moved away, drifting towards the front entrance. 'I'll get changed and help.'

He grabbed her arm and she looked back.

'Are you OK?' he said, seeming to pick up on her tone. He knew her so well.

She shrugged. Should she tell him? 'I don't think I am, if I'm honest.' Her eyes filled with tears. 'I thought I saw Carl Jeffery.'

'What?' His expression darkened. 'Where?'

'At the supermarket.'

He worried his bottom lip. 'But there's no way, Isla . . .'

'I know,' she said. 'It just unnerved me, that's all.'

'Yeah, it would do.' He let go of her arm, wiped his hands on a rag, and slammed closed the car bonnet.

Once in their apartment he made some coffee, and they sat together on the sofa in silence. It was as if neither of them knew what to say.

'There's something I need to tell you,' Isla said eventually, placing the empty coffee cup on the table in front of them.

'That sounds a bit ominous,' Jack said, eyes narrowing.

'The thing is . . .' She paused. 'There was an appeal.'

'An appeal.'

'Carl Jeffery was granted an appeal. His sister campaigned for it.'

'What? When?'

'In September.'

'Oh God, how long have you known?'

'I received a letter. I could have gone to the appeal, but . . .'

'And you never thought to tell me?' He rose and began pacing the room.

101

'I thought you would worry.' It sounded pathetic.

'Yeah,' he said, voice rising, 'too right, I would have worried. Oh God, Isla. He didn't win, did he? Is that why you thought you saw him?'

'Calm down, please, Jack.'

'Jeez, could it be him?'

'I don't know.' Tears filled her eyes.

'You don't know?'

'I never found out. I couldn't face it. I didn't want him in my head, Jack, but it turns out he's there anyway.' Tears rolled down her face. 'What if he's out and in England?' Isla continued, her fears catching in her throat.

Jack dropped on the sofa next to her and rubbed a hand over his beard. 'They wouldn't let him out, Isla. There's too much evidence.'

'But they said there were sufficient grounds for an appeal.' She paused, her head in her hands. 'I hate that his sister did this. What kind of woman would think he's innocent? First the book, and now this.'

'We need to know if he's out, Isla,' Jack said. 'Although I'm sure he can't be. Everything was stacked against him from the start. You know that. Remember Bronwyn?'

She could suddenly see her friend's freckled face, the excitement in her eyes as she'd taken off for New Zealand, and more tears rolled down her cheeks. She knew what Jack meant. They had found Carl's DNA on Bronwyn's body, and that had gone a long way with the prosecution. But what if they'd argued again that he'd been in a relationship with Bronwyn, and that would account for the DNA?

'Sometimes I wish I'd killed him that day,' she whispered. 'Is that awful of me? To wish he was in hell, where he could never hurt me again.'

'Well, if I could get hold of that bastard, I'd rip his head off, and fuck the consequences,' Jack said, eyes flashing with anger, as he took hold of her hand and squeezed. 'God, I hate what he did to you.'

He let go of her hand and leant forward to pick up his laptop. 'We need to look him up, Isla. Find out the results of the appeal.' He locked her into a stare. 'We have to.'

She nodded.

He opened the laptop and began searching. Moments later, he'd found an article. 'Thank God,' he said, placing the laptop on her knees. 'Serial killer Carl Jeffery loses appeal,' he read from the screen.

There were photos of Carl, and a grainy black and white study of Darleen and Carl as children. Isla knew Darleen was much younger than Carl, but she was almost as tall, and far too skinny. They looked forlorn in tatty dungarees with no T-shirts. Sad creatures that made Isla sick with sorrow – if someone had only seen how dreadful their lives were, maybe Carl wouldn't have ended up a psychopath.

'I reached out to Isla Johnson,' Jack read from the screen. He looked at Isla. 'What's this about? It says here you rebuffed her. Blocked Darleen Jeffery's messages.'

Isla covered her face with her hands.

Jack continued to read from the screen. 'I only wanted to discuss the truth about what happened that night. I believe Isla Johnson is a liar, and I have no doubt, even now, that my brother is innocent.' He paused for a moment. 'She contacted you?' Jack said, bewildered.

Isla looked up and nodded. 'Just once.'

'And you didn't think to tell me? You kept that from me too?' His eyes darted her face, as though he was searching for the Isla he knew.

'I didn't want to worry you, that's all,' she said. 'I didn't tell anyone.'

'And that's meant to make me feel better?'

'Jack, please can we keep this to ourselves?' she said, closing her laptop. 'There's no point in worrying my parents or Roxanne.'

He rose and, without replying, headed into the kitchen. She could see him leaning against the worktop in the darkness, taking long gulps of lager. She wanted to go after him, try to explain again that if she'd told him, he would have worried, and it would have changed everything, but her brain was whizzing too fast. Who had been standing outside the supermarket and her apartment? Who had pressed her buzzer? Followed the taxi? Who put the butterfly on her doorstep and the flyer on her car? If Carl Jeffery was still locked away, who was it?

# Chapter 18

**Facebook:** *Much needed girlie night with the lovely Roxanne Furaha at La Fábrica.*

'Ooh, try the asparagus, Isla,' Roxanne said, chewing and pointing at the grilled vegetable and feta cheese wrapped in prosciutto. 'It's totally yummy.' Her brown eyes rolled in ecstasy, as she made orgasmic sounds that caused a laugh from two blokes at the next table.

'I want what she's having,' one of them said.

La Fábrica, a recently opened tapas bar, had a modern, trendy feel, with live music and great food. Isla and Roxanne had been sitting by the window for about an hour, their table heaving with half-eaten bowls of tapas.

'I love these little pork and apple thingies,' Isla said, tucking in. 'They're to die for.'

'God, I'm stuffed,' Roxanne said, finally leaning back in her chair and rubbing her slender stomach. She stared at Isla. 'So you're really, really OK?'

Isla had told her about what happened at the supermarket, in case someone had seen her and mentioned it, but now she wanted to wipe the subject away, like an annoying smudge on a worktop. 'I'm fine,' she said. 'Honestly. I'm totally, totally OK.' She took a gulp of her lemonade, wondering what her friend would think if she knew Isla had kept the appeal from her, and a surge of guilt ran through her.

Roxanne slipped off her copper-coloured silk jacket and hung it on the back of the chair. She looked amazing: her black hair spiralling to her shoulders, her narrow-legged jeans and tight white T-shirt hugging her lanky figure. Her heels were like stilts. It was a look Isla wouldn't even attempt to pull off.

'It couldn't have been him. You know that, right?'

'Yep. I just feel a bit of a numpty wailing like a fool in front of all those customers at the supermarket. They must have thought I was crazy.'

'Nobody would ever think that.'

But Isla wondered if her friend thought exactly that. After all, she'd been there. Seen her at her worst. The way she'd refused to go out. Her bursts of anger. She needed to put Roxanne's mind at rest, before she thought she was taking a step backwards. She took a deep breath. 'I do know it must have been some random person at the supermarket dressed like Carl Jeffery,' she began, trying not to let it show how much she was struggling. 'I mean, the bastard isn't the only person to wear a beanie and scarf.'

'Exactly.'

'And he's in prison,' Isla went on, wishing there was alcohol in her glass, and she hadn't opted to drive.

'Where he belongs,' Roxanne said, reaching over and touching her friend's hand.

Isla shuddered, needing to change the subject. Trying to smile through the tension building in her neck and shoulders was impossible.

'Thank you,' she said. 'You know, for caring, and for being the best friend anyone could wish for – for never letting me down.' Tears gathered close to the surface.

'I'll always be here for you, Isla,' Roxanne said. 'No matter what – you know that.'

'Right, subject change, methinks,' Isla said, taking another deep breath to ward off tears. 'So how's work?'

'Yeah, pretty good.' Roxanne picked up a green olive and popped it into her mouth. After leaving university, Roxanne had flitted from job to job, and later spent time in Africa doing voluntary work. Recently, she'd taken a job in marketing, although it didn't stop her devoting every spare moment to working with charities, and a stream of good causes. 'A new intern started this week who's rather cute. Only eighteen though, and even I draw the line at cradle-snatching.' She laughed. 'Although . . .'

'Roxanne, you're a bad, bad lady.'

'I know. I can't help it.' She giggled.

'Maybe you'll meet a nice bloke at my sister's fortieth.'

'I don't want a nice bloke, Isla,' she said, licking her fingers and winking at the man at the next table. 'You know that. I like things the way they are.'

'But you could be missing out—'

'Enough!' Roxanne put up her palm. 'Talk to the hand . . .'

Isla laughed, picked up a spicy corn kernel, and nibbled on it.

'Ooh,' Roxanne blurted. 'You haven't told me how the reunion went. Did you meet up with Trevor Cooper?'

Isla shook her head, thoughts of his last message, and the way she'd blocked him on Facebook, filling her head. 'He didn't turn up,' she said, deciding not to tell Roxanne about the message. She would only say she was a fool for going near him. 'In fact, only Sara Pembroke came.'

'I saw her picture on your Facebook. She looked amazing.'

'I know. Stunning.'

'So, nobody turned up but her?'

Isla shook her head.

'That's well weird.'

'Uh-huh, little bit. Still it's probably for the best. I shouldn't have gone in the first place.'

'Did say.' Roxanne pulled a smug face.

'Yeah, I know.' Isla paused, not wanting to talk about it any more. The subjects she actually wanted to chat about were dwindling. 'And talking of Millie's fortieth . . .' she said.

'Were we?'

'Have you any idea where I can get a Minion cake by Saturday? Apparently I agreed to get one a while back. I can't remember saying I would, but I guess I must have. Millie says she has the text to prove it, and she's not afraid to use it.' A grin stretched across her face. 'Plus Jack's already got his Spider-Man costume,' she said, hoping he would have forgiven her by then. He'd seemed so distant that morning. 'And I haven't even thought about what I'm going to wear.'

'Well, there's a fancy-dress place in Hitchin. Maybe try there. And I'm pretty sure I've seen Minion cakes in almost every supermarket I've been in.'

'Cool,' she said. 'Sorted.'

'Dessert?' Roxanne picked up the menu.

'Silly question,' Isla said with a laugh.

Later, outside in the car park, they hugged goodbye. 'See you Saturday,' Roxanne said, as they got into their cars. Isla waved from the driving seat, as her friend pulled away, before turning the key in the ignition. The engine didn't even attempt to whirr.

'Christ,' she muttered. They'd managed to jumpstart her car the day before, and it was working fine earlier.

She pulled her phone from her bag. There was no signal, so she climbed out of her car. A light breeze tickled her cheek, and there was a mizzling rain in the air. She glanced about her, suddenly aware how lonely the car park was, and took a few steps before getting a signal. She knew Jack well enough to know that even though things were a bit rocky between them, he would be there for her.

'Hey, Jack,' she said when he answered, raising her voice to make herself heard, as the line was poor. 'You'll never guess: my bloody battery has died again.' The thought of walking the short route home across the park made her uneasy, and the long way would take over an hour. She hadn't even brought an umbrella with her.

'Where are you?' He sounded a bit off, and she hated the way that made her feel.

'La Fábrica, standing in the car park.' She moved from foot to foot, feeling chilly and damp, as she looked around her once more. 'Listen, forget it, don't worry. I'm fine. I'll call a taxi,' she continued, her anxiety rising. 'I shouldn't have called you. I'm a big girl now.'

'No, it's fine. I'm on my way. I was in the shower. Just need to get dressed. Go back inside, until I get there.'

'OK. If you're sure. Thanks. I really appreciate it – see you soon.' She ended the call and went back inside.

It was even more crowded than earlier, as a new wave of customers had arrived, and a bloke with a guitar was doing his best Ed Sheeran impression.

She'd been standing by the door for several minutes, when a waitress approached. 'Are you Isla?' she said, blowing her fringe from her forehead, flustered.

Isla nodded.

'There's been a message to say—' she looked down at a Post-it in her hand '—you're not to wait for Jack. He'll walk to meet you the park way. Does that make sense?'

'I think so.' Maybe jumpstarting her car had flattened Jack's battery too. The woman disappeared into the busy restaurant, and Isla looked down at her phone. There was no signal.

She left the bar, and walked in the direction of home, trying not to look over her shoulder at the quiet darkness swallowing her. The rain had eased off, and she'd been walking for five minutes, when she reached the park entrance. It was quiet, and she stepped from foot to foot, feeling uneasy as she waited for Jack. She pulled out her phone and tried to call him, but it went to voicemail.

The houses close by were in darkness, and she suddenly felt sure someone was standing in the shadows. Without a second thought, she set out at speed across the park, certain she would bump into Jack coming in the other direction.

In truth, she hadn't realised how thick with darkness the park would be. Towering trees blocked what little light there was, throwing shadows across the path. A few more steps and she would be able to see the road that ran by her apartment in the distance, and the lights from the steady flow of traffic would be sure to settle her anxiety.

She pulled out her phone again, and flicked on the torch, casting a beam of light that picked out the deserted playground. She'd played in the park as a child, and could almost hear her childhood self squealing, 'Higher, higher,' as Millie pushed her on the swing. Now the swing, a trendy, brightly coloured netted effort that could hold more than one child, creaked, swinging in the breeze.

Suddenly her mobile rang, making her jump. It was Jack.

'Isla, where are you?' he said, as she answered.

'I'm walking home, like you said. Almost there.' Her tone was brighter than she felt.

'Why? I'm in the car park standing by your car.'

'What? But you said to walk home.' She looked around her at the silent, lonely park, and picked up speed.

'Why would I say that?' He sounded confused. 'What's going on? Where are you?'

'I told you, I'm almost home.'

A noise behind her, and the sudden sound of footsteps pierced her ears. Was someone following her? She glanced over her shoulder. The darkness was total, impossible to see. 'Oh God, Jack, I think someone's behind me,' she said into the phone, but the signal had died.

Isla took off like a sprinting athlete, thanking her sensible side for wearing flats. She didn't look back, and was out of breath by the time she got to the main road. She'd never been so relieved to see the flow of noisy traffic.

At the apartment block, her hand shook as she keyed in the code.

She opened the door and finally dared to look behind her at the huge expanse of park. A young couple walked along the road arm in arm. But there was nobody else about. Had she imagined the footsteps?

Isla was sitting on the sofa trying to gain control, when Jack's key turned in the door. She jumped to her feet, blinking away tears. As soon as he appeared, a look of confusion on his face, she raced into his arms.

'What's going on?' he said, holding her close. The argument of the night before seemed to be forgotten.

'I don't know,' she said into his shoulder. 'The waitress at the tapas bar said you'd called. That your car wouldn't start, and I should walk home.'

'But I didn't call, Isla.'

'I don't understand.' Her brain felt as though it was closing down.

'Let's go back,' he said. 'We can talk to the waitress and jumpstart your car.'

'No!' She paused. 'Sorry,' she said, quieter. 'I really want to stay here.' She tugged from Jack's arms and moved towards the window. She looked out at the park. She'd loved it there as a child, but now it looked almost sinister.

'I had a feeling someone was watching me,' she said quietly. 'I heard footsteps and ran.' She closed the curtains across the window, her heart thumping. 'It was horrible, Jack. I haven't felt like this in years. What if we're wrong and Carl Jeffery is free? Or he's somehow managed to escape?'

'Isla, he's locked away.'

She turned. 'OK. Fine. But what if he's got someone on the outside trying to scare me, maybe even planning to kill me? Like that series you watch about serial killers with Kevin Bacon.'

Jack's eyes widened. 'You think Carl Jeffery has disciples on the outside willing to murder for him?' He approached and touched her arm. 'Isla, this is silly.'

She flinched and moved away. 'Why? Why is it silly?'

'Because that's fiction, Isla, and this is real life.'

'It's not fiction, Jack. I read about it on a website.' She was talking too fast, her cheeks wet with tears. 'People like him have groupies.'

'Please stop, Isla. You sound . . .'

'Crazy?'

'No, but you're winding yourself up. It was probably just a misunderstanding at the restaurant, that's all. You need to put Carl Jeffery out of your head, or . . .'

'I know.' She said softer now. 'I know. Yes. Ignore me. I'm fine, honestly.'

But she knew she was far from it.

# Chapter 19

**Wednesday, 2 November**

'Shall we ask at the bar first, or jumpstart your car?' Jack said, dropping down gears as they arrived at La Fábrica. It was just after seven, and the car park was already rammed.

Isla was relieved that any talk of the wedding, and her keeping things from him, had disappeared after the shock of the night before, and Jack seemed focused on supporting her.

'Let's try to find the waitress,' she said, unclipping her seatbelt. 'Get it over with.'

'I'm sure it's some kind of misunderstanding,' Jack said, getting out of the car.

'Yes, I'm sure you're right. I just need to be sure, that's all.'

Even though Jack had found the article, Isla still couldn't get Carl Jeffery out of her head. Someone *had* called the restaurant and asked the staff to give her a message. She needed to know who it was. Felt her sanity depended on what the person had said. What they sounded like.

The restaurant was heaving, and a waiter in black trousers and a crisp white shirt stood near the entrance, a book open on a stand in front of him.

'Table for two?' he asked with a smile, as they approached.

Jack shook his head. 'No thanks, mate. We're looking for one of your waitresses. She was here last night, and we'd like to talk to her.'

'We have a lot of staff,' the waiter said, as Isla scanned the area, searching for the woman who'd spoken to her the night before. 'Could you be more specific?'

'She gave me a message last night,' she said. 'Told me my boyfriend had called saying I should walk home.' Her eyes flicked from Jack to the waiter. She knew she wasn't explaining herself very well.

'OK.' The waiter's eyebrows furrowed.

'It's important we speak to her,' she went on, running her finger over the band on her wrist. 'It was a lie, you see.' She hadn't really noticed it last night, but now the place felt far too crowded. And although the food tasted good when she was with Roxanne, now the spicy smells made her queasy.

'O-K,' the waiter repeated, but with more emphasis. He tilted his head, and screwed up his face. 'Sorry, I confess, I'm a tad confused.'

'One of the waitresses told me to go home last night,' Isla said, the noise making her head throb. 'But I should have waited for Jack, because it couldn't have been him. Do you see? Because Jack hadn't called. His car was OK.' She was talking way too fast, her phrasing clipped. 'And when I walked home, someone followed me. Or I think they did.'

'The bottom line is,' Jack cut in, taking Isla's hand and squeezing, 'I didn't call the restaurant. We think someone called here pretending to me. We just need to speak—'

A deliberate cough came from behind them, and Isla and Jack turned to see a middle-aged couple, tight-lipped with impatience.

'I won't keep you a moment, sir,' the waiter said, peering round Jack and Isla.

'We've booked a table,' the man said. 'We'd like to be seated, please.'

'I'll be with you shortly.' The waiter threw them a forced smile and sucked in a sigh. He glanced over his shoulder into the busy restaurant, and then back at Isla and Jack. 'We've got about a dozen

114

staff on tonight, but they're pretty much a different bunch than last night, I'm afraid. What did this phantom waitress look like?'

Isla looked at Jack. Was the waiter being sarcastic? Did he think she was crazy? 'About forty, I think,' she said, realising she could barely bring the woman to mind.

'Hair colour?'

'Mmm . . .' She touched her own hair. 'I'm not sure, brownish.'

'Maybe we should go somewhere else,' the man behind said, sounding irritated.

'Excuse me,' the waiter said to Isla, as he grabbed two oversized menus. He beckoned the couple forward and escorted them into the restaurant.

'This is a waste of time, Jack,' Isla said, as the waiter disappeared. 'I'm not even sure I'd know her if I saw her.' She paused. 'And what can she really tell us? In fact, maybe I imagined someone behind me in the park. Or maybe it was someone innocently walking their dog, or something.' Tears were close to the surface.

He wrapped his arm around her shoulders. It was as though he didn't know what to say.

Isla gave the restaurant one last sweep with her eyes. It didn't matter that Jack had found the article saying Carl Jeffery was still locked up. He was still haunting her – just as he had six years ago. 'Let's get my car sorted,' she said. 'I want to go home.'

Once they were on the road, she followed in the wake of Jack's taillights, eyes darting from the pavements either side of her – imagining Carl there, lurking behind every tree and in every shadow – and back to the small red light on the dashboard that told her all the doors were firmly locked. He couldn't get in. She was safe – for now.

### Six years ago

Isla had been working in the bar the day she heard Bronwyn was dead. She hadn't known it was her feisty friend. Not then. Not at that moment when the news grabbed her attention.

It had been a long day. Rowdy between seven and nine, but now it had quietened down, and the TV above the bar boomed out over the low muffled chatter of stalwart punters. Isla had been talking for the last ten minutes with a relatively sober Ernie, sipping a glass of wine he'd bought her, when news of the death was broadcast.

Isla's skin prickled at its close proximity. Less than a mile from the hostel.

'What's a young sheila want to go and top herself for?' Ernie said, banging down an empty glass. 'Stick another schooner in there, Isla, would ya, love?' He sighed. 'Life's so fucked up, and my missus wonders why I drink.'

Robotically, Isla filled his glass and handed it over, her eyes fixed on the screen.

'The young woman was found hanging from a tree, like an ancient execution,' the newsreader, a woman in her thirties, was saying. She was at the scene, holding a mic, dense forest all around her. 'Although police say there are no suspicious circumstances at this point.' It was clear the news channel thought otherwise.

Isla grabbed the remote control. 'Let's put something more cheerful on, shall we?' she said, flicking through the channels, and landing on a repeat of *Neighbours*. 'That's better,' she said, but she couldn't get the thought of the woman out of her head. What would drive someone to take their own life? Didn't she have anyone to turn to? A friend? Family? She brushed away a tear. She couldn't begin to imagine being so desperate. But then her life was pretty good. She was one of the lucky ones.

It was Carl who later told Isla it was Bronwyn. The police had contacted him. His details were in her backpack.

'I should have known,' he said, through tears, as they sat in the corner of the bar. 'Abused by her father, she told me. Never really came to terms with it. The signs were there. Just wish I hadn't missed it.' He shook his head, tears filling his eyes. Seeming different. Genuine. Gone were the charms, the flirting. It seemed the shock of Bronwyn's death had stripped away the fake layer.

And Isla cried too, sobbed until her stomach hurt, before covering her mouth with her hand, attempting to quieten her emotions. 'I didn't know,' she said, the helplessness of being that friend who Bronwyn had never turned to biting into her.

'We were never serious,' Carl said after a while. 'But close, if you know what I mean – had fun. I had no idea she was so desperate.' A tear rolled down his face, out of place on his tanned cheek. 'No idea at all.'

She took his hand and squeezed, her fingers damp from dashing away her own tears.

'Don't beat yourself up, Carl,' she said, as another heavy tear dripped off her chin. 'Neither of us could have known.'

The following day Isla had headed into the woodland behind the hostel, the sun hot on her back. It was as she was taking a photograph of a Blue Triangle butterfly that she spotted Carl in the distance. He was taking a photograph too.

'Hey,' she called, but he didn't seem to hear her. So she made her way towards him, her footfalls crunching on the dry fauna. 'Hey,' she said again as she approached, and he looked up.

'Isla,' he said, with a smile that brightened his eyes. 'It's great to see you. Listen, I'm sorry about last night. My emotions were all over the place. I still can't . . .'

'No, nor me,' she said, biting back her own emotions. She nodded towards his camera. 'I didn't know you were into photography.'

'Yeah, have been for years. I find it therapeutic.'

'Me too,' she said, her eyes wide, pleased to find someone else who shared her passion. She looked over her shoulder. 'I was taking a few photos of butterflies.'

He smiled. 'You like butterflies, Isla?'

'Love them.' She nodded. 'There's just something amazing about them, don't you think? They're like fairies.'

'Well, I'd never seen them like that, but OK.' He laughed. 'I tend to think of the butterfly effect when I see one.'

'The smallest step can change everything.'

'Yeah, something like that.' He smiled. 'I read that the tiny flutter of a butterfly's wing can cause pandemonium on the other side of the world.' He paused, looking almost shy. 'Listen, I don't suppose you fancy a drink tonight? Ignore me if you think my timing is out.'

She wasn't sure. Bronwyn's death was so fresh in her mind. But wouldn't she want them both to be happy? To find comfort in each other? After all she had been heading off to New Zealand. It was over between them. *The smallest step could change everything.*

'No worries,' he said, seeming to pick up on her delay. He aimed his camera at a Sacred Ibis.

'I'd like that,' she said.

He turned and met her eye. 'Yeah? That's great. I'll pick you up at seven, Butterfly Girl.'

# Chapter 20

www.travellinggirlblog.com
*0 followers*
*Wednesday, 2 November, 11.55 p.m.*

Somebody pretended to be Jack last night. I know they did. I can barely type these words, as my fingers are shaking so much. Tears blur my vision, and splash the keyboard, like tiny pools of sadness, magnifying the letters.

I don't know what to do. I feel as though I'm losing my mind. I need Andy more than ever now. If he loved me, he'd be here, wouldn't he?

He still texts – sometimes. Says he'll see me in Sweden. But the messages are becoming less frequent. I feel so let down. In fact, I wonder sometimes what the point of it all is.

*Comments* *disabled.*

# Chapter 21

'Ahhh, for Christ's sake, go away.'

Jack's cry woke Isla from a nightmare where she was being chased by a superhero with a machete, his Spider-Man ringtone piercing the darkness of the early morning. She turned to see him staring into the brightness of his phone screen, hair ruffled.

'Jeez, Jack, who the hell is it?' she said, rubbing her eyes with her fingertips.

He pulled back the duvet and sat up, twisting his legs round so they dangled off the bed. 'Hello,' he said, pressing the phone to his ear, as he rose and left the bedroom.

He returned five minutes later. 'I've got to go down to Dorset,' he said, face flushed, eyes hard to read. He didn't give her time to respond, hurrying into the bathroom without looking back.

Once he'd showered, he returned. Shoving on his black jeans, and a round-neck jumper.

'You're going now?' she asked, dragging herself up to a sitting position, and cradling her knees.

'My mother's had another heart attack,' he said. 'She's back in hospital.'

120

'Oh God. Is she OK?'

He shrugged. 'I don't know.' He turned to look at her. 'Are you going to be OK? I won't go if you need me, you know that.'

'I'll be fine, honestly. I've got a feature due in tomorrow. What I need is to get my head down, and fingers on keyboard.'

She watched as he packed. 'I hope to be back for Millie's party,' he said, zipping his holdall. 'Hopefully before that.'

After kissing her gently on the lips and touching her cheek, he headed for the door, glancing back once as he left the room.

From the window, Isla watched him drive away, and an annoying snag of worry at being alone niggled at her, followed by a surge of anger that she was letting the fear in. Even though she knew Carl Jeffery was locked away, she felt unsettled. Unleashed horrors of her past danced a manic dance in her head. But she was stronger than this, surely. Capable. She would lose herself in her book and finish her feature. She hadn't worked so hard to mend herself, only to fall apart.

\* \* \*

Isla spent the afternoon in Hitchin choosing a costume for Millie's party. It was a choice between Daffy Duck or Marilyn Monroe. She chose the latter. The blonde wig was a bit straw-like, but she felt sure she could do something clever with her own hair on Saturday.

Later, she picked out a gift for Millie – an ornament that depicted sisters holding each other close that she knew her sister would love – and she grabbed a Minion cake from the supermarket.

It was around seven, after she'd microwaved a ready meal and pushed it around her plate, barely eating any of it, that she began tapping away on her laptop, a glass of wine on the table in front of her. She needed to finish the article she'd been working on – a piece about tiny houses. She'd been gathering photos and information for a while now on houses she'd seen in Islington and Wales, another on the Rue du Chateau in Paris, and now the Little House in Toronto she'd seen so recently – a tiny white house built in 1912, the smallest in that area. How strange it must be to live somewhere so small. 'Would you feel trapped?' she typed. 'Or would the size make you feel safe?'

Perfect memories of Canada bashed against all that had gone wrong since her return, and her hands stiffened on her keyboard, as though she had arthritis. She had to beat this. She had to.

She put down her laptop and picked up her wine. A long gulp went some way to soothing her senses, and Luna's purr, from where she was sprawled near the radiator, helped too. She closed her eyes, but moments later the sound of her phone vibrating across the coffee table prevented her from drifting into a doze.

It would be Jack, letting her know he'd arrived safely. But, as she leant over and picked up her phone, she saw that it was from Trevor.

*Isla. I know we're not friends on Facebook any more – but that's OK, I'm a bit of a dinosaur in that department anyway. I just wanted to say sorry for my last message. I'd had a bottle of wine, and you know how it is – I just spilled it all out. And I'm also sorry I didn't turn up at the reunion. I guess the nerves got the better of me. I'm trying to organise another, if you fancy it. Text back soon, and we'll sort something out. Trevor X*

She'd forgotten he had her mobile number. She should have blocked that too. She pressed reply.

*Hi, Trevor, I'm afraid I won't be able to come to another reunion. And please don't contact me again. I'm in a relationship.*

After a few seconds, guilt took hold, so she added – *I hope you understand. Isla*

Within moments her phone pinged again.

*You really think you're something special, don't you?*

Heart racing, she bit down hard on her lip, looking at her phone screen. Hand shaking, she typed a final message.

> *I don't know why you're being like this, Trevor. I never meant to hurt you. You have to understand I'm deeply in love with someone else.*

Once the message had left her inbox, she took several long gulps of wine, before blocking him from her contacts.

She got up Jack's number. Should she call him? No, it wouldn't be fair. He was with his mother. She had to deal with this herself.

It was much later that she closed her laptop, her eyes growing heavy and sore from constantly looking at the screen. She hadn't noticed the quiet stillness of the apartment while she'd been working, but now it was pawing at her, reminding her Jack wasn't there. That she was alone.

She curled up on the sofa, resting her head on a cushion, and dragged the throw over her. She knew she should get up and go to bed, but the trip to the bedroom seemed a long way – too hard somehow. She would sleep where she was.

It was gone 2 a.m. when she woke with a start. Something had crashed to the floor in the kitchen, but now all was quiet. She sat upright, grabbed her phone, and pulled the throw round her. 'Luna?' she called into the darkness.

Within seconds the cat leapt onto the back of the sofa.

'Jesus, cat,' she cried, reaching for the band on her wrist, noticing Luna's feline face was covered in the cream she'd left on the worktop earlier. 'You'll be the death of me.'

### Friday, 4 November

'Yay, you're back,' Isla said, looking up from her laptop as Jack walked through the door with his holdall. It was gone eight, and he looked so tired. 'How was your mum?'

123

He flopped down onto the sofa next to her, and she felt the touch of his lips. 'She's not great, but stable.' He paused. 'She's given me my dad's address. Apparently she's had it all these years.'

'What? So you could have been in contact with him all this time?'

'Pretty much.' He bent to pull off his trainers. 'She had an epiphany, apparently.' He sounded flippant. 'Suddenly realised I should be in touch with my father. She never did tell him where we'd moved to, when he walked out.'

'Well, at least you know where he is now.' She rested her hand on his arm. 'Will you get in touch with him?'

He nodded. 'I called him on the way home.'

'And?' She felt excited for him.

'To be honest, it was a bit stiff and awkward, but he asked me to come down to see him next Friday after work.'

'When I'm away?'

'Yeah, he lives on the east coast.'

'The east coast is pretty big.'

He smiled. 'Sheringham.' His eyes met hers. 'I can't wait for him to meet you. I know he'll love you.' He touched her cheek. 'You know I'd do anything for you, Isla, don't you?'

'Blimey, Jack, what's brought this on?'

'Oh, I don't know.' He pulled her to him. 'I suppose I look at the mess my parents made of everything, and feel so lucky I met you.'

# Chapter 22

*Saturday, 5 November*

**WhatsApp:** *HAPPY, HAPPY 40TH BIRTHDAY, MILLIE. YOU'RE THE BEST SISTER EVER! LOVE YOU XXX*

**Facebook:** *Heading to my sister Millie Bailey's 40th at Crabthorn Community Centre, Letchworth Garden City with Jack Green. That's me without the mask trying Marilyn Monroe on for size! Feeling excited.*

**Email:**
From: ISLA Johnson islajjohnson@windlemail.com
To: SARA Pembroke saraapembroke@windlemail.com

*Hi Sara,*
*So sorry for taking so long to reply. It was lovely to meet up with you. Yes, a shame nobody else turned up to the reunion, but, like you say, their loss.*
*Anyway, I may not be in touch for a while as I take off for Abisko on Wednesday, but will email you after that. Isla x*

*       *       *

Isla pummelled her temples, the thrump, thrump, thrump of the disco's bass making her head pound – not helped by a same-day hangover gathering momentum. She regretted the wine she'd already knocked back since arriving at Millie's party three hours ago.

But she'd needed Dutch courage. She didn't like parties at the best of times. But then she couldn't have coped with Millie's sad face if she'd backed out.

She hadn't even liked parties at university, when Roxanne used to drag her along. Roxanne had been different to Isla, dabbling in anything that would make her high, whereas Isla wouldn't touch drugs, and often ended up getting her friend out of scrapes.

'Come on, Isla. Dance with me.' It was Millie dressed as a rag doll, with red circles on her cheeks, and a blonde wig woven into plaits and tied with pink ribbons. She placed her hands on her curvy hips and wiggled.

'Where's Julian?' Isla asked, eyes searching the room for her brother-in-law. 'Can't you dance with him?'

'Julian can't dance,' she said with a giggle. 'Anyway I have no idea where he is, and I don't care.' There was a hint of rebel in her voice. 'I want to dance with you, my lovely sister.' She grabbed Isla's hand and dragged her from the corner of the hall, where she'd been hiding for the last hour, taking photographs she would upload onto Facebook later. In fact, she'd caught a great study of Jack and Roxanne messing around on the dance floor. She hadn't realised Jack had so many dance moves.

'Do I have to?' Isla protested, sticking out her bottom lip. But Millie continued to pull her towards the disco lights.

'Yes you do. Please. It's my birthday.'

Once there, Millie began spinning on the spot and singing along to 'Sex on Fire', arms stretched above her head as she danced in front of pulsating lights. Roxanne was gyrating like a pole dancer without a pole, wearing a clinging leopard-skin jumpsuit with a long tail attached, and a headband with orange ears, seeming blissfully unaware of the line of men at the bar ogling her.

Millie grabbed Isla's hand, and swung her back and forth. But Isla had always danced like a toddler, bouncing on the spot, fists clenched – her body barely moving. Not a dance style that went with the Marilyn-Monroe-in-her-famous-white-dress look she was trying to pull off.

A group of Millie's friends pulled her away from Isla, and into their huddle, and a muscular black man approached Roxanne and took hold of her waist with a playful jerk, as though they were about to tango. She put up no resistance, a seductive smile crossing her lips, as she looped her arm around his neck.

Surely Isla could sneak back into the corner, unnoticed. She was about to head away, when a short woman in her seventies, dressed as Cher, tried to make herself heard above the music. 'Are you Isla?' she yelled.

Isla nodded.

'Spider-Man is looking for you outside.' She nodded towards the exit door, which was constantly being opened and closed, as people went outside for a smoke, or a breath of air.

'Oh, OK, thanks,' Isla said. 'Where is he?'

But a Colin Baker-era Dr Who had grabbed the Cher almost-lookalike, and she was now being whipped up into a 'Dancing Queen' frenzy. In fact, the dance floor had filled up, lights pounding the darkness. Isla searched the throng of dancers, but she'd lost sight of her sister and Roxanne, and she couldn't see Jack.

She moved away from the crazy dance routines and pushed open the hall doors. The freezing air hit her like a slap, and goose pimples rose on her arms. She hadn't realised the temperature had dropped so low. How cold it was.

'Jack,' she called, stepping outside, searching the dark car park.

The sky burst with bright lights, and the bangs of rockets exploding overhead made her jump. She'd forgotten it was fireworks night.

A snake of smoke drifted on the air, and tobacco tingled her nostrils. She moved away from the entrance and turned a corner to see a Pokémon, a Power Ranger and someone dressed in pyjamas chatting. The Power Ranger was tapping his foot to the music that floated from the hall through an open window.

There was no sign of Jack.

'Have you seen Spider-Man?' she asked, knowing she sounded a bit silly, and they all turned to look at her.

'Is it a bird? Is it a plane?' Pyjama-man said with a slur, blowing smoke towards Isla, making her eyes sting.

'That's Superman,' she said, mildly irritated.

Pokémon dragged hard on his cigarette. 'Yeah, he was here a while ago. Went back inside, I think,' he said with a sniff.

She glanced through the window to see Dr Who twirl Cher like a spinning top, causing her to stumble and fall flat on her face. Dr Who pulled her to her feet and handed her a coat.

'OK, thanks,' Isla said, eyes back on the smoking trio. She turned to go inside.

'Hang on, Marilyn,' the rotund Power Ranger said, throwing down his cigarette and extinguishing it with the heel of his boot. 'Isn't that him?'

She turned and looked to where he was pointing. Someone dressed as Spider-Man stood in the darkness on the far side of the sprawling car park, beckoning her.

'Jack?' she called, stepping away from the gathered smokers, and squinting. 'Jack? What are you doing over there?'

The figure gestured again for her to come over, and she walked towards him. But, as she got closer, struggling to walk on heels she wasn't used to, he swung around and took off into a dark alley.

'Jack, where are you going?' she said, picking up speed.

She reached the entrance to the alleyway. It was long and dark. Even the light from the hall didn't illuminate it. She screwed up her eyes, peering so she could just about make out a figure in the distance standing still. 'Jack? What's going on?' she called, stepping into the darkness, fumbling with her phone, trying to turn on the torch as she walked.

Someone came up behind her and grabbed her arm. 'Isla?'

128

She turned and shone her torch into Jack's face.

'Jesus!' she cried, falling into his arms. He wasn't wearing his mask, and he smelt vaguely of cigarettes. 'Oh God, I don't understand. I thought . . .' Her throat closed. None of it made any sense. 'I thought it was you,' she stuttered.

'Who?'

'Someone dressed as Spider-Man called me over here. He disappeared into the alley.' She trembled, eyes darting everywhere.

Jack released her and flew off, heading towards where she was pointing. She stood alone in the darkness, heart pounding, shivering.

Within minutes he reappeared, breathless and holding his stomach as though he had a stitch.

'Did you see him?' she asked.

He shook his head, puffing, bent double.

'You do believe I saw someone, don't you, Jack?'

'Of course, why wouldn't I?' he said. 'Hang on . . . let me get my breath back.'

'You don't believe me.' She stared into his face. 'I can see it in your eyes. You don't believe me.'

'What? Isla, don't be daft. Why wouldn't I believe you?' He took her in his arms once more, pulling her close, and she rested her head on his chest.

'What if Carl Jeffery *is* here messing with my head?' she stuttered, her eyes stinging with tears. She knew she sounded ridiculous.

'Isla, it can't be him,' he said, his voice concerned.

'But . . .'

'Isla, it must have been someone dressed like me. It's a pretty common fancy-dress costume.'

'Yes . . .OK . . .maybe.' Her thoughts skittered. Had she seen another Spider-Man at the party? But even if she had she would have thought it was Jack, wouldn't she? 'But he beckoned me over.'

'Are you sure? It's really dark out here.' He looked towards the night sky, lit up with more fireworks. 'I'm not saying you didn't see someone, Isla. Really, I'm not. But maybe whoever it was, was calling over someone else.'

But she was certain he hadn't been. As memories of Carl Jeffery flooded back, she knew she needed Jack to take her seriously. She felt sick, limbs trembling, as she glanced across to the smoking area. There was nobody there. Pokémon, the Power Ranger and Pyjama-man were getting into a yellow Volkswagen Beetle on the far side of the car park.

'They saw him,' she cried, pointing towards them. 'I need to speak to them.'

She pulled away from Jack and went to run, but he grabbed her hand. 'I believe you, Isla. Really I do.'

'Yes, but they saw him beckon me. I need them to tell you that.' She was talking way too fast. 'Please, Jack.'

He released her hand, and she ran towards the car, tripping on her heels. But the engine of the VW was running. They were about to leave.

'Wait,' she cried, tripping and crashing to the ground, the coarse gravel of the car park stinging her hands and making them bleed. 'Please wait,' she whimpered.

'Isla!' It was Roxanne with the man she'd been dancing with. She raced over and crouched down beside Isla. 'God, lovely. Are you OK?'

Isla sat up, gasping, hands bleeding, and tears sprang from her eyes and rolled down her face. She hooked her arms around her knees and rocked. She could hear Jack's footsteps and glanced back to see his worried face as he approached. The VW sped away, passengers and driver oblivious.

Jack bent down next to Roxanne. 'Oh God,' he said, pulling Isla into his arms, and she buried her wet face in his shoulder.

'Isla, whatever's wrong?' Roxanne said. 'What's happened?'

'Someone tried to lure me away,' Isla cried, noticing her tights were laddered and bloody from a surface wound. 'My dress is ripped,' she said in a small voice, pushing her finger through a hole in the fabric. A tear dripped off the end of her chin, and her nose streamed.

'Who, Isla?' Roxanne said, brown eyes wide as she took hold of Isla's hand. 'Who tried to lure you away?'

But Isla was no longer sure. Had someone really been there in the darkness? Had someone really beckoned her over? Maybe it *was* just another guest at the party.

'I'm OK,' Isla said, dashing her tears away with the back of her hand, as Jack pulled her to her feet, and wrapped her in the comfort of his arms once more.

They headed back to the party, Isla leaning her head on Jack's shoulder. As she limped beside him, she said, 'By the way, what did you want?'

'Sorry?'

'You asked Cher to come and get me.'

'Do you know how weird that sounds?' He tried for a smile. It was just Jack doing his best to make things right.

'But what did you want?' she persisted.

'I'm off, Isla,' Roxanne called from where she was getting into a car with the man she'd been dancing with. Isla turned to see her blowing kisses. 'I'll call you before you leave for Sweden, yeah? Are you sure you're OK?'

'I think so,' Isla called back.

As she watched Roxanne go, Jack took her hand. She flinched – it was sore – but she didn't pull away.

'So, Cher?' she said seriously, turning to look into his eyes.

He shook his head. 'I didn't talk to any Cher, Isla.'

Isla gulped, her eyes darting around the car park once more. Was this the way whoever it was worked? Was he passing on messages, pretending to be Jack, in an attempt to lure her away? Or was she simply losing it?

'But I'll tell you what I did see,' Jack went on. 'At the end of the alleyway, a sports car was pulling out of the street at speed.'

# Chapter 23

www.travellinggirlblog.com
*0 followers*
*Saturday, 5 November, 11.55 p.m.*

Someone was out there in the darkness. I can't bear how helpless that makes me feel. How afraid I am. Thoughts of him trip over themselves inside my head – thoughts that Carl Jeffery is back to finish what he started.

A scream explodes inside my head. How the hell am I meant to sleep?

Am I *really* losing my mind? Has my sanity packed a case and left? My eyes sting with tears, but I cling to the fact I've heard from Andy. I found the text when I got home from Millie's party. He's going to meet me in Abisko on Friday. He's promised he'll be there.

I pray he will be. I need him more than ever now.

*Comments* *disabled.*

# Chapter 24

Isla spent the next two days in bed, with Luna curled asleep on the pillow next to her.

Jack had tried to coax her out of bed on Sunday, his ploys ranging from sympathy to making jokes. 'You know I'd do anything for you, Isla,' he'd said. 'A takeaway?' 'A glass of wine?' 'A strawberry milkshake?' He'd even offered to watch *The X Factor* results show.

'Or,' he'd said, tugging at the duvet, 'you can have my body, if you want.'

He'd tried so hard to make her smile, but she'd pulled the duvet further over her head, and said, 'Just leave me alone, Jack. Please.'

On Monday she'd rung the magazine she was currently writing for feigning a stomach bug, and asking for her deadline to be extended, but it was her head that was a tangled mess. Jack had sat on the edge of the bed and, with worried eyes, he took hold of her hand and squeezed. 'Maybe you need to see someone,' he'd said.

'What?' She looked up at him and pulled her hand away. 'A shrink, you mean?'

'No, no . . . just the GP.'

'I'm fine,' she snapped, although she knew she was far from it. 'I challenge anyone not to feel like crap after the weird things that have happened.' She burst into tears, and he wrapped his arms around

133

her. 'You do believe me, don't you, Jack? That I saw . . .' She wanted to say Spider-Man, but it almost sounded funny. Well, it wasn't a funny place inside her head.

'I believe you saw someone,' he said, releasing her. 'Listen, maybe we should contact the police.'

She shook her head. 'And say what? That Carl Jeffery, who is locked up in Australia, is stalking me?'

Jack shrugged helplessly. 'I don't know, Isla. I want you to be OK.'

'I am, Jack,' she said. 'I probably just need a few days to reset.' She leant into him, sniffing against his shoulder. 'That's all.'

'And you're sure you still want to go to Sweden?'

'Yes!' She dashed away her tears. 'I need to finish my book, and it's more than that – if I don't go, Jack, he's beaten me, hasn't he? The bastard's won.'

That evening, as Jack watched *Captain America* in the lounge, she wished she had the strength to drag herself out of bed and go to him. To snuggle up next to him on the sofa, breathe him in. Pretend everything was OK. But instead she lay alone and lonely, eyes tightly closed, tears seeping through sealed lids, wondering if she was going crazy.

### Tuesday, 8 November

The postman arrived early, and Jack placed a pile of letters and a cup of coffee on Isla's bedside cabinet next to her battered teddy bear.

He kissed her head. 'Why not go to your mum's today?' he said, before setting off for work, still urging her to get back to normal.

Once he'd gone, she pulled herself to a sitting position and took a sip of coffee. The inside of her head felt like a maze with high hedges she couldn't see over, but she had to get out of bed, get past this awful feeling that life was slipping backwards.

She grabbed the pile of mail: a circular from Virgin, a reminder that her tax was due on her car and a greeting card addressed to her and Jack in a spidery hand she recognised. She ripped it open and pulled out a floral engagement card that smelt of lavender, and smiled as a ten-pound note fluttered onto the duvet.

> *To our darling Isla and Jack. Congratulations to you both, Gran and Granddad xxx*

Fresh tears filled her eyes. She hadn't seen her grandparents in a long time, and a surge of happy memories filled her head of visiting them in Devon, reminding her of the child she'd once been.

She pulled her legs round, tucked her feet into her slippers, and padded into the lounge where she fired up her laptop. She needed to find out if there had been two people dressed as Spider-Man at Millie's party. If she could only find a picture with both of them in it, Jack would have to believe her, and it would prove she wasn't losing her mind.

But then Jack had never said she was losing her mind. He'd said he believed her. He was just worried about the effect it was having. *Wasn't he?*

She trawled through the photographs she'd taken, finding a couple of Jack, the one of him and Roxanne dancing making her smile. But there was only ever one Spider-Man in each picture. She sighed. That didn't necessarily mean there hadn't been two. Maybe Jack's doppelganger hadn't been caught on camera.

It was pointless. She snapped her laptop closed and thrust her pounding head into her hands. Once in Abisko she would feel better. The cold quietness of such a remote place would help her get her head straight. Everything would be OK once she was there.

Showered and dressed, she went back into the bedroom and began throwing things into her case, realising she was short of jumpers. She took a deep breath, went into the kitchen, and grabbed her car keys from the hook on the wall. She tickled Luna's chin, and, with her jacket over her arm, she stepped out into the brightness of the chilly day.

She drove to Hitchin. She loved the market town with its abundance of crowded cafés, where she often sat outside, sometimes with

Jack – him playing games on his phone, her writing and sipping on a cappuccino, and eating blueberry muffins – sometimes alone. She'd written a few articles for her local paper about Hitchin, and a feature for a woman's magazine called 'The Real Parminster' about the series *Doctor Foster* being filmed there.

Now, she strolled towards the market. It reminded her of her childhood, when she would push through the crowds, gripping her mum's hand. Listening as fruit sellers yelled that their strawberries or bananas were a bargain at twice the price, while the smell of hotdogs and burgers from a van had made her young tummy rumble.

After wandering from stall to stall for some time, she finally bought two jumpers from a woman selling hand-knitted woollens, and was on her way back to her car when she heard a voice she recognised.

'Isla?'

She turned to see Sara crouched in front of a flower stall, a spray of pink roses in her hand, her perfect face lit up with a bright smile. She was wearing jeans, a green woollen poncho and suede ankle boots, her blonde hair scooped into a high ponytail.

'Oh my God,' Sara continued, thrusting the flowers back into the bucket of water. She rose, raced towards Isla as though they were long-lost friends, and air-kissed Isla's cheeks, her distinctive perfume wafting on the air. 'How lovely to see you again.'

Isla wasn't sure it was. She wanted to get home. Pack. And get out of England as soon as she could.

'How are you?' Isla said, always polite. 'How's your dad?'

Sara screwed up her nose. 'If I'm honest, not so good – I'm really worried about him.' Her chin fleetingly crinkled. 'He relies on me so heavily, which I don't mind. But I just want him to be OK.'

'I'm so sorry. It must be so hard for you.'

She shrugged. 'Enough about me, or it'll set me off,' she said with a sniff. 'What are you doing here?'

Isla lifted her bulging carrier bag. 'Shopping for woolly jumpers,' she said.

'Ooh, yes, you're off to Sweden tomorrow, aren't you?' She gave a gleeful whoop. 'I got your email. Sorry I haven't replied. I've been so busy at work.'

Isla's forehead furrowed. She hadn't expected her to.

'I'm so jealous, by the way,' Sara went on. 'I've always wanted to see the Northern Lights.'

'Me too,' Isla said. A twinge of excitement ran through her body. The first she'd felt since she returned from Canada. 'Although I guess there are no guarantees I'll see them.'

'Fingers crossed. Listen, I don't suppose you fancy a pot of tea and maybe some cake, or something?' Sara tilted her head. 'I spotted a lovely little tea room in Bancroft.'

Isla glanced at her watch. 'Maybe another time. Sorry. I need to get back to finish packing. I've barely started—'

Sara put up her hand like a traffic cop. 'No excuses necessary,' she said. 'Totally understand.'

'So what about you?'

'Me?' Sara pressed her chest.

'Hitchin's a bit of a trek for you, isn't it? What are you doing here?'

'Well, you're never going to believe this,' she said with a grin. 'Trevor Cooper got in touch and asked if I'd like to meet up with him.'

*So he did organise another reunion.*

'We had lunch at the restaurant in the Market Square,' Sara went on. 'They do a great beef Wellington.' She glanced about her. 'In fact, Trevor's about here somewhere.'

A shudder ran through Isla. He was the last person she wanted to see.

'Are you OK, Isla?' Sara asked, as Isla's mind drifted. 'Isla?' she repeated.

'Sorry, I'm miles away. Yes, I'm fine.'

'Trevor said he wanted to invite you, to make up for the Spoon's fiasco. He's so embarrassed by that, poor chap, but his messages didn't seem to go through.' She tilted her head, the cool, bright sun highlighting the strands of gold in her hair. 'He even tried to call you several times when we were in the restaurant.' She paused for a moment. 'He's still got that yellow Nokia he had at university, would you believe? It did make me laugh.'

'What do you think of him?' Isla said, trying to keep her tone even.

'Trevor?' She shrugged. 'He seems nice. Just like he was at uni, really.'

Isla's legs felt unsteady, her head muzzy. Should she mention the odd messages? 'It's just . . .' She paused. No, she really didn't know Sara well enough. 'Did Veronica and Ben come?'

'At lunchtime?'

'Mmm.'

'Ben was there.'

Isla's heart sank. If Trevor hadn't been so odd, she might have met him.

'He couldn't believe how much I'd changed,' Sara continued. 'Pretty sure he was flirting with me.'

'Some things never change,' Isla said with a smile. 'He was a bit of a player at uni, wasn't he?'

'I wouldn't know. Nobody but Trevor spoke to me much back then.' She laughed as though it didn't matter. 'I told Ben about your book.'

'You did?' Isla felt her cheeks flush.

'Uh-huh. I gave it my best shot, told him what a great project it was, about the cats in France.'

'Italy.'

'Yes, sorry. Although I'm not sure he really listened.' She paused and stuck out her bottom lip. 'Sorry.'

'Well, thanks for trying,' Isla said, wishing the ground would open up. 'Was Veronica at the restaurant?'

Sara shook her head, her ponytail swinging to and fro. 'Trevor invited her, but she couldn't make it. Rude, if you ask me,' she said, playfully, a slight snort expelling from her nose. 'Trevor said Veronica messaged an apology both times. Mind you, he said he couldn't really complain, having blown us all off in Cambridge.' She put her hand on Isla's arm and narrowed her eyes. 'Isla, there's something I probably should have told you when we met up last time, and it's been eating away at me ever since.' She paused for a moment. 'Especially as you said how close the two of you are.'

'The two of us?'

A woman with a hessian bag barged past, banging Isla's leg. She winced.

'You and Roxanne,' Sara said.

'What about us?'

'Listen, can we sit down? It's so crowded here.' Sara pointed to a bench near the river, and they strolled out of the market, and sat down. A man with a toddler laughed as they fed ducks. The little boy flapped his hands and stomped his feet as the ducks approached. The rushing sound of the fountain should have been therapeutic, but despite that, the stunning view of the ancient church and the sun's rays glinting on the water, tension began to build in Isla's shoulders. What was she doing here sitting with Sara? She needed to get home.

'The thing is,' Sara began, screwing up her face so a thin line formed in the centre of her forehead, 'when it came to sharing a Bunsen burner, or a laminated list of chemical formulas, Trevor and I were a great team back then.' She bit her bottom lip. 'Sometimes, he would tell me things. Things he didn't tell other people. I think he saw me as a kind of confidante. I mean, I wasn't about to blab about what he told me, as I barely spoke to a soul during my three years there.'

She let out a strange little laugh, followed by a silence as Isla scrutinised her. There was no doubting she'd had work done. Everything about her was far too perfect. There was no trace of the girl she'd once been, and she wondered what insecurities had led Sara to change her appearance so drastically.

'What kind of things did he tell you?' Isla said, not sure she wanted to know.

Sara turned from Isla's stare and looked up at the sky. 'Oh wow, look,' she said as a noisy flock of Canadian geese came in to land. 'Amazing, aren't they?' Her eyes were back on Isla, and she sighed deeply. 'He said that the day Roxanne told him it was over between you . . . well . . .' She rested her hand on Isla's knee. 'She made a pass at him, and in a weak moment he slept with her.'

'What?' A surge of blood raced through Isla's veins. She got to her feet. 'That can't be true. You must have it wrong.'

The toddler stopped flapping and stared over.

'Roxanne would never do that,' Isla said, lowering her tone.

'Well, I suppose you weren't technically with Trevor at the time.' Sara shrugged. 'On a break, as Ross in *Friends* would say.'

'Even so, she wouldn't have.' She glared at Sara, who pulled a tissue from her poncho pocket. 'Trevor must have lied.'

'Please don't shoot the messenger, Isla. I'm only telling you because I don't like to think of you still being friendly with someone who let you down. I know it's none of my business, exactly.'

'No, no you're right. It isn't,' Isla said, stepping backwards and touching the band on her wrist. 'In fact, I barely know you, Sara. And why would I take Trevor's word above Roxanne's? And even if Roxanne did sleep with Trevor, which I'm sure she didn't, you're right – it was over between us.'

'I'm only thinking of you, Isla.' Sara patted her eyes with the tissue. She rose too. 'You're such a nice person, but you need to choose your friends carefully.'

Isla zoned out, her mind flashing to the past. The way it had ended with Trevor. 'He's so clingy, Isla,' Roxanne had said a few weeks before she broke up with him. 'He just won't take a hint that you don't want to be with him any more. I don't know how you can bear it.'

'But I love Roxanne, Sara,' Isla said, as a flock of pigeons took off, flapping their wings. 'She's been my best friend for over ten years. She couldn't have . . .'

'OK, OK. I'm sorry I even brought it up. I've clearly upset you, and I'm sorry for that.' Sara dabbed her eyes once more. 'I feel so stupid.'

'No, no it's fine,' Isla said, softening, and touching Sara's arm. 'Let's just forget about it, shall we?' She shook her head, confused. 'Anyway, I've got far too much going on in my head right now. I can't worry about this as well.'

She turned to leave and, as she did so, Sara blurted, 'Isla, please, please keep in touch.'

Isla didn't reply. She just walked away through the busy market stalls, head down, not looking back.

# Chapter 25

www.travellinggirlblog.com
*0 followers*
*Wednesday, 9 November, 6 a.m.*

It was when I left Sara yesterday, after her awful accusations about Roxanne, that the text from Andy appeared on my phone.

*There's someone else. There's always been someone else. I'm so sorry.*

The shock was too much.

He'd told me on Saturday that he would come to Sweden, and now this. Is he trying to send me mad? Confuse me? Has he forgotten the way we made love so intensely? Has he forgotten the way he touched me? How he trailed hot kisses over my body, so I heard fireworks, felt sparks land on my skin?

'I love you, Isla,' he'd said so many times in Canada.

I've replied to his text. Told him I refuse to believe his words. Begged him to be there on Friday in Sweden like he promised.

He has to be, because if he isn't, there's simply nothing left to live for.

If he doesn't come, I will die out there in the cold.

*Comments*                                                    *disabled.*

# Chapter 26

'You're such a sweetheart taking me to the airport,' Isla said, looking across at Jack, who braked to turn a corner. It seemed like a lifetime ago that he proposed, since he last mentioned it. 'I do appreciate it.'

'No worries, I've got to drop a game off at Matt's anyway.'

'In Baldock,' she said. 'It's another half an hour or more to Stansted. I know you're going right out of your way, Jack. Thanks so much.'

'Well, it'll save you paying parking fees.' He glanced her way, his face creasing into a half-smile. 'Isla, listen, if you want us to take a step back with the engagement, that's OK. Maybe I rushed you.'

Her heart sank; she didn't want to think about it. 'Let's not talk about this now.'

'OK. Well. Just give it some thought while you're away.'

'I will. I promise.'

'And you're sure you're going to be OK? You're certain you want to go?'

She nodded. 'It'll be good to get away.' She paused, wondering if he would think she meant from him, but he didn't react.

'I wish I could be there with you.'

143

'Really? In the snow?' She smiled, knowing he'd hate it.

'Well, maybe not.' He smiled too. 'I hope you can get that bastard out of your head, Isla.'

'I hope so too.'

Jack pulled into a space by the side of the road opposite a church and grabbed an Xbox game from the glove compartment. 'Won't be a minute,' he said, getting out of the car.

She watched him go, thinking how handsome he was, as he jogged along the pavement, wishing with every part of her that she wasn't putting him through so much crap. He was one of the best. He'd be happier without her.

Once he'd turned the corner, heading to where Matt lived on the High Street, she pulled out her phone and occupied herself for several minutes trawling through Facebook updates, adding loves and likes and wows to friends' posts.

As she slipped her phone back into her bag, she spotted someone in the graveyard opposite. She narrowed her eyes, a shot of adrenaline pounding her body. The man was too far away to see clearly, but he was wearing a green hat. She pulled out her phone again and, with shaking hands, snapped a picture. If she could show people the picture, it would prove she wasn't going crazy. But when she looked at the screen, the picture was a blur. Whoever it was had moved.

She climbed out of the car and, vaguely aware of a car braking sharply as she crossed the road in front of it, she walked towards the church. She ran her finger over the band on her wrist as she made her way under the ancient porch and into the grounds. Surely it was safe enough. The vicar must be about somewhere. But, as she weaved her way between the headstones, getting further away from the road as she went, and into the still silence of the graveyard, she became unsettled. What was she doing? What if it was Carl Jeffery? What if the article had been wrong? What if it was one of Carl Jeffery's disciples?

'Isla. What are you up to?' She startled, and turned to see Jack behind her, looking pink-cheeked as though he'd been running.

'Nothing,' she said, realising how stupid she was being. 'It's just . . . nothing.'

'We'd better head off. You don't want to miss your flight.'

As they drifted down the path towards the car, she glanced over her shoulder. A man wearing a green hat was placing flowers on a grave. It wasn't Carl Jeffery. It wasn't even a beanie. It was a cap, and the man was elderly, and had now been joined by a woman, who linked her arm through his. Was everything that had happened really just delusions brought on by her fear of Carl Jeffery?

'You know what?' Isla said to Jack once they were in the car, and she was trying to calm her anxiety. 'I wonder sometimes if what happened in Australia messed with the wiring of my mind. I just don't feel like me lately. I feel like I'm going crazy.'

'You're not crazy, Isla,' he said, starting the engine, and thrusting the car into gear. 'You just need some time out. You said so yourself. Anyone who went through what you went through would have bad times.' He made it sound as if it was something and nothing. An off day because someone nabbed her parking space, or pushed in front of her at the supermarket.

'But why now? Why after six years?'

'You know why. It's because of that bloody appeal. Just go to Sweden, relax, and when you get back, everything will be OK.'

She didn't reply, unsure if that was even possible.

\* \* \*

Departures at Stansted Airport was crowded, and Isla's plane being delayed made her restless. She got up, left the café, where she'd been watching her coffee go cold for almost an hour, and made her way through the throng of people, searching for a quiet space.

Relieved, she spotted a row of seats next to a huge window, just a man on the end seat reading a Dan Brown book, and a woman doing a crossword. Isla could cope with that.

She sat down, gazing through the window at a stationary plane

145

being refuelled by what looked like Playmobil people, and her stomach tipped. Not long now, surely.

She pulled her phone from her carry-on bag, opened up her email account, and began typing.

To: SALLY Johnson sallyjohnson@windlemail.com
From: ISLA Johnson islajjohnson@windlemail.com

*Hi Mum,*
*I'm about to take off. Please don't worry about me. I won't be gone long. I'm going to take loads of photographs, but mainly get my head down. Maybe I'll complete* Isla's Journey *— you never know.*

*The details of where I'm staying can be found here: www. camp-arctic.com. There's a phone number, and pictures of the place. They provide snow wear, so I won't freeze, and I've bought some of those little hand-warmer thingies, which I can also use to keep my camera battery warm. I'm hoping the weather will be perfect for the Northern Lights. Love you lots and please give my love to Dad too. Isla xxx*

She closed her emails and clicked on the text message icon:

*Hi, Jack. I'm so sorry I've been acting so odd. Forgive me. Isla xxx*

Next she pressed the Facebook icon.

*At Stansted Airport waiting for my flight. Camp Arctic, Abisko, here I come — WHOOP!*

She stopped herself from messaging Roxanne. Even though she knew she shouldn't believe what Trevor had told Sara, Roxanne had been a wild card at university, sleeping with everyone on campus. Taking drugs. Was it possible she'd slept with Trevor? It wasn't that she cared now, of course. It was more that their friendship had been based on a lie.

Before she switched off her phone for the flight, she registered that Ben Martin still hadn't accepted her friend request, even though Sara had mentioned her to him. She sighed deep and long, trying to summon the girl she'd once been. It was time to head to Scandinavia, write, and live the final chapter of *Isla's Journey*. She hoped it would be special, and she could leave the UK and the stress of the last week behind her.

But as her phone screen buffered and went black, she felt small and lost. The giant toad of Stansted Airport overwhelmed her. She glanced about, pinged the band on her wrist, and took a deep breath. She looked down at her passport and boarding pass in her hands, and up at the sign that now told her to go to her gate. The first flight with Ryanair would take her to Stockholm. From there, Norwegian Air would take her to Kiruna.

In four hours she would have reached her final destination.

She rose to her feet, her stomach leaping, her subconscious screaming, 'Go home, Isla.'

But she had to go.

She couldn't give up now.

# Chapter 27

*Five and half years ago*

For six months Isla had been cocooned in her old bedroom at her parents' house. It hadn't changed since she'd left for university five years before. Her old paperbacks jostled for space with Disney videos on a cheap bookshelf. And as she burrowed herself under her duvet, like a rabbit down a hole, scared of life, the Spice Girls and Take That looked down from posters Blu-Tacked to her butterfly wallpaper, reminding of the person she had once been.

Over the months following the attack, she'd eaten just enough to keep alive, showered when her mum told her politely that the smell was getting too much. Her hair hung long and greasy. Her skin had an unhealthy grey tinge.

She'd had a job lined up for her return from Australia in a café by the River Hiz that a friend of her mum's owned. She'd planned to work there while she thought about her next step. Eventually it was given to someone else. *They can't wait for ever for you, Isla, love.*

Her mum had kept her updated about the constant flow of people calling – asking after her. They'd seen what had happened, on the news, in newspapers, online. 'They care about you, darling,' her mum would say, reeling off names she didn't take in. She didn't want or

148

need anyone. They meant nothing. And anyway, all they wanted was to pick over the bones and walk away.

Through the months her mum had pinned on a smile, as though she thought Isla might catch it and wear it too. She never did. She couldn't smile. In fact, the pills had made her feel so numb her face felt like it was set in a plaster cast. Her body a shell carrying around half the person she once was.

Roxanne would turn up with piles of glossy magazines and paperbacks – rom-coms to cheer her up. Isla never read them.

'She's doing OK, Roxanne,' she would hear her mum say, and Isla wondered if her mum believed her words. Whether she was in that much denial.

'I'm thinking of going to Africa,' Roxanne said one day, full of smiles as she plonked yet more magazines on Isla's bed. 'I want to help out out there – be useful, you know.'

'Great!' Isla said.

'Really?' Roxanne said. 'I won't go until I know you are OK,' she added.

'I'm fine. Go. Fuck off,' Isla said, voice rising. 'I don't need you.' She grabbed her battered bear from the bedside unit, her skull tingling, a feeling of panic rising at the possible loss of her best friend, and she disappeared under the duvet. 'Just leave me alone.'

'You need to eat more,' Millie said, staring at the uneaten cod and chips on the floor. 'It's been over five months, Isla. You look so thin.'

Isla was sitting up in bed, bolstered by pillows, her dirty hair tied into an untidy ponytail. She was flicking through the TV channels at speed, the noise blaring out.

Millie snatched the remote and turned off the TV.

'I was watching that. God's sake, what do you want, Millie?'

Millie sat down on the edge of the bed, turning the remote in her hands. 'I'm worried about you, Isla.'

'I know. You've told me a thousand times. I'm fine.'

Millie placed the remote on the bed and tucked a straying tendril of Isla's hair behind her ear. 'You pop so many pills. You never go out. You never eat. You won't see a counsellor.' She tilted her head, furrowing her forehead. The *I'm worried about you* look. 'I just want my sister back, that's all. I miss her.'

'Life's hard, Millie,' Isla whispered. 'Too hard.'

'Everyone's life is hard, Isla.'

'What?' She glared, catching Millie's eyes for a long moment.

'It is, Isla,' Millie said, looking away. 'Everyone has problems.'

A bubble of anger rose. 'So you think being almost killed by a serial killer is the same as having a beautiful, funny, amazing daughter with Asperger's?' she spat.

'I didn't say that. But my life isn't exactly easy. It's all relative, Isla.'

'Jesus, Millie.' She closed her eyes. Her sister could be so stupid at times, barging in with her big feet.

'I know there's no comparison. I realise that. But . . .' She rested her hand on Isla's, her voice soft and caring. 'Julian thinks maybe you should take the bull by the horns. Get out of bed and get on with it. Try to get your act together.'

The slap was hard and tears shot to Millie's eyes. The print on her cheek was instant. *Julian. Why did you have to mention bloody Julian?* Isla's body began to shake, and tears prickled at the reality of what she'd done. 'Oh God, Millie, I'm so sorry.'

The door opened and their dad peered round. 'Is everything OK, girls?'

'Dad,' Isla said, sinking lower down her bed, tears streaming her cheeks.

'I heard raised voices,' he said.

'It was nothing.' Millie got to her feet and fumbled for a tissue in her pocket.

'I'm so, so sorry,' Isla sobbed, burying herself under her duvet, her shoulders heaving, hysteria setting in – and as she cried she felt the weight of her sister on the bed once more, cradling her body through the duvet, the summery floral smell of her giving her comfort.

'Don't cry, little sis,' Millie said through her own tears. 'Please don't cry. I can't bear it.'

\* \* \*

150

And then Isla had no choice. She'd dragged herself from under her duvet. *He may go free if you don't.*

The journey to Australia was long and tiring. Two flights. A stop-off in Singapore, where they'd grabbed a burger, and dozed, stretched on the floor in the airport like they were homeless.

'You OK?' Sally gripped her daughter's hand.

Isla nodded, but she was far from it. To go back to where it all happened was horrendous, scary, what nightmares were made of.

'We'll be landing soon, love,' Sally went on, peering through the window at the fluffy white clouds above Sydney. 'Won't be long now.'

Johan Arnold, the prosecution lawyer, was confident, his Aussie twang strong. It had made Isla flinch when she first heard it. Sad. She'd always loved the accent before.

'What Jeffery did to you that night, Isla,' he'd said over Skype a week before they took off, brushing a hand over his silver-grey beard, 'along with his DNA on Bronwyn's body, the fact he admitted to you that he killed Sophie Stuart and Clare Simpson, topped up,' he'd gone on as though he was filling a glass of fizz, 'with the eyewitness accounts. It's enough. But we need you here, Isla. We can't do this without you.'

Once in the courtroom, dressed in a drab brown skirt suit, it hadn't taken Isla long to realise the defence's tactics.

'Yeah, too right Isla Johnson's violent.' It was Coral Reynolds from school talking over a live link to the UK. 'Nearly gave me brain damage.'

Isla stared at the woman on the screen – still thin with cropped blonde hair – but now she had a tattoo of a windpipe on her neck. Isla placed a shaking hand on her own neck. Tears burned.

'Isla threw me across the classroom,' Coral went on with a shrug. 'I banged my head on a desk, and there was, like, blood everywhere.' Isla turned away from the screen, the memory of Coral, a girl she'd barely known, insulting Millie pushing its way into her head. 'Your fat-arse sister's been knocked up by a creep,' Coral had spat back then.

She had gone around winding people up, lighting touchpapers, and getting off on their reactions – the chaos. Anyone would have retaliated. But it was such a long time ago, they'd been kids – thirteen, fourteen maybe? Why was she dredging up ancient history, defending a man who'd killed three women? In fact, how had they even found her? But it was simple. She'd found them. She hadn't changed.

'The defence are clutching at straws, Isla. We've got this in the bag,' Johan said, when she expressed a desperate need to go home. He'd looked harassed, eyes dull, frustrated. 'They're dredging up stuff to make it look as though you attacked Carl. It's pathetic. We will win this.' He hadn't given her a chance to respond, just walked away with his briefcase, his expensive suit creased.

Day after day, the defence picked over Isla's life. And, day after day, she watched on as the prosecution held up the green beanie, the scarf, photos that made her stomach turn. Day after day, she shared the courtroom with Carl Jeffery. Went over and over what had happened that awful night, knowing his eyes were on her.

It was a Friday – Isla remembered because it was the thirteenth – when her dad climbed onto the witness stand, visibly shaking.

'Mr Johnson,' the defence began. 'Are there any moments when, growing up or even more recently, Isla has been prone to violent outbursts?'

Gary looked over at Isla, no longer shaking. There had been moments – teenage tantrums when Isla rebelled a little. Threw things. But more recently there had been that awful moment when she'd lost control and slapped her sister – hard – bruised Millie's cheek. He'd known about that. He may not have seen it, but he'd known.

'Never,' he said, always fiercely protective of his daughters.

The turning point came when Carl was questioned about his mother. Isla couldn't be sure if Johan had expected the reaction he got, but his eyes went from dull to bright in moments. He began firing cleverly crafted questions, shooting them at his victim.

'Talk to my sister,' Carl Jeffery cried, his eyes searching the many faces of the public gallery as though he hoped she was there. He began stuttering over his words, crumbling like a child. 'Me and Darleen went through hell when Mum left.' His eyes darted around the courtroom, and he began to cry. Helpless tears. 'Mum knew what he did, but she still left us with him.'

Suddenly he wasn't the Carl Jeffery who'd attacked Isla, or even the Carl Jeffery she'd fallen for. He was the lost child his mother walked out on, and a wave of pity consumed her, bashing against the revulsion and hatred, causing a concoction of confusion.

Isla should have felt elated when Carl Jeffery got three life sentences, but it wasn't elation she felt that day. There was some relief, but the truth was she knew she would continue to share her journey with Carl Jeffery. He would always be there. Riding trains with her. Buses. Planes. Walking a few steps behind. Lurking in the shadows on dark nights, among the crowds on bright summer days, Just hidden enough that she couldn't quite see his face. The fear would always be there; she would just have to learn to live with it.

# Chapter 28

*Now*

Isla's eyes ached as she gazed out at the miles and miles of freshly fallen snow, the bright sun reflecting off its brilliant whiteness. It was quiet, nobody for miles, and she felt so absorbed by the silence that sitting in the back of a taxi felt unusually easy.

A moose in the distance wandered, slow and lumbering, and Isla pulled out her camera. She lowered the window, the bitter cold air making her face tingle.

'Are you staying here long?' the taxi driver asked, as she rested the camera lens on the glass, zoomed in on the moose and snapped a picture.

'A week,' Isla said. 'I wish it was longer.' She slid the window to a close, and the driver dashed a look over his shoulder. He was about thirty, with a friendly smile.

'I live in Kiruna,' he said, his English good, although there was no doubting he was Scandinavian.

She glanced out once more at the miles and miles of endless snow. This was perfect.

'Kiruna's the most northerly town in Sweden,' he continued, as though proud of his home. 'Although it will all move eventually.'

'What will?'

'Kiruna.'

'Really?'

'Yes.' He nodded. 'The area will one day be swallowed up by Kiirunavaara.'

'Kiirunavaara?' She imagined a monster gulping down the small mining town.

'Kiirunavaara is the mountain,' he continued. 'It has one of the world's largest iron-ore mines, but the ground below is becoming rickety.' He took his hand off the steering wheel and mimicked a rocking gesture.

'Oh God.' Her startled eyes met his in the rear-view mirror.

He laughed. 'It's fine right now,' he said, continuing to chuckle. 'It will be many years before we need to worry – long, long time before that happens.' He laughed again, throwing his head back. 'You see, I'm a good tour guide, yes?'

'You are indeed,' she said, smiling and making a mental note of all he'd told her for her book.

Apart from the roads, the whole area was buried under eight feet of snow, but the taxi driver seemed oblivious to the weather conditions, driving at a fair speed. At home in the UK, a sprinkling of snow caused havoc, Isla thought, and yet here he was, taking it in his stride.

They pulled up in front of Camp Arctic, a sprawling one-storey, wooden lodge in Abisko. The driver unloaded her case, and she paid him.

'You want more good tour, you call and ask for Erik, yes?' he said with a smile, pocketing her generous tip.

'Yes, thank you,' she said, as he got back into the taxi, leaving her alone.

Inside the building, she stomped her booted feet at the entrance to shake off the snow. Two huge, shaggy dogs bounded over to greet her, their claws clattering on the wooden floorboards. She ruffled their heads with gloved hands.

'*Bry dig inte om dem, de inte bita,*' a woman with wiry, red hair called from behind a small, wooden counter, although Isla had no idea what it meant. 'Tindra! Max!' The woman slapped her thigh, and the dogs scooted off and disappeared behind the counter.

Isla collected the key to her room from the woman, who told her the timings for breakfast and dinner.

Her room was tiny, reminding her of the hostel in Sydney. Her parents had sent extra money back then, so she didn't have to share a dorm. 'It will be safer,' her mum had said. The irony hit her now, but she battered down the memory.

She turned on her phone, noticing the battery was low. After heaving her case on the bed, she opened it, hunting for the charger.

'Crap,' she muttered, as she rummaged further in her case, realising she'd forgotten it. She picked up her mobile and, with the phone's last breath, texted Jack and her mum, telling them she was a numpty, and if they needed her in an emergency to call the hotel. She would attempt to borrow a charger, but needed them to know all was well, in case they worried.

She tugged her teddy bear that she took everywhere from the case and sat it on the bedside table.

Wasting no time, she grabbed her camera and made her way back to reception, where she hired a snowsuit, thermal gloves and a pair of boots from the red-headed woman. She pulled them on and dived out into the frosty air.

After walking for half an hour, the silence and sheer peace clearing her head a little, and the pleasure of snapping photographs soothing her senses, she spotted someone in the distance. The sun glanced off the snow making it hard to see. She stopped, pulled down her goggles and squinted, trying to make out the figure standing against the whiteness wearing a dark snowsuit and holding walking sticks.

She looked about her. There was nobody else around. *It's just a tourist*, she told herself, but with everything else that had happened, a desperate need to turn back, to run, was overpowering.

The figure lifted a snow stick, as though greeting her, and she spun round and attempted to walk at speed. Her boots were heavy in the deep snow, like walking in treacle, but she kept on going, looking back every few seconds. Whoever it was didn't move; just watched as she ploughed on, snow crunching under her feet, her emotions on hyper alert.

As the figure grew smaller in the distance, another figure appeared, dressed in pink. The two figures appeared to talk for a few moments, before turning, and moving off in opposite directions.

Once back at the lodge, Isla almost fell into the doorway out of breath.

'Is everything all right?' the red-headed woman asked. She was large, with a rather bohemian look.

'Yes,' Isla said, feeling ridiculous, and angry with herself that he was still there – even in the quiet of Abisko – Carl Jeffery, messing with her head. How had he done that? How had he crawled back under her skin and set up home?

# Chapter 29

www.travellinggirlblog.com
*0 followers*
*Wednesday, 9 November, 9 p.m.*

My brain races too fast, rushing past what's happened. It's as though everything is sunny and perfect on the other side of a window, but the glass is covered with frost. I can't see through, so I rub my hand over the glass. The ice burns my flesh, and I cry and cry in pain, helpless as the ice thickens, getting colder and colder.

The only person who can save me now is Andy. He has to come on Friday, or I don't know what I'll do. Maybe I'm going crazy. Maybe I imagined someone outside my window that day, or at the supermarket, or at Millie's party. Is it possible nobody else can see him but me? That he was never there at all? That Carl Jeffery is haunting me from the other side of the world, lodged in the workings of my mind for ever, deep inside my head, mocking me?

*Comments*                                                    *disabled.*

# Chapter 30

**Thursday, 10 November**

Isla knelt in the snow and zoomed in the lens of her camera for a close-up shot of Nomad. The husky's eyes were velvet-black. White fur bled into grey.

'You're absolutely gorgeous,' she said, rising and ruffling the dog's head, as his tail swished to and fro. She brushed snow from her knees, aware the minibus was waiting for her. The other guests from Camp Arctic, all wrapped in snowsuits, seemed to scowl at her from the iced-over windows. They'd been on a husky ride, and clearly wanted to head back. Isla hadn't joined them on the ride, instead taking pictures of the dogs, and the surrounding countryside and wildlife.

Earlier she'd spent time with Sami people, learning about their culture and history, while sitting in a tepee around an open fire eating game soup. It had briefly helped to free her mind.

Snow began to tumble from the pale sky, flakes stinging her cold cheeks.

'Please come now,' the minibus driver called, pulling his white, woolly bobble hat further down over his ears and stomping snow with heavy boots.

'Coming – sorry.' Isla tucked her camera away, and hurried towards

159

him, almost slipping over. She climbed aboard, sensing a hostile environment. 'Sorry for holding you all up,' she said, as a young man looked at her from the back seat. 'Sorry,' she said again, scrambling into a seat, as they set off.

The woman next to her finally smiled. 'Did you have a good day?' she asked, her American accent strong. 'Beautiful here, isn't it?'

Isla nodded and smiled back. 'Yes, yes it is.'

The minibus's temperature gauge registered minus seventeen Celsius, and the windscreen wipers, despite whipping across the glass at speed, were no match for the falling snow. Out of the front window, she could just make out the road stretching ahead of them, chalk-white.

Back at the hotel, the reception buzzed with people leaving and arriving. Cases were everywhere, and a suffocating feeling of chaos replaced her earlier sense of wellbeing. Jittery, she pushed through the throng, and headed past the reception desk.

'How was your day?' the red-headed woman called to her, smiling, before turning back to her computer screen.

'Good, thanks.' She itched to open the door that led to the sanctuary of her room.

'What are your plans for your stay?'

Isla placed her hand on the doorknob. 'I'm going to the Aurora Sky Station tomorrow night.'

'You'll enjoy that.' The woman's eyes were still fixed on the screen in front of her. 'Make sure you wear thermals.'

*Please stop talking.* 'I will.'

Isla eased open the door and stepped into the corridor, the woman's voice trailing after her: 'The weather conditions are looking good for the Northern Lights, so you might be lucky.'

Isla spent the next few hours jotting down the string of things she'd done and seen that day, before heading for the restaurant, where she sat alone. She ate herring-three-ways, and drank two glasses of wine, while writing up more notes, and somehow managed to block out any unwanted thoughts.

It was around ten o'clock that she returned to her room. But despite the day being full, tiring her to the point of exhaustion, she couldn't sleep. Her brain whirred, and Carl Jeffery darted into her head like a phantom. She couldn't switch off.

At midnight the wind got up. She squeezed her eyes shut, listening as it howled and whistled, ebbing and flowing outside her window like a roaring waterfall. She imagined snowflakes twisting and turning in the black night, whipping up like a tornado. It must have lasted an hour before silence resumed.

Her brain finally began to close down, and she was in a place between asleep and awake, when there was a tapping sound on her window. Her eyes shot open, her body drenched with sweat as her mind tumbled back to that terrible night.

### Six years ago

Isla's eyes sprang open. It was the tapping sound again.

Carl had laughed the day before. Said she worried too much. That the sound was nothing more than a tree branch moving in the light breeze, brushing against her ground-floor window. Or perhaps she was imagining it. That's what he'd said too.

But this was the second night it had woken her, and last night she'd felt sure someone was out there in the darkness. Just like Bronwyn had mentioned. It couldn't be her imagination.

She threw back her duvet, too hot in the Australian climate anyway, got out of bed and padded to the window. Hands shaking, she eased open the blind.

*Thank God.* Maybe Carl had been right – that the nearby tree, silhouetted against the night sky, was the culprit. But, as she peered closer, a full moon brightening the area, she knew the branches couldn't reach her window. And, as she peered closer to the window, she saw a movement. Someone was out there, standing twenty feet away, where the hostel grounds morphed with the neighbouring forest. A place she'd spent so much time taking photographs of the wildlife.

161

She squinted into the darkness, trying to make out the figure. He was standing so still. A hat pulled low over his forehead and a scarf wrapped around his face, despite the heat of the night. She closed the blind and rushed back to bed. It was all very well travelling to India, New Zealand and Australia alone, independent, but what happened now? What happened when fear crept in?

She'd already decided that she would go home, that she'd had enough. The last six weeks had been great with Carl; she liked him, but it was nothing serious. And Bronwyn's death still played heavy on her mind – especially as there was an ongoing inquiry. The police no longer believed it was suicide. The thought had made her uneasy.

Her final trip to Canada could wait. She'd already booked her flight home and would be leaving in a few days.

The tapping stopped, but it was several hours before she drifted into a doze, and it was almost eight o'clock when the chattering laughter of a kookaburra startled her, and the sun's rays burned through the blind. She forced herself to get out of bed and into the shower, and was lost in the bliss of the soapy water, when the knock came on the door of her room.

'Are you ready, Isla?' It was Carl. He hadn't really been the same since she'd told him she was going back to England. That she missed her family. Said he'd thought she might stay. Be with him for ever.

She turned off the water, wrapped her towel around herself, and raced to open the door.

'Not ready yet?' he said, coming into the room. 'I thought we'd agreed eight.'

She smiled, as he perched on her bed. 'You OK?' she asked.

'Yep, just thought you'd be ready.'

The truth was, apart from knowing he worked and lived in Sydney, she knew little about him. They'd never really got to the place where they told each other their life histories, mainly having fun – and great sex.

'Sorry. I did say eight.' She stepped towards him, bent down and kissed his lips. He smelt of sun cream, and the musky, distinctive aftershave he always wore. 'Give me five minutes. I'll be right with you.'

Carl dragged his fingers through his hair as he watched Isla dash around, putting on her pants and bra, a pair of khaki-coloured shorts and an orange vest T-shirt. She tied her hair into a ponytail, and slapped sun cream onto her face, shoulders and arms.

'Ta da! Ready,' she said with a bright smile, putting on sunglasses and grabbing her camera. But he didn't smile. He was acting odd. She hated seeing him this way.

He'd promised to take her to the Blue Mountains, as she desperately wanted to go before she returned to England. 'I know a great place,' he'd said. 'You'll get some great shots of the Three Sisters.'

Outside the hostel, the sun burned down from a clear blue sky at around thirty degrees, despite it still being early. They climbed into Carl's truck, and he stepped down on the throttle, and sped along the highway. Should she tell him she'd seen someone outside the window? But then he'd been dismissive before.

'I heard it again,' she said finally, her voice small.

He changed gear, his shirtsleeves hugging his muscular forearms, the tick-tock, tick-tock, tick-tock of the indicator seeming loud, as he slowed to swerve round a corner.

'Sorry, what?' he said, as though he didn't understand, looking at her from the corner of his eyes.

She leant back, the headrest vibrating under her head, as he sped up again along the straight, lonely road. She turned to look at him. He seemed relaxed, one hand on the steering wheel, the other fiddling with the CD player, finger jabbing through tracks until he reached Aerosmith's 'I Don't Want to Miss a Thing'.

They continued for some way, before Isla tried once more. 'Someone tapped on my window.' Why had her voice taken on a timid tone? She wasn't timid. She had never been timid. Was it Carl? Was he making her uneasy?

He twisted to look her way. 'Isla, you couldn't have.' He smiled. 'Who the hell would tap on your window in the night? It's like I said before – a tree, I reckon.'

'There is a tree outside. I looked.'

'There you go then.'

'Except it's too far away from the window.'

He gave a grim laugh. 'You've been watching too many thrillers.'

'No,' she said, the makings of a foggy headache nagging at her temples. 'I never watch thrillers.' She sighed. 'Carl, there was someone out there,' she continued. 'Or at least I think there was.'

'You *think*. Can you hear yourself, Isla?' He took both hands from the wheel and threw them in the air in a shrug. He turned to face her. 'There's nobody out there, Isla,' he said. 'You've got an overactive imagination.'

He pulled off the road, tyres bouncing over bumpy ground, and screeched to a stop in a clearing. 'There's a great place to take photographs through there.' He pointed towards some eucalyptus bushes.

She would have to let things go for now.

They got out and made their way through the bushes to an area that looked out over the Three Sisters. The sheer drop below made her stomach leap.

'Don't go near the edge,' Carl whispered, standing so close she could feel his warm breath on her neck. 'I wouldn't want to lose you.'

'It's absolutely stunning,' she said, pulling out her camera, and snapping pictures of the sun glinting off the mountain range giving it a magical purple and blue tinge. She turned and crouched beside a redback spider scurrying across a web, and zoomed in her camera lens.

'Jesus, Isla, keep back from him,' Carl said, placing a hand on her shoulder and squeezing. 'He'll kill ya as soon as look at ya.'

She rose once more and tucked a straying hair behind her ear. 'Everything is so amazing,' she said, but she was feeling unsettled. 'Thanks for bringing me here.'

'Pleasure.' He scuffed the undergrowth with his boot. 'And, yeah, it is pretty awesome. A great country, even if I do say so myself.'

'Are you from Sydney originally?' she said. It was the first time she'd asked.

'Melbourne,' he said, crossing his arms over his broad chest.

'Do your parents live there?'

He shook his head. 'Not any more – Dad died a while back, now. I've got a younger sister, but when Mum left, she only stayed with me and Dad for a few years, before being taken into foster care.'

'I'm sorry. You must miss him.' Her dad had tried so hard not to cry at the airport, when she first set off on her travels, and she had tried too.

'He wasn't a good 'un, Isla.' Carl's expression darkened. 'Let's leave it at that.'

'Sure, sorry.' She raised her camera and aimed it at his face. 'Can I take a photo of you to show my mum? I've told her all about you.'

He grabbed her wrist. 'Hey, that hurts,' she cried, as he jerked it downwards.

'I'd rather you didn't,' he said, those dark haunting eyes that had won her over now cold. He was barely recognisable.

'OK,' she said, as he released her. She pushed her camera into her rucksack. 'Is everything all right? You're acting really weird.'

His face flashed red. 'We should get back.'

'But we've only just got here. I thought we'd take a walk. Maybe see Wentworth Falls.'

'Wentworth Falls is miles from here,' he said, taking off, without looking back.

She followed to find him sitting behind the wheel of his truck, the engine running. She climbed in beside him, and before she could clip her seatbelt, he reversed out of the clearing at speed. Tyres skidding on dry earth. She wanted to ask again if he was OK. Had she done something wrong? Was it because she was leaving? But it was as though her throat had tightened around her words, and she couldn't speak, afraid of how he might react.

That evening they went to a restaurant near the hostel. Carl, in front of the waiters, was back to his charming self, as though nothing had happened earlier, but Isla's stomach felt too knotted to eat. They talked and drank wine, as Carl ate pasta. He told her more about how he'd travelled Australia over the last couple of years, been to Canberra, Brisbane and Perth. 'Everyone should see the Great Barrier Reef, Isla. Dive down there among the amazing fish, see the corals. You need to see more of this wonderful country,' he said, not for the first time. 'You should stay with me. We could travel together.' He leant forward, taking her hand. 'I'd really like that.'

'I can't,' she said, pulling away. 'I'm homesick as hell.' And now, on top of everything else, she couldn't get out of her head the way he'd looked at her earlier, spoken to her. It was time to head back to the UK. Begin a new chapter in her life.

That night she told him again she had to leave, her head resting against his back. His muscles tensed as she spoke, and he exhaled a long breath, making her uneasy.

'We can keep in touch. I don't want to lose you from my life,' she said, but it was far from the truth. It was over.

He left her room around eleven, and she curled like a question mark on the bed, hugging her teddy bear, her eyes open, thinking about home.

As she drifted into a fitful sleep, a nightmare latched on to her subconscious. She was falling fast, grasping at the still, hot air as she tumbled from the Blue Mountains. She woke with a gasp, sweating, the sheets twisted beneath her. There was no doubting that she'd made the right decision to leave as soon as possible.

At around 4 a.m. the tapping on her window began again. At first she lay still, trying to ignore it, hoping it would stop. But a sudden sound, as though fingernails were scraping the windowpane, made her shoot upright.

She pulled back her duvet, heart banging against her ribcage, and moved towards the window. She eased open the blind, hands shaking, and let out a strangled scream.

A man stood so close that her reflection morphed with his image. He wore a green beanie hat. A scarf covered his face. She fumbled the blind closed, raced across the room and turned on the light.

She checked the door was locked and pressed her body against it, holding her chest, her breathing erratic.

She grabbed her mobile phone from her bedside cabinet and tapped in 000.

'Someone's out there,' she cried, as the phone was answered.

'Try to keep calm, love.' A woman on the other end. 'What's your name?'

'Isla Johnson.'

'And where's there, Isla?'

'Bristol Hostel. There's someone outside. You have to help me.'

A rap on the door. 'Isla!' *Thank God. Carl.* 'Are you OK in there?' he called. 'I heard you scream.'

She raced to open up, fumbling with the lock. *Did I scream?*

'Carl?' As she opened the door, her phone slipped through her fingers and clattered to the floor. He was wearing a green beanie, a scarf draped around his neck. There was a thick rope in his hand. Her body froze. 'What the hell are you doing?'

'I can't let you go, Isla,' he whispered, stepping into the room and closing the door behind him. 'You can't leave me.'

She went to scream, but he covered her mouth, grabbed her, and slammed her so hard onto the bed that the cheap mattress creaked, and the metal frame bounced on the floorboards. Stars danced in her head, as she fought back panic and pain.

'Please, Carl, stop,' she attempted through his heavy, sweaty hand. But his eyes were wild as he wrapped the rope around her slim neck.

He was unreachable.

*Now*

Tap, tap, tap.

Isla leapt out of bed, darted across to the window and, beating down the fear that someone would be standing behind the glass, yanked back the curtain. A branch, heavy with snow, swayed back and forth in the wind. Tap, tap, tap.

'Thank God,' she whispered, closing the curtains. She hugged her chest, her heartbeat strong under her fingers. 'Get a grip, Isla,' she muttered, rushing back to bed and covering her head with the duvet.

# Chapter 31

Deep snow surrounded Aurora Sky Station, the temperature around minus ten. The wind chill caused pain in Isla's temples, as though the blood in her veins was slowly freezing. The inside of her bones hurt, her teeth ached, and her toes had gone from painful to feeling as though they weren't there at all. But still she'd stayed, mesmerised by the sight of the Northern Lights through her lens.

'The Aurora Borealis.'

She turned, the fur around her snowsuit hood tickling her cheeks, and lowered her camera.

'Beautiful, isn't it?' the man, early fifties at a guess, continued, stomping from foot to foot, snow crunching beneath his boots. He rubbed his gloved hands together. 'I'm Alex.'

Isla stared, unsure whether to enter into conversation. He was tall and slender, with feathers of silvery-white hair poking out from beneath his hood. He smiled, his sparkling blue eyes appealing in his tanned, lightly lined face. He seemed to pick up on her apprehension. 'I believe we're both staying at Camp Arctic.'

He looked suddenly familiar. She'd seen him when she first arrived, and several times the day before. He was sharing a room with a much younger woman.

Isla smiled. 'Ah, yes,' she said, a slight stutter in her voice, a misty cloud leaving her mouth as she spoke. She looked towards the sky. 'It's stunning – indescribable – although I'll give it a jolly good try.'

'Ah, you're a writer, yes? I did wonder when I saw you on your laptop back at the lodge. What do you write?'

'Articles, mostly travel.' She smiled. 'I'm on the final chapter of my book.'

'Amazing. Will we see it in the shops?'

She shook her head and shrugged. 'Perhaps, one day.' An embarrassed tingle rose in her neck, as the words tripped off her tongue. Jack had always been behind her, encouraging her to finish her book, been so full of praise, but now, as she stood in the darkness, she wondered if she'd been naive. She'd devoted so many hours to it, but perhaps she'd been a fool. Maybe it had simply been her way of dodging reality through the years.

'We should head back,' came a voice through the darkness. It was the younger woman she'd seen with Alex, now standing by the chairlift in a pink snowsuit. Isla knew instantly that *this* was the couple she'd seen on her walk the day she arrived. That Alex was the man who'd waved at her with his walking stick. The man she'd fled from in such a rush, stupidly afraid.

'Well, however beautiful this all is,' he said with another smile, 'I'm more than ready for bed.'

'Goodnight,' Isla said.

He went to step away. 'To be honest, I'm not looking forward to the chairlift down.'

Isla laughed. 'No, it's quite wobbly, isn't it?'

He nodded. 'But I guess we have to suffer these things, if we want to see the wonders of the world. It was nice meeting you . . . sorry, I don't know your name.'

'Isla,' she said.

'Well, Isla, perhaps we'll see you again,' he said. 'What are your plans?'

'I may go to Narvik tomorrow. I want to get some photos of the Norwegian Fjords.'

'We're hoping to see them too,' he said. 'I'm sure you'll enjoy it.'

He trudged away, and Isla turned and raised her camera towards the sky once more. The liquid greens drifted across the cloudless, star-filled sky, like a fantasy creature let loose from captivity, weaving psychedelically on its way to another planet. She wanted to stay, up there she could pretend everything was OK, but her fingers ached with the cold, and it was getting late. She searched the darkness. The mountain had been alive with people earlier, all gasping with excitement as they witnessed the phenomenon, but the throng had now whittled down to a few stalwarts.

She stayed a few more minutes before putting her camera in its case and collapsing her tripod. She had so many photographs. Two or three would be perfect for her book. One might even be right for the cover.

She walked across the mountain, paraffin lanterns lighting her way towards the chairlift. Once there, a chair glided in and thumped onto the platform.

A young lad steadied the swaying metal chair. He held out his arm and guided Isla into it. The bar locked down over her and he pushed the chair onwards.

At first it moved swiftly downwards, heading away from the mountain, before coming to an abrupt stop midway down. The sky looked even greener than it had been up above, and the circulating freezing air clung to her like a fog. She was glad to be swaddled in the snugness of her snowsuit.

As she swung to and fro in the gentle breeze, the vacant chairs around her creaking in the darkness, the neon lights bending and stretching in the low sky, she caught sight of someone standing in the darkness below, staring up at her.

# Chapter 32

www.travellinggirlblog.com
*0 followers*
*Saturday, 12 November, 9 a.m.*

At first, last night was amazing, like something from a romantic novel. He was there looking up at me as I came down on the chairlift, searching me out in the darkness. Even from a distance I knew it was him. He'd come. Even after saying he wouldn't. He'd come. Andy.

As the chair drifted down, I could see him clearly, wrapped in a thick, dark coat, hood up covering his auburn hair, brown eyes on me as I drifted down my final descent, before thudding to the ground.

He helped me out, pulled me close and started kissing me. I felt as though I'd been injected with a powerful drug. I couldn't speak I was so excited. The weather was so cold it felt as though my breath had frozen in my lungs. I couldn't believe he was there.

He said sorry for not answering my calls, for not coming to England. But said he was here now. I was close to tears when he told me it was me he loved. That he'd always wanted to be with me.

We went back to my room and made love. I wasn't cold any more after that. The ice on that window I couldn't see through before had melted.

Later, as we drank gin, he told me again that there was someone else in his life. But it was more than that. He was married, and he hadn't been able to bring himself to leave her. But he said his love for me had been too overpowering. He'd known he had to come to Sweden. The draw was too much. 'I'm here now,' he said again, stroking my cheek, his hot breath on my neck.

I didn't think about Jack. Does that make me a horrible person? Am I cruel? Cruel in the same way I was cruel to Trevor all those years ago?

This morning I woke at eight, expecting to find Andy's warm, naked body beside me. But he wasn't there. I glanced around the room, straining my ears, wondering if he was in the shower, but there was no sound, just silence.

'Andy,' I called, getting out of bed, grabbing my robe and slipping it on. And then I saw the note.

*My darling Isla,*

*I've been awake all night thinking – tormenting myself for coming. I thought this was the right thing to do, as I missed you – I really did miss you. But this morning, I found a text from my wife. She's having our baby, and I realised I'd made a terrible mistake coming here. I can't leave her. I thought I could, but I can't. I'm so sorry.*

*I love you, Isla, but I'm returning to Canada. I'll be changing my phone number, so you can't contact me – not because I don't want to hear your voice, but because it's easier this way. I'm sorry for the pain I've caused you. The mess I've made of both our lives.*

*Forgive me, Andy*

I'm not sure how long I sobbed for, or how loud. But now the tears have gone. I know what I have to do.

The truth is I never got over what happened in Australia. Never got over Carl Jeffery. For a time those around me thought I had. And why not? I suppose even I thought I had control. Then came the appeal, stripping away the protective layers, revealing soft, bruised flesh. I felt those spindly cracks under the surface widen.

Going to Canada was the perfect escape, far away from reality.

Then *he* appeared – so strong. A man who made me feel so much safer than Jack ever could – Jack who played at being a man as he tried to fix me. When I was with Andy, thoughts of Carl Jeffery dissipated. I talked. I cried. Nothing new, but so different than the talks I'd had with Jack and Roxanne, my parents. Millie. When I was with Andy, everything was OK.

Then I came back to England, his promises echoing in my head. Things began to fall apart. Odd things started happening. Andy seemed to melt away like an ice cube on a hot day. And as he made excuses not to talk to me, not to see me, my fear grew. Nobody could help me but Andy. Without Andy, Carl Jeffery would haunt me for ever.

When someone you love lets you down, loves someone else, the world turns on its axis. Nothing looks the same any more, and a distorted image of life appears before you like a scene from a horror movie. I know nothing will ever be the same again.

Now I grab the bottle of gin from last night and pour the dregs into a glass and swallow hard. I need something to give me courage.

Life isn't worth living without Andy.

There will be no more posts here.

I'm sorry. I can't go on.

*Comments*                                                              *disabled.*

174

# PART 2

PART 2

# Chapter 33

## Roxanne

**Saturday, 12 November**

Isla's phone went straight to voicemail. Roxanne had tried to call and text her several times over the last few days, with no luck. It was odd that her friend hadn't even messaged her from the airport, like she always did.

She glanced over her shoulder to see Leo, the bloke she'd met at Millie's party the week before, heading down the stairs, two at a time.

'Hey,' he said, rubbing sleep from his eyes. He came up behind her, pushed her hair from her neck and trailed her with warm kisses. He smelt good. 'You OK?' he said, dropping down onto a chair at the table next to her and grabbing the box of cornflakes.

She watched him, mesmerised, a surge of panic rising inside her. He ticked far too many boxes – boxes she didn't even know were there to tick. 'Fine thanks.'

She put down her phone and opened Facebook on her laptop and began sharing links to various petitions.

'Can I see you again?' Leo asked, tipping golden flakes into a bowl. 'I'd like to.'

She stared into his eyes. *No, no, no. I hadn't meant to see you this time.* 'Why not?' she said, as her phone vibrated across the table.

'You going to get that?' he said, in his easy way.

She picked up the phone. It was Isla's mum. Sally never normally called. Her number was only in Roxanne's phone from a time when Isla was going through hell.

She was about to answer, when the call ended.

'Everything OK?' Leo said, dark eyes narrowing. 'You look worried.'

'I'm good. I'm sure everything's fine.' She rose from the table, a weird sense of doom washing over her. 'Excuse me,' she said, turning her back on him and pressing Sally's number.

'Hey,' she said into the phone, when Sally picked up.

'Roxanne.' Her voice was jittery. 'I . . . well . . .'

'What's up? You OK?' Roxanne turned a curl of her hair around her finger.

'No, no I'm not. The thing is, Isla has emailed and . . .'

'Sally, what is it?' Roxanne's pulse quickened as Sally burst into tears. There was a rustle on the other end of the line, voices in the background. 'Sally?'

'Roxanne.' It was Gary. His voice low and even. 'The thing is, love . . .' He paused. 'God there's no easy way to say this.'

'Say what, Gary? What's going on?'

'The thing is,' he repeated. 'We think . . . we think Isla may have taken her own life.'

\* \* \*

Sally and Gary's dining room had dropped into a painful silence, when the shrill sound of the doorbell pierced the still air.

'That'll be Jack,' Millie said, rising and rushing to the door.

Within moments, Jack dashed into the room, pale and bewildered, Millie behind him.

'Thank God you're here,' Sally said through tears that hadn't stopped since Roxanne arrived. She rose and pulled him into a hug.

He freed himself from her grasp, yanked off his jacket and threw it onto the sofa in the adjoining lounge. 'I came as quickly as I could.'

'I'm so sorry to drag you away from your father, Jack . . .'

'It's hardly important, Sally, in the scheme of things,' he said, not meeting her eye.

'No, no, of course it isn't. My mind is a complete mess.'

'Why would she have done this?' Gary's elbows were on the table, the heel of his palms pushed into his eyes. 'My girl would never take her own life.'

Sally sat back down next to him. 'We can't make sense of any of it.'

Jack glanced at Sally's pink laptop open on Isla's blog in front of her. The words 'Travelling Girl' headed the home page, typed in a swirly lilac font on a background of blue skies and butterflies, and a photo of Isla smiled from the screen.

Sally must have read all the blog posts twenty times since Roxanne arrived, taking her glasses off and on, as if hoping, each time, the later posts might say something different.

'I keep trying her mobile, even though there's no point,' Jack said, eyes flicking from Sally to Gary.

Gary sighed. He was wearing a polo shirt, and there was a mud stain on his cheeks from gardening. Sally was in the navy skirt suit and white blouse she wore to her part-time job as a travel agent.

'We've all tried to call her,' Gary said, shaking his head. 'If she'd only taken her phone charger.'

Roxanne hadn't seen Gary cry since she arrived. But he'd left the room several times, and his red-rimmed eyes told of private tears. He stood up, pushed his chair back and left the room again, leaving the door open.

Millie sat down next to Roxanne, and Jack dropped into the seat next to Sally.

'So what did her email say?' he asked, fingers entwined on the top of his head, pressing down on his skull as if suppressing unwanted thoughts. Roxanne knew he was already aware of what Isla's email said. Well some of it. Sally had blurted it out on the phone when she'd called him earlier.

179

Sally grabbed a tissue from a box and blew her nose.

'Isla said she was sorry, Jack,' Roxanne said, trying to sound calm, but she was far from it. She'd created a tough, strong image, but wasn't sure that's who she was any more. 'She said she couldn't go on.' She paused for a moment, deliberating whether to say more. He would know soon enough. 'It seems there was someone else, Jack.'

'Someone else?' His eyes flicked to Roxanne's. He lowered his hands and held her in a stare.

She nodded. 'Andy.'

'Andy?' Jack's eyes widened. 'Who the hell is Andy?'

Roxanne shrugged and looked down. 'She met him in Canada, and . . . well . . .'

'She fell in love with him,' Millie cut in.

Jack screwed his hands into fists, his face distorting, as though someone had rammed a blade in his back. He got to his feet and began pacing. 'But we just got engaged,' he said, voice rising. 'How is that even possible?'

'Jack, please. Try to keep calm,' Millie said, eyes doubling in size, her acne inflamed. She pushed her fringe from her forehead. 'We're all trying to make sense of it. We're all in pain here.'

'Sorry,' Jack said. 'Sorry,' he repeated. 'It's just . . . I'm sure I would have known if there was someone else. I know Isla.' But Roxanne picked up on the doubt in his voice. The doubt she felt too.

'We all thought we did,' said Millie, dashing a tear from the corner of her eye. 'But she hasn't been herself lately.' She rose too. 'I'll put the kettle on again.'

Roxanne glanced at the half-empty mugs and screwed-up tissues that littered the table. The strong smell of lilies in a vase in the centre of the table punctured the air, making her nauseous. 'Not for me, Millie, thanks,' she said, pushing her fingers through her hair, a sudden tightness in her chest. 'You got anything stronger?'

'Mum?' Millie looked at Sally.

'There's your dad's gin in the cupboard,' she said.

Silence fell as Millie left the table, tugging up her pink tracksuit bottoms. Her dark hair hung lank and loose to her shoulders, and she wasn't wearing make-up. She crouched down and opened the cupboard door.

Roxanne looked over at the framed photographs that jostled for space on the many surfaces: Isla's graduation; Millie and Julian's wedding; Abigail growing from a cute toddler to a teenager, no evidence of her Asperger's syndrome.

How could this happen to such a strong and happy family? But then Roxanne had asked the same question six years ago, when Carl Jeffery came into Isla's life, and changed her from a carefree young woman to a frightened rabbit refusing to leave the comfort of her parents' house. And now this had happened – an affair gone wrong, and a suicidal impulse. How the hell had she missed that?

Millie pulled out a bottle of gin and a clutch of glasses, and returned to the table.

'Did she mention me? In the email, I mean,' Jack asked, grabbing a glass as Millie filled, knocking back the gin in one gulp.

Roxanne dragged a glass across the table towards her and shook her head. 'I'm so sorry, Jack.'

'She didn't mention me either,' Millie said, as though they'd joined the same club. 'She sent Mum an invitation to read the blog she'd been writing since the beginning of August, said it would explain everything. But . . .'

Jack looked at everyone in turn, grabbed the bottle and filled his glass once more. 'But what?'

'Please don't read the blog, Jack. No good will come from it,' Millie continued.

'Millie's right,' Roxanne said. She'd seen the photo of Isla and Andy sitting in a café together. She'd read Isla's posts – the things she'd said about Jack – and felt sick that her friend had been leading a double life. 'She's said some odd things.'

Sally let out a wail like a strangled cat and pushed her head into her hands. 'What were you thinking, Isla?' she cried, as though her daughter was in the room.

'I want to read it.' Jack sat down once more. 'I need to.'

Roxanne leant across the table and placed her hand over his. 'It's as if none of us really knew her. I wonder if she ever truly got over six years ago, and she mentions an appeal that none of us even knew about.'

'It doesn't make sense, Jack. I can't understand why she didn't tell us about it,' Sally said, dabbing her cheeks with a screwed-up tissue. 'I never even noticed how much pain she was in.' She grabbed a glass and knocked back the drink, pulling a face as the liquid ran down her throat, wincing as she swallowed.

'She said she didn't want to worry you,' Jack said softly, rubbing his forehead.

'You knew about it?' Roxanne glared at Jack. 'And you never said anything.'

'How long have you known?' Sally said, grabbing another tissue.

'She only told me recently.' Jack didn't meet Sally's eye. 'Darleen Jeffery tried to get her brother acquitted back in September.'

'The bitch who wrote that awful book?' Roxanne said.

Jack nodded. 'She didn't win, but it unsettled Isla.' He sighed deeply. 'She wasn't herself.' He looked about him as though trying to find the right words. 'We should contact Camp Arctic.'

'Done that,' Gary said, drifting back into the room, his cheeks red and blotchy. 'She's not in her room. They said they'll make enquiries. Call us back as soon as possible.' He glanced at his watch. 'That was a couple of hours ago. If she's not there, I don't know what else they can do.'

'Maybe it's an awful mistake.' Sally rubbed her face. 'Please let it be a terrible mistake.'

'Have you called the police?' Jack asked. 'Would the cops be able to help?'

Sally nodded. 'They're sending someone round to talk to us.'

At that moment the doorbell rang, and Millie rose once more. 'It must be them,' she said, her voice dull and lifeless, as she left the room.

* * *

Roxanne looked on as two police officers introduced themselves, and sat down at the table, opposite Sally. PC Samantha Langton was young, with dark hair and a large nose; Inspector Blackstone older, with a crumpled, battered look, as though he'd been dragged through the last forty years tied to the back of a police car.

Jack was on his feet once more, pacing in front of the French doors, an unlit cigarette clenched between his fingers.

Roxanne had got up and drifted to the corner of the room, where she was now leaning against the magnolia wall, beneath a print of a field of poppies. To an onlooker she probably looked calm, too nonchalant perhaps, but it was far from the truth. Someone had to stay strong, and looking at the state of everyone else, it had to be her.

'I understand your daughter has sent you an email, claiming she intends to take her own life,' Inspector Blackstone said to Sally, rubbing his chin.

Roxanne couldn't help feeling as if she'd been transported into one of the crime TV shows her mum watched: the bumbling older cop, who was actually a super-sleuth, and his young sidekick.

Except it wasn't, was it? This was her best friend: her lovely, funny Isla. The girl she thought she knew so well, but it seemed she didn't know at all.

Sally stared at the inspector, her bloodshot eyes vacant, as though her brain had shut down, unable to cope any more. She nodded and patted her cheeks with a wad of brightly coloured tissues. 'She just got engaged, seemed happy. I can't believe she would take her own life.' She paused for a moment. 'I should have noticed what a state she was in, especially after what happened before.'

'Carl Jeffery?' The inspector rubbed his forefinger across a deep

183

crevice in his chin, his bushy grey eyebrows rising. He'd clearly done his research. 'Targeted hostels over in Australia.'

Millie nodded. 'Isla was one of his victims,' she said, pouring another gin, and swigging it back in one gulp.

'He killed three backpackers,' the inspector went on, as though he was telling them something new.

Roxanne eased away from the wall and moved towards the table. 'He's rotting in prison, although it's nowhere near enough. He deserves to be strung up by his balls, and a red-hot poker shoved up his arse.' She met Sally's watery eyes. 'Sorry, I just . . .'

'Isla thought she saw him recently,' Millie said.

Jack's forehead furrowed. 'But it couldn't have been him. He had an appeal recently, but it was refused.'

'She was left scarred and shattered, after it happened,' Sally said with a sniff. 'But surely this can't have anything to do with that. It's been six years.'

'She'd been behaving odd lately, Mum,' Millie said.

Gary placed his hand over Sally's. 'The police need to know everything, love,' he said. 'It will give them an idea of the kind of person Isla is. You know yourself how long it took her to even go out after it happened.'

'Yes, but that's the point, Gary. She did in the end,' Sally said. 'Things had been going well for her over the past few years. She'd been like her old self. Why would she let some man ruin that?' She let out a small sob, and whispered into her hands, 'It's heartbreaking.'

'And why get engaged to Jack?' Millie said, meeting the inspector's eye. 'Why would she do that, if there was someone else?'

'Jack?' The inspector scanned the room.

Jack stopped pacing and raised his hand as though he was back at school.

'She met Jack two years ago,' Sally said, voice croaky now from crying. 'She was so happy.'

'But everything changed when she went to Canada,' Millie said.

'She didn't seem herself when she got back. And now we know why. She met someone else.'

Roxanne glanced over at Millie. Was that anger or sadness in her bloodshot eyes?

'You said on the phone that she's in Sweden,' the inspector said.

'Yes, Abisko. She set off on Wednesday.' Sally rubbed her forehead.

'And nobody's heard from her since she arrived? Apart from the email, obviously.'

They all shook their heads.

'She forgot her phone charger,' Jack said. 'So couldn't get in touch.'

'She didn't think to borrow one?'

Jack shrugged. 'Isla often gets lost in her work as a travel writer. She probably didn't think.'

The inspector looked at Jack. 'She never called you from a landline, no emails?'

'No.' Jack shook his head, his expression hard to read. 'She's only been gone since Wednesday.'

'Except she's been blogging, as it turned out,' Millie said, refilling her glass, the gin splashing on the table. 'She found time to do that.'

'Millie, please,' Roxanne said. 'That isn't helpful. This is hard enough for Jack, for all of us.'

'But it's the truth.' Millie brought the glass to her lips. 'I'm only saying it like it is. She couldn't ring up or email us, but she was typing away on that stupid fucking blog of hers.'

'Stop that now.' Sally glared at her daughter.

'I'm not five, Mum,' Millie said under her breath.

The inspector's eyes were back on Sally. 'So Isla's email came in early this morning.'

Sally nodded, now shredding a tissue, its pieces drifting onto the table.

'And Isla said in this email that she was going to take her own life.'

'Not in those words exactly, but . . . yes.' A tear rolled down her face.

'May I see the email?'

185

Sally rubbed her eyes dry, put on her glasses, and opened the email. She pushed the laptop across the table towards the inspector.

To: SALLY Johnson sallyjohnson@windlemail.com
From: ISLA Johnson islajohnson@windlemail.com

*Dear Mum*
*I'm sorry I can't go on living.*
*I fell in love for the first time in my life in Canada, but I was let down so painfully. Andy is my everything. Without him, I can't go on.*
*I've been writing a blog since August – www.travellinggirlblog. com. It began as my travel blog, but later it was where I privately wrote my thoughts. I've sent you an invitation to read it, in the hope that, when you do, it will help you to understand what I've been through and why this has to be goodbye.*

# Chapter 34

'I still can't believe she didn't mention me in her email,' Millie said, her chin crinkling.

Roxanne cleared her throat. 'Or Jack,' she whispered.

Jack drifted behind the inspector and leant over his shoulder. Even the police officers were silent, as Jack's sad eyes skimmed the words.

Finally, he ran the back of his hand over his eyes, turned and, with glass in hand, padded into the lounge, and dropped, helpless, onto the sofa.

'Who is Andy?' Inspector Blackstone asked.

'We have no idea.' Sally rubbed her neck. 'Isla never mentioned him.'

'To any of us,' Roxanne added.

'There's a lot about him on the blog she was writing,' Sally said, reaching over and gently touching her laptop, as though Isla was trapped inside. 'It seems she loved him.'

The inspector began clicking through the blog posts, eyes flicking over the words, thick fingers awkward on the keyboard, as he read Isla's upbeat posts from August and early September, telling of things she and Jack had done together – places they'd been to – and later the desperate ramblings.

'Did any of you know she felt this way?' the inspector asked, eyes narrowing as he focused on each of them in turn.

A pang of guilt ran through Roxanne. Could she have done more? Had she been so preoccupied with her job, her causes? Her mind flashed from Isla pinging the rubber band on her wrist, to her friend collapsing at Millie's party, sobbing. And why hadn't Isla messaged her the day she left for Sweden? Isla always texted before she took off abroad.

They all shook their heads. Isla had been acting odd, but not suicidal.

'So you haven't heard anything from her since the email?' the inspector asked.

Sally shook her head.

'And you've tried her mobile?'

'Of course, a hundred times.' There was mild irritation in Gary's voice. 'Her battery's flat. She forgot her charger.'

Inspector Blackstone grunted as he heaved himself out of the chair, as though his body wasn't agreeing to the movement. 'We'll contact the police over there. See if there have been any reported suicides.'

Sally burst into tears. 'Oh God, my darling, darling girl,' she cried, burying her face in her hands.

Roxanne rarely cried, but at that moment the pain was unbearable. Tears stung the backs of her eyes. It took all her willpower to beat them back.

'We'll be in touch, Mr and Mrs Johnson,' the inspector said, heading for the door. 'Rest assured, we will do everything we can to find out what's happened to your daughter.'

Gary saw the police officers out, thanking them. But what could they do? What could anyone do but wait?

Ten minutes later, Sally was upstairs lying down, and Gary was deadheading flowers in the garden, snapping the shears with force. He was a gentle man normally, but today it was as if he wanted to kill someone.

Jack was outside too, smoking, looking on, one hand deep in his trouser pocket. Roxanne could see through the window that they weren't talking. That neither had anything to say.

'I should head off,' she said, turning to see Millie pour another gin.

'No, no, no, please stay,' Millie begged, her voice slurred. She picked up the bottle and glass, and stood up. 'Let's talk,' she added, staggering into the lounge, where she dropped onto the sofa.

Roxanne followed. 'But I'm not much use here, Millie,' she said. 'My phone's on, just call me if you hear anything.'

'None of us are any use, Roxanne, but it's good to know we're all here together, supporting each other, supporting Isla.' She put the gin bottle on the coffee table in front of her and patted the seat next to her. 'Sit with me for a bit,' she said. 'Please.'

Roxanne felt she had no choice and lowered herself onto the edge of the sofa. 'OK, I'll stay a bit longer,' she said. 'But I really should go soon.'

Millie knocked back the drink and filled the glass once more. 'I'm not a drinker, as a rule,' she said, pulling a face.

'I know you're not, so maybe you should go easy, aye?'

'Julian doesn't like me drinking, says I show myself up.'

Roxanne had noticed he wasn't there when she first arrived and had been relieved. The last time she'd seen him was at Millie's party, where he'd refused to dress up, finding the whole thing ridiculous. He'd made a comment about Roxanne's costume being far too tight, and that she should be careful as the men were ogling her. She'd ignored him. He wasn't worth her energy.

'Where is he?' she said, watching as Millie continued to pour drink down her throat.

'Julian?' It was as though she'd forgotten her train of thought.

Roxanne nodded.

'Miniatur Wunderland.' Millie's attempts at German weren't good, especially after so much drink. She shrugged. 'Somewhere in Germany . . . Hamburg, I think. It's this huge model railway attraction he wanted to see.' She flung one arm in the air. 'So I'm home alone at the moment.'

'No Abigail?'

'Staying with a friend. She's taken Larry.' She took another gulp of gin. 'Do you know what? I don't even like this.' She held up the glass and stared at it, furrowing her forehead. 'But these are unprecedented circumstances, don't you think?'

'They are,' Roxanne agreed. 'But maybe you should slow up a bit. You won't be much use to Isla pissed.'

'I'm not pissed.' Millie's eyes widened, and then she laughed. 'You know what, Roxy? Do you mind if I call you Roxy?'

Roxanne hated it, but she kept quiet. It seemed petty.

'You know what, Roxy?' Millie repeated. 'Isla has always been my pretty little sister. So lovely. So perfect.' She flopped her head back on the sofa with a thud and closed her eyes. 'I'm afraid I was left behind the door when God gave out all the good things. He forgot about me, and later gave them all to Isla.'

Roxanne looked at Millie. She wasn't unattractive – struggled a bit with her skin and weight, perhaps, but Roxanne knew when Millie put the effort in, she looked good.

'You're both beautiful,' she said. 'And anyway, looks mean nothing. It's about who you are on the inside. And you've always been the best sister to Isla.'

'Do you think so?' Millie said, eyes still closed.

'Yes, and let's face it, Isla's life has hardly been perfect.'

Millie opened her eyes. 'I know. I know. I'm drunk. Ignore me.' She flapped her hand and took another gulp of her drink. 'It's not exactly been a normal day, has it?'

'You can say that again.'

'I guess it's hit me that Isla has so much. She's beautiful, clever, and has the most amazing man in her life. A perfect life.' She glanced out through the window at Jack, and he turned and met her eye. 'And she's snuffed it out like a candle . . . just like that.' A tear rolled down her cheek and dripped from her chin.

'We don't know that for sure.' Roxanne's words seemed hollow. What more proof did they need? All they could really hope for was that Isla's suicide attempt had failed. 'And you have a lovely life too, a great job . . . Abigail . . . Julian.'

'Ha! A husband who barely looks at me, let alone wants sex with me, and he always pick, pick, picks away at everything I do; and a daughter who struggles to interact, bless her heart. Yeah, my life's a bed of roses, Roxanne.' She sighed deeply. 'Don't get me wrong, I love my Abigail, and would kill for her, but sometimes it would be nice if someone in my house actually had a proper conversation with me. I get more interaction from Larry.'

Roxanne took hold of Millie's hand. 'I'm sorry. I didn't know that's how you felt. Isla always told me you were happy.'

'Isla thinks I am, I suppose. I keep it all in here, you see.' She tapped her head three times. 'I pretend to the world that all is fabulous in my life, but it's a big pile of steaming crap.'

'I'm sorry,' Roxanne said again, a little stunned by how self-absorbed Millie was being in the circumstances. But then emotions were running high, and she was drunk. 'Just try to remember Isla's had it far from easy. Don't forget what she went through . . .'

'Oh no, we mustn't forget that, must we?' She rolled her eyes heavenwards.

'She could have died that day.'

'Yes, but she didn't, did she? And then she met lovely Jack.' Millie's eyes were back on the window. 'How could she?'

Roxanne didn't have an answer. 'We all thought they were happy.'

'Mmm, but she decides Jack's not enough, and sleeps with some Canadian Mountie, or whoever he is—'

'I don't think he's a Mountie, Millie.'

'—and because that doesn't work out she gives up on life, without thinking of the effect it will have on us all. Nobody saw that coming, did they?' She turned from the window, and screwed up her nose, wobbling her head as though struggling to focus. 'Why would she do that to us, Roxy?'

Roxanne felt helpless. People who take their own lives feel they have no reason to live. Millie had a reason to live, even if she couldn't

191

see it at that moment. She lived for Abigail. She said herself she would kill for her. But it seemed Isla thought she had nothing to live for any more, narrowing her life to a pinpoint where only Andy was important. She'd lost sight of the people who loved her. She saw no reason to carry on.

'She's stupid, stupid, stupid. Couldn't see how much I adore her,' Millie cried, her high-pitched tone jabbing into Roxanne's thoughts, then she gulped and swallowed, colour draining from her face. 'Actually, I feel a bit sick.'

'I'm thinking you've probably had enough to drink.' Roxanne took the glass from her and put it on the table.

Millie didn't resist and leant her head on Roxanne's shoulder. 'I almost had an affair once, Foxy Roxy,' she said, 'with a teacher at the school where I work. He asked me out for a drink and I went. I liked him – still do, in fact. I was so close to saying yes to going away with him, but, unlike my sister, I didn't jump into what looked like greener grass, only to find a swamp. I just bit down hard and got on with it with Julian.' She paused for a moment, her face wet with tears. 'Do you think my sister's dead, Roxanne?' she said, her voice cracking, as a fat tear rolled down her blotchy face. 'Because I couldn't bear it if she is.'

There was a silence before Millie fell asleep. Roxanne eased her from her shoulder, and slipped off the sofa, lowering Millie's head onto the cushion and covering her with a throw.

Roxanne returned to the dining room to find Jack had come in from the garden and was now sitting alone at the table, reading Isla's blog on Sally's laptop. His eyes had landed on a photograph of Isla and Andy outside a café together. They were looking towards the camera. Isla, in a black jacket with a grey fur collar, hair twisted into a messy knot, her fingers gripping a cup, her laptop closed in front of her. To Roxanne, Andy looked ordinary. Neat, red hair, average build, around thirty – not cute and quirkily handsome like Jack. No, this Andy, whoever he was, was nothing special. Ordinary. He was dressed in a dark jacket, a green-checked scarf looped around his neck, and there was a cup in front of him too.

'How did he win her over?' Jack whispered, as though he could read Roxanne's thoughts. 'How the hell did he steal her from me?'

'I'm sorry,' she said. 'I wish I knew.' She moved closer and rested her hand on his shoulder. 'I'm going to Abisko now,' she said, on impulse. 'I need to know what's happened to her. Find out for myself. I can't just wait around here for Policeman Plod.'

Jack snapped the laptop closed and turned to look at her. 'I'll come with you. Luna's already in the cattery as I was supposed to be spending the weekend at my father's.' His face crumpled with uncertainty. 'I can't sit around here and do nothing.'

# Chapter 35

'I wasn't sure what to throw in my holdall,' Roxanne said, as she and Jack headed down the aisle of the aircraft looking for their seat numbers. She'd managed to book tickets for an afternoon flight to Stockholm from Stansted Airport, and a continuing transfer to Kiruna. 'It can be well into the minuses over there this time of year.'

It was small talk, and she didn't blame him for not responding. In fact, he'd barely said a word as they'd waited in departures for their gate to open, his head in his hands.

She spotted their seats and shuffled in next to the window. Jack shoved his coat in the overhead compartment, and plonked down next to her with a thud, before pushing his carry-on bag under the seat in front of him. He looked pale under his beard, his eyes bloodshot. He clipped his seatbelt on, pulled up the hood of his sweatshirt, a Heath Ledger 'Joker' on the front, and shut his eyes, closing himself off. It was clear his sadness had deepened to another level, and Roxanne wished she could take him in her arms and squeeze. How could her friend have done this to such a nice guy?

She didn't attempt any further conversation. There would be time enough for that once they arrived in Sweden, when he would have to talk about the blog and face up to the fact that there'd been another man in Isla's life. For now, silence was probably the best option.

She pulled a book from her carry-on bag and settled down to read, but her mind wouldn't absorb the words. Instead it buzzed and fizzed, her body restless as the plane took off, and the UK was reduced to the size of a model village.

* * *

In Kiruna, they climbed down the metal steps of the plane, and onto the icy ground. Roxanne slipped on her ski jacket and bobble hat, and Jack tugged on his long, grey woollen coat. He looked as though he was about to go into the trenches in World War I. He lifted the collar as a strong gust of wind cut across them.

'Jesus,' he said, voice low and sad, as they dashed through the darkness towards arrivals. 'This is a nightmare from hell.'

They took a taxi to Abisko, and the driver, Erik, tried, in upbeat fashion, to fill them in about the history of the area, but Roxanne barely took in his words, and she knew Jack was struggling, his gaze focused on the huge expanse of white, under the night sky.

At Camp Arctic, Roxanne brushed snow from her shoulders, as they stepped through the double doors into reception, and banged snow from their boots. They approached a red-headed woman sitting behind a counter.

'Hi. Do you speak English?' Roxanne asked, clapping her hands to try to warm them.

'Of course. How may I help?' The woman smiled.

'I think it was you I spoke to on the phone earlier. I'm Roxanne Furaha. I'm looking for my friend Isla Johnson who appears to have gone missing. She was . . . *is* staying here.'

'That's right, yes. I'm afraid your friend hasn't returned.' She looked at the screen in front of her. 'You've booked two single rooms. Is that right?'

Roxanne nodded and, as the woman searched for keys, she glanced over her shoulder. The reception had a cosy feel. There were a couple of armchairs, and three sofas heaped with mismatched cushions and draped with fur throws. There were a few people dotted about reading newspapers or looking at their phones and iPads. A floor-to-ceiling window looked out into the darkness, and a rather dated-looking computer was on a desk in the corner for guests to use. On a table near the restaurant was a jug brimming with loganberry juice and several glasses.

The woman handed Roxanne and Jack the keys. 'Once you're settled in we can talk if you like.' She eyed Jack, who was shivering, his face rosy-red from the cold. 'We have snowsuits and boots,' she said, nodding towards a wooden rack near the door, as the fluffy face of a dog appeared on the counter. She stroked its head.

'I'm fine as I am,' Jack said, his eyes darting around the room, as though searching for Isla.

'You're in rooms twelve and seventeen. Easy to find, they're just through there.' She pointed towards a side door in the corner. 'Dinner is from seven to nine, and breakfast is served from eight.'

The corridor was narrow – doors on the left-hand side heading into the near distance, windows on the right. Jack led the way past a cleaning trolley.

'God kväll,' a housekeeper called from inside room nine.

They continued along the corridor in silence until they reached room twelve. 'I'll see you in five minutes in reception, shall I?' Roxanne said, as she opened the door. 'We can talk to the woman and decide where to go from there.' But in truth, she had no idea where 'there' was. What the hell did she think she could do here, snowed in and far from anywhere?

'OK,' Jack said, carrying his holdall further along the corridor, shoulders slumped as he entered his room.

Roxanne's room was like a cupboard. She propped her bag in the corner and pulled out her phone. It had reset an hour forward, and her Internet roaming had attached to a Swedish network. She had hoped there would be a message from Sally with news from the police. How hard could it be to find out about a suicide attempt in this quiet, out-of-the-way place?

196

She took off her jacket, pulled free her scarf and woolly hat, and sat down on the edge of the bed. 'Isla,' she whispered, legs sprawled almost touching the wall. 'Where the hell are you?'

She left her room and walked towards reception, where the dogs bounded to greet her.

'Hi, there,' she said, ruffling their heads, as she made her way towards the sofa.

It was some time before Jack appeared. He was still wearing the same sweatshirt, but his hair was damp, and his face had drained to the colour magnolia. He joined her on the sofa, and Roxanne picked up on a slight smell of cigarettes. The red-headed woman came from behind the counter and made her way over, heavy boots clonking the hardwood floor.

'I'm Alma,' she said, sitting down in one of the armchairs. 'So what do you need to know?'

Roxanne bit her lip as a jumble of incoherent words gathered in her head. Nothing sounded right. She didn't know where to start.

'So you've checked Isla's room,' Jack said, and Roxanne threw him a wide-eyed look. Of course they'd checked her room. They'd said that on the phone. It was clear he had no idea what to ask either. This was ridiculous. They were like two school kids playing detective.

Alma nodded. 'Your friend's belongings are there. Although I must tell you it was cleaned this morning before we got your call. Do you need to take a look?'

'That would be great. If that's OK,' Roxanne said, looking at Jack, who nodded.

'Did you see Isla talk to anyone while she was here?' Jack asked. 'A man with red hair, maybe?'

Roxanne wanted to reach out and hold his hand, but stopped herself.

Alma's brow furrowed. She shrugged. 'Not that I recall. Your friend spent most of her time alone, writing on her laptop, or taking photographs.'

'Typical Isla,' Jack said, a crack in his voice.

'She went to the sky station at Abisko National Park last night, I believe. A couple who are staying here, Alex and Maddie Grimes, mentioned they'd been there too. They may have seen her, spoken to her, perhaps. Is that helpful?'

'Could be,' Roxanne said. 'They may have seen her with someone.' She didn't catch Jack's eye, but imagined his thought process. Isla had said on her blog she met Andy at the foot of the chairlift.

Alma looked around her. 'I don't think Mr and Mrs Grimes are here at the moment. They said something about going to the Ice Hotel in Jukkasjärvi, but they should be back later. Perhaps speak to them then.'

'Yes, yes we will.'

'So when was the last time you saw Isla?' Jack asked.

'Well . . . as I say . . . she went to the sky station, but I didn't notice her return. All our guests have passes for the rear door, for when they arrive back after ten o'clock. We close the front entrance around that time, so she may have come back after that.' She paused, looking straight at Roxanne. 'Maybe you need to give it a bit more time before you panic too much. It's normal for a grown woman to take off.'

'Yes, but I told you on the phone, she sent us an email saying she was going to commit suicide.' Roxanne's voice had risen in volume and smacked of anger. She hooked Alma into a stare. 'Hardly normal.'

'Can we see her room now?' Jack said, getting up and shoving his hands into his jean pockets, as though he wanted to defuse the moment.

'Of course.' Alma rose, and threw Roxanne a concerned glance. 'I'll get the key.'

She led the way, and stood in the doorway of Isla's room, as Roxanne and Jack stepped in. But they were no sooner through the door, when the dogs started barking in reception.

'Tindra! Max!' Alma yelled down the corridor. She screwed up her face. 'I shouldn't really leave you,' she said, tapping the door key on her palm three times. 'But I guess you look honest enough.' And with that she dashed away yelling, '*Stoppa buller!*'

They wandered aimlessly around the tiny room for a few moments, before Jack dragged Isla's case from the corner. He threw it onto the bed and unzipped it.

'I should have known there was someone else,' he said, his voice a whisper. 'She wouldn't talk about the wedding or set a date. I must have pushed her into the engagement. I'm such an idiot.'

'Not an idiot, Jack.'

He stood for some moments, staring into space. 'She would flinch sometimes when I went to hold her.'

'She was like that after Carl Jeffery, Jack. I reckon that was as much to do with her worrying herself silly about him and the appeal, as anything else.'

He shrugged and shook his head, as though he didn't believe her words, then began rummaging in Isla's case. He tugged out a jewellery box, opened it and pulled out a St Christopher medal. 'She's not wearing it,' he said. 'Maybe she hasn't travelled far.'

Roxanne couldn't help thinking Isla might not have wanted the luck of the saints where she'd said she was going. She swallowed down her sadness.

'Did you buy it for her?' Jack asked.

'What?'

'The necklace, did you buy it?'

'Uh-huh.' She nodded. 'Just before she went to Canada.'

His lips fleetingly turned up at the corners. 'Well, at least she didn't lie about that,' he said, putting it back in the box, and closing the lid.

'Oh, no,' Roxanne muttered, spotting a photo propped on the shelf. She cleared her throat. 'It's the picture of Isla and Andy,' she went on, picking it up and turning it over. There was nothing written on the back. 'It's the one on her blog.'

Jack closed his eyes for a second, as though mustering strength, before stepping towards her and taking it from her hands. He dropped down hard on the bed. 'Shit,' he said, his eyes filling with tears. 'How did I get it so fucking wrong? She even said I was trying to fix her. I wasn't trying to fix her. I just loved her.'

'Jack. I'm so sorry.'

'You know what, I've just remembered, there was this guy called Andy on her Facebook – you don't suppose . . .'

'Facebook.'

'Yeah.' He paused, scratching his head. 'Andy . . . I can't even remember his surname, that's how little notice I took. But he's on her Facebook. His profile picture was a maple leaf. It's got to be him – the bloke from her blog – talking to her on social media, right in front of me.'

'We have to contact him, Jack,' she said, pulling out her phone, but she had no signal.

'No. *You* contact him, Roxanne. There's no way I want to talk to the slimy shit.' He got up and straightened his shoulders. 'I don't even know why I'm here, if I'm honest,' he said, waving the photo in the air. 'This!' His voice had grown in volume and smacked of anger. 'This isn't who I thought Isla was.'

Roxanne took the picture from him and put it in her pocket. 'None of us did, Jack,' she said.

The sudden silence that fell between them was painful.

'We must find her,' she said, eventually, pulling Isla's teddy bear from the bedside cabinet and hugging it to her chest. 'She had this at uni. Never goes anywhere without it.'

'Until now.' Jack covered his face with his hands.

She put the battered bear back on the bedside cabinet, kissed her fingertips, and pressed them against it, before looking around the room once more. 'There's no gin bottle,' she said.

'What?'

'Isla said on her blog she was drinking gin last night, didn't she? So where's the empty bottle?'

He shrugged. 'Alma said the cleaner's been in. She would have emptied the bin.' He was on his feet again, pacing. 'I didn't even know she liked bloody gin. Or that she was writing a blog. I didn't know her at all.' A tear rolled down his face, and Roxanne pulled him into a hug and patted his back as if she was comforting a child.

'But we still have to find her,' she said, releasing him and gripping his upper arms, snagging him into a stare. 'We need to know what's happened, even if it's the worst possible news.'

'You're right,' he said, pulling away and rubbing the back of his hand across his face. He turned and opened Isla's case. 'We need to find her.'

He tugged out a couple of jumpers and her laptop.

'Do you think she wrote her final blog post on that?' Roxanne asked. 'Her email to her mum?'

Jack shook his head. 'No, this is just for writing. Isla hated the Internet distracting her when she was working. She must have used the guest computer in reception.' He threw the jumper and laptop back in the case, a look of defeat on his face. 'Roxanne, what are we doing here? We're not Sherlock and Doctor Watson. What the hell do we think we'll find?' He pulled a packet of cigarettes from his pocket and pulled one free.

'You can't smoke in here, Jack,' she said.

'No, no, God, I'm really not thinking straight.' He shoved the cigarette back into the pack.

'Try to keep calm, please. We need to be strong, for Isla.'

'How, Roxanne?' He shook his head. 'I would have done anything for her, and she cheated on me.' He lowered himself back onto the edge of the bed. 'I thought we were good, you know. I thought she loved me.'

'She did, Jack.'

'No!' He shook his head again. 'No, you don't do this to someone you love. And now she's gone, and I've lost her in the worst possible way.' He paused. 'I just don't know what to do.'

Roxanne's eyes stung. Jack was one of the best, always making everyone laugh – brilliant to be around. *How could you do this, Isla? This is beyond cruel.* Why had Isla led him on, when she was crazily in love with someone else? She sat down beside him and took hold

201

of his hand. 'Oh, Jack,' she said, 'this is about what Carl Jeffery did to her. The damage he did.'

He looked up, silent now, his face damp, eyes intense green. 'I need to go back to the UK,' he whispered. 'This is killing me. I don't know what I was thinking saying I'd come.' He tugged his hand away, got up, and left the room.

Roxanne hurried after him. 'Jack, please,' she called, racing down the corridor. 'I can't do this alone.'

'I can't do this at all, Roxanne. I'm sorry,' he said, not looking back. 'Please, Jack.'

He put the key in his door and turned to face her. He was shaking. 'I thought I could, but I can't,' he said, stepping into his room. 'I'm sorry.' He closed the door with a gentle snap.

Roxanne rested her forehead on the wood, biting down hard on her bottom lip to stop her tears.

Ten minutes later he'd gone.

Roxanne was alone.

# Chapter 36

Back in her room, Roxanne flopped onto her bed, folded the pillow and shoved it under her head, her mind spinning. Where the hell was she supposed to begin?

Why hadn't Isla turned to someone? Surely after all their years of friendship, she should have known Roxanne would have been there for her. Why hadn't Isla said something? Given someone a clue to her state of mind. Or had she, and Roxanne had missed it?

There were ways back from the edge. Choices. Someone would have helped her – listened. Even if Isla didn't want to mention Andy to Roxanne or Jack, there were suicide helplines – The Samaritans – a doctor. Why hadn't she cried for help? *Why, Isla?*

Edgy, Roxanne pulled herself to a sitting position and leant against the wall. Twirling a curl of her hair around her finger, she bit down on her sadness, refusing to let it drop deeper, determined not to let her friend down. She had to do something – anything. Surely the fact there had been no news was hope enough that Isla could still be alive.

Propelled by that hope, she leapt from the bed and headed to reception. She would question the guests. Ask if anyone had seen Isla.

The dogs were sprawled on the floor in reception, and a blond lad of about fourteen, wearing a thick-knit sweater and a woolly hat, was tapping away at the computer.

A young couple had followed Roxanne through the side door, and the woman smiled. 'Beautiful here, isn't it?' she said, with an American accent.

'Yes, yes it is,' Roxanne said. Keen to begin her questioning, she pulled out her phone and found a picture of her and Isla – a photo of them attempting to ice-skate last Christmas, holding each other up, cheeks pink with the cold. They'd been useless on the ice, but the day had been fun. They'd had doughnuts and Prosecco for lunch, pizza and Prosecco for dinner, and they'd laughed until they hurt.

She showed the couple the picture. 'I don't suppose you've seen my friend.'

They leant in as one, to glance at the photo. 'Yes, I saw her a couple of times,' the woman said. 'Once on the minibus after we'd been on a husky ride, and another time here in reception.'

Roxanne pulled the photograph of Isla with Andy from her pocket. 'Did you see her with this man?'

They shook their heads, glancing at each other. 'Sorry,' the woman said.

'Well, thanks anyway,' Roxanne said, doubting how useful she was being.

As the couple walked away, she dropped down on the sofa next to a man in his sixties reading a newspaper. 'I don't suppose you've seen this woman?' she began again, as someone wearing a bright blue snow jacket with a mountain scene on the back, got up and disappeared into the night.

'I think I may have seen her in the restaurant,' the man said, studying the picture. 'But young blonde women all look the same, don't they?' He paused. 'Are you a policewoman? Has she been murdered?'

Roxanne shifted away from him, the thought turning her stomach. 'No, no, of course not.'

'Well, who is she then?'

Roxanne rose without responding, noticing the teenage boy was no longer at the computer. She turned, spotting him through the window, where he scooped up a handful of snow and lobbed it at the glass, before racing away, and disappearing into the darkness.

Roxanne headed for the screen and rested her fingers on the keyboard. After a few moments' thought, she signed into Facebook, and got up Isla's profile. Her last update was the one she'd put on just before leaving England.

*At Stansted Airport waiting for my flight. Camp Arctic, Abisko, here I come – WHOOP!*

Roxanne had commented, telling her to have a great time, but Isla hadn't replied, or even liked her words. She'd had several likes, but she couldn't see any comments from anyone called Andy.

She clicked on Isla's friend list. There was only one Andy. Andy Fisher. His profile picture was a maple leaf, and his cover photo a picture of Niagara Falls. Could this be him? The man who Isla fell in love with? There was nothing else to see. No updates to view. And although he'd changed his profile picture a few times over the last couple of years, they were all generic photos of places and animals. His friends list wasn't visible either. And there was no way of sending him a private message. She couldn't contact him. The most she could do was attempt to add him as a friend. Although she didn't hold out much hope that he would accept. He wouldn't know who she was, so why would he?

She would tell Sally about him and hope the police could get hold of him.

She sat for some moments, struggling to believe Isla would lose her sanity so quickly over a broken relationship. But maybe it was possible. After all, Andy had seemed to be the only person who could stop Isla's fear of Carl Jeffery. Roxanne dragged her fingers through her hair. Or had something snapped in Isla's mind? If she could find out what, maybe it would help her find her.

A memory drifted in of a schizophrenic man she'd once worked with, who tragically threw himself under a train. She keyed in 'schizophrenia' and 'symptoms' and millions of websites flashed up. She clicked on a few. *It usually begins in early adulthood. Hallucinations. Schizophrenics have a higher than normal chance of committing suicide.* Roxanne pushed her hair flat with the palms of her hands, as she stared at the screen. Was Isla suffering with schizophrenia?

She was about to key in Dissociative Identity Disorder, but her fingers froze on the keyboard. What the hell was she doing? How was this helping? She wasn't a psychologist, and even if she was, how would any of this find Isla? She stifled a desperate cry, tears blurring her vision.

Her pulse throbbed in her temples, as she closed down the row of website tabs she'd opened, at speed – ashamed she'd even gone there. A pain settled deep in her chest. *Be alive, Isla. I'll be there for you, always. Just be alive.* She rubbed her eyes, her head solid – heavy with confusion. She'd been so close with Isla over the years, but now she wondered if she'd known her friend at all. She clenched her fist against her forehead, her mind flashing back to university. Isla was happy and carefree – a little shy at first, perhaps, but she'd grabbed life and run with it. She'd been kind too. In fact, the only person she'd ever hurt was Trevor Cooper, and she'd felt awful about that.

Roxanne impulsively keyed 'Trevor Cooper' into the search engine. Rolling her eyes at her own stupidity when thousands of websites appeared. She tried 'Trevor Cooper Chemistry', knowing he'd studied the subject, but Cooper was a far too common name. She signed into Facebook, and ploughed through hundreds of pictures of strangers, unable to find anyone who even vaguely resembled the Trevor Cooper she remembered.

Suddenly she felt uneasy, as though she was being watched. She swung round, but nobody in the reception area seemed to be paying her any attention. She turned back to the screen, and on impulse searched Facebook for Sara Pembroke. She scrolled through several profiles before she came to one that seemed to bounce off the screen. Her stomach flipped. There was no doubting she'd found the correct Sara Pembroke. Her profile picture was the one of her and Isla, taken in Cambridge.

Roxanne took a deep breath, battling down a surge of – what was that? Envy? She was being silly. Sara had every right to have a picture of her and Isla as her profile picture. Maybe Isla had become friendlier with Sara than Roxanne had realised. She may even know something about Andy.

She wasted no time in sending her a friend request, a spark of hope rising. The most important thing was finding Isla, not her petty jealousies.

She flung her head back. Oh God, was she clutching at nothing?

Again on impulse, she keyed in Darleen Jeffery, and quickly found her Twitter account. She had over five thousand followers, a photograph of her book as her cover photo, and her profile was a picture of two children Roxanne assumed were her and Carl.

'Good God,' she whispered, as she read tweet after tweet around the time of the appeal. Darleen had been so outspoken, calling Isla a liar. But the last tweet was on 1 October. It was as though the appeal being rejected had finally silenced her.

'Hi!'

Roxanne turned to see the lad from earlier by her side, his chubby, freckled cheeks pink with the cold.

'I heard you say you're looking for someone,' he said in broken English.

'Yeah, that's right,' Roxanne said, grabbing her phone, and bringing up the picture of Isla. 'Have you seen her?'

He stared at the screen for some moments, before saying, 'Yes, last night, they were coming through the back door, when I was returning to my room.'

'They?'

'She was with a man.'

Roxanne's pulse throbbed in her neck. 'Do you remember what he looked like?'

'He had red hair. They were kissing.' His cheeks reddened further.

Roxanne took the photo from her pocket. 'Is this him?' she said. 'Yes, that's him.'

'Did you see her after that?' Roxanne asked, trying to control her emotions.

'No. Just the one time,' he said, and he turned and took off through the side door.

Roxanne's hopes quickly petered away. What did that prove, other than what she knew already?

She turned back to the computer, and stared at the screen, her mind drifting to all the strange things that had happened to Isla before she came to Sweden. It started with the reunion. Why had Trevor Cooper bottled at the last minute? *I hope you've made the right decision*, he'd written on Isla's engagement update.

But then none of this was helpful, or even relevant. Her mind was jumping like a grasshopper without a leaf to land on. Jack was right. He wasn't Sherlock, and she certainly wasn't Doctor Watson. But then what else had she got to grab on to?

Later, in her room, she drifted into a fitful, nightmare-fuelled sleep. Through solid darkness, Isla was running towards her, screaming, slipping and sliding on icy ground. 'Help! She's going to kill me.'

'I'm here, Isla,' Roxanne called back, holding out her arms, but she was wedged knee-deep in snow. It clung to her legs like cement. She stretched forward and Isla grabbed her, exhausted, her face streaming with tears.

'Thank you,' Isla said, falling into Roxanne's arms like a rag doll.

Microseconds later, a knife was plunged deep into Isla's back.

'Nooooooooooo,' Roxanne cried, as her friend fell to the floor, just as she had that day in the car park at Millie's party, her blood spreading in the whiteness like red wine into a carpet. Roxanne dropped to her knees and cradled her friend in her arms.

'I had to get rid of her.' The voice was some distance away. Roxanne looked up to see another Isla, eyes ice-cold, face bleached white. 'She wasn't really me.'

Roxanne's eyes shot open. Gasping for breath, she scrambled to a sitting position and cradled her knees. Her body was hot and sweaty, despite the cold, her sheets twisted beneath her.

The curtains at her window were half-open, revealing the night sky. It was snowing again, and she longed for home, or just a familiar face to appear behind the glass – although, at times, home could be a lonely place too.

She sat for some moments, taking deep breaths, stilling herself and trying for calm. Finally, she got out of bed and pulled on her snow-suit, gloves, hat and boots. She had never understood Isla's craving for space and air, always loving loud places and crowds, but she thought she understood now. The desire to dive outside into the quietness of the cold night, and not look back, and the need to piece together her thoughts where nobody could hear them, was overwhelming.

She made her way through reception, moving silently past the sleeping dogs, but the entrance was locked. It was gone ten o'clock. She turned back and returned to the long corridor. She passed the rooms, and left through the back door, where the boy had said he'd seen Isla with Andy.

It had stopped snowing, but the freezing air made her cheeks tingle. She wrapped her scarf around her face, and walked away from the lodge, heading under a bridge and out into open countryside, her mind turning everything over.

Perhaps she should have stayed in the UK. It had been an impulsive, stupid decision to come, when emotions were running high. The kind she always made. But then she wanted to be there. She needed to be there.

She walked for a long time, using her phone torch to guide her way. Eventually her nose and fingertips became numb, and her toes, despite a layering of socks and her fur-lined boots, felt as though they might snap off. And now, the many footprints in the snow around Camp Arctic had dwindled to one set of prints stretching into the distance like chocolate buttons on royal icing. There were animal prints too – a moose or perhaps a bear.

She took a deep breath, and let it out, mist forming in front of her lips. She was about to turn back, when a sudden noise in the trees caught her attention. She sprang around and pointed her torch towards the sound.

'Hello!' She flicked the light across the leafless, snow-heavy trees. 'Is anybody there?'

There was another rustle.

She spun around to see that the route she'd travelled was a tunnel of darkness. She'd definitely come too far. She'd walked for almost an hour, trying to clear her head.

A snake of green whipped across the black sky. *The Northern Lights*.

Her heart raced and she felt angry with herself. She didn't do afraid. And yet here she was gripped by fear.

She began to head back, shoulders hunched to her ears as she stepped in her own footprints. In her haste, she stumbled, falling face down in the snow. She lifted her head to look back over her shoulder, her cheeks freezing, and shone her torch into the darkness. *What if it's a bear?* Suddenly a hare darted from the trees where she'd focused her light a few moments ago. It bounded across the path, its back legs leaping as if on springs, and into the bushes on the other side.

She scrambled to her feet and brushed the snow from her suit with gloved hands. 'Bloody hare, you nearly gave me a heart attack,' she muttered, close to tears as she hurried back to the lodge.

There was no doubting that it had been stunningly beautiful out there in the cold, dark night, far away from everything and everyone. But it was a place for those who absorbed the heavy silence and loneliness without fear. It might be something Isla craved, but Roxanne knew now, it wasn't for her.

### Sunday, 13 November

It was still dark when Roxanne woke at 6 a.m. She lay for a few moments before grabbing her phone from the bedside table and staring at the screen, blurry-eyed. The battery was dead from using the torch the night before. She got up and plugged it in to charge.

After showering, she headed to reception and asked Alma for the key to Isla's room.

'Just to see if there's something I missed, if that's OK,' she said, tilting her head apologetically. She needed to do something.

Alma led the way. 'I need to give the room to someone else, soon,' she said, opening the door, and folding her arms. 'Your friend left a credit card number, but if she's not coming back . . .'

Roxanne growled inside at the woman's lack of tact, but decided to shrug it off. 'I guess so,' she said. 'In fact, stick her things in my room, if you like.' She stepped through the door. Isla's room was as it had been when she and Jack looked around the day before. She knew she was wasting her time. She left within moments, closing the door behind her. Alma locked it and headed back to reception, swinging the key by her side.

Roxanne leant against Isla's door, noticing the door to the next room stood open. She peered inside to see a housekeeper singing as she puffed up pillows.

Roxanne stepped in. 'Hello.' The woman didn't look round, so Roxanne moved closer. 'Hello,' she repeated, tapping her on the shoulder.

'Skit!' the woman said, dropping the pillow and pulling out her earphones.

'Sorry, I didn't mean to startle you,' Roxanne said. 'Do you speak English?'

'A little.' The woman gestured a small amount with her thumb and forefinger. 'Is this your room? I can come back later.'

Roxanne shook her head. 'No, I just wondered if you remember the woman who was staying in the room next door?' She pulled out the photograph of Isla with Andy and showed it to her.

She shook her head, 'Sorry.'

'What about the man?'

She screwed up her nose, as though thinking, before shaking her head again.

'Did you clean her room on Saturday morning?'

The cleaner looked puzzled.

'On Saturday.' Roxanne grabbed her feather duster and wiggled it in the air. 'Did you clean her room?'

The cleaner laughed. '*Ja, ja.*'

'Did you see anything odd?' Roxanne had no idea where she was going with her questions. She pointed at the photo again. 'Did this man spend the night with her?'

She shook her head, brow furrowed. 'I clean and make bed. That is all.' She shrugged. 'Is everything OK?'

'I don't know . . . we think . . .' She stopped, frustrated for not knowing any Swedish. There was no point in carrying on. 'Thank you,' she said, leaving the room.

* * *

'That's right, we saw Isla on Friday at the sky station,' Alex said as he tucked into his breakfast. He was a bit of a silver fox, the kind that might give Paul Hollywood a run for his money.

Alma had pointed the couple out to Roxanne, saying they'd been to the sky station on the night Isla was there, and she'd approached and shown them a photo of Isla. Alex had invited her to sit down, to the clear disapproval of his much younger, and very beautiful wife.

'The Northern Lights were incredible, weren't they, Maddie?' he went on, turning to smile at her.

Maddie flicked her dark hair over her shoulders, and sipped her Buck's Fizz, her eyes boring into Roxanne. She didn't respond.

Roxanne snatched her eyes away from Maddie's and glanced around the restaurant. It was heaving. Waiters and waitresses buzzed to and fro with pots of tea and coffee, and the tables were crammed with visitors. She returned her attention to Alex. 'So did she seem OK?'

He nodded. 'Well, she was taking lots of photos, and seemed to like

212

it up there in the darkness. She was still there when we left. Although I noticed her heading down as we climbed into the minibus.'

'Did you see her talk to anyone? A man with red hair?'

Maddie leant forward. 'What's this about, exactly?' She was Scottish, and there was a hint of aggression in her voice.

'I just expected my friend to be here,' Roxanne said, not wanting to talk about the email. 'I'm worried about her, that's all. I don't suppose she mentioned where she might be heading.'

'Well, I didn't speak to her.' Maddie looked at her husband and folded her arms across her slim body. 'I just wanted to get back to the hotel that night. It was fucking freezing up there. But Alex just *had* to say hello.'

'I thought she looked lonely, needed a friend.'

'Yeah, well, you're meant to be with me, remember? It's our honeymoon, for Christ's sake.'

Roxanne sensed Alex was a bit of a ladies' man, and Maddie didn't fully trust him. Whatever it was, their marriage looked destined to fail.

'She said she might go to Narvik – take in the Fjords,' Alex said, ignoring his wife. 'There's a direct train.'

Maddie unfolded her arms, pulled her phone from her bag and began thumping the screen. She glanced up and met Roxanne's eye. 'What?' she said. 'Do you want to be in my Facebook update too?'

'Well, thanks for your help,' Roxanne said, rising, knowing it was time to leave.

'I hope you find her soon,' Alex said.

'Me too,' she called back over her shoulder as she left the restaurant.

Back in her room, she found her phone was fully charged, and that she'd missed several calls from Sally. She pressed her number.

'Sally. Hi, it's Roxanne,' she said, when she picked up, keen to tell her about Isla's planned trip to Norway, and about the Andy she'd found on Facebook.

'Oh thank goodness, Roxanne,' Sally said, before she could get

213

the words out. Her voice was anxious and jerky, not helped by the poor signal. 'I've been trying to get hold of you.'

'Is everything OK? Is there news about Isla?'

'Yes, yes there is.' She was close to tears. 'A woman was struck by a car in Narvik in the early hours of this morning. They think it's Isla.'

# Chapter 37

Sally took a deep breath and went on. 'They can't be certain it's Isla,' she said. 'But the description fits. They got her details from her bag, and my name and number were on her passport.' She snatched another breath, clearly struggling to get the words out. 'We're at Stansted now, waiting for a flight over. She's not good at all, Roxanne.' Sally let out a stifled sob. 'She's in a coma.'

'Oh God, that's awful.' She gripped the phone tighter to her ear, tears flooding from nowhere.

'They said she's opened her eyes once, and mumbled something they couldn't make sense of.'

'That's good, right? She's at least attempted to speak.' Roxanne gulped, trying to compose herself, fighting the tears.

'I really don't know,' Sally said, through her sobs. 'I feel at a loss being so far away.' She paused, clearly trying to calm herself. 'The driver of the car that hit her said she leapt out of nowhere. He swerved and crashed into a wall. Lucky to be alive, they said.'

'This is too awful.' Roxanne dashed away her tears with the back of her hand.

'What was she doing wandering the streets of Narvik at gone midnight?' Sally said. 'I thought she was in Sweden.'

'She did tell a couple here in Abisko that she hoped to see the Fjords. There's a direct train to Narvik.'

'But it doesn't fit, Roxanne.' Sally sniffed. 'Why would she tell people she wanted to see the Fjords, only to . . . to do this?'

'You're right, it doesn't make any sense at all.' Roxanne picked up her pyjama top and wiped the tears from her face with it.

'They said it happened in a side street where youngsters often hang out. Druggies, some of them.' Sally paused, as though trying to compose herself. 'What was she doing hanging out somewhere like that? It's not Isla's style.'

Roxanne began pacing the room, and a silence hung between them for a few moments.

'People stay in comas for years sometimes, don't they?' Sally said. 'What if she never comes out of it?' Her voice was growing in volume.

'But she's alive, Sally.' Roxanne sat down on the edge of the bed, searching for her inner strength. 'We have to see this as positive news. She'll come out of the coma, and we've been given a second chance to help her.' She lowered her head, letting her hair fall around her face. 'Everything will be OK,' she added, wishing she believed her own words. 'And *when* she comes round, she'll need our help. We must be there for her.'

'We need to be strong for Isla, don't we?' Sally's voice was shaky, but resigned.

'She'll be counting on us.' There was a brief silence before Roxanne added, 'Listen, I'll catch the next train to Narvik. I can be at the hospital in about two hours.'

'OK, well, we'll be a lot longer, but hopefully we'll be there before nightfall.' Sally told her the address. 'I've tried calling Jack, but he didn't pick up. Is he still with you?'

'No . . .' Roxanne recalled the dreadful state he'd been in the night before. 'He said he was going back to England.' She paused and tugged one of her curls until it hurt her scalp, then released it so it pinged back like a coiled spring. 'He wasn't coping, and who can blame him?'

Sally sucked in a sigh. 'Well, I've left a message on his phone. Told him all we know.'

'Good. Well if you hear from him . . . or anything else . . . just call me.'

'I will.'

'Oh, hang on a sec, there's one other thing,' Roxanne said. 'There's an Andy Fisher on Isla's Facebook. It looks as though he's from Canada, going by his profile and cover photos.'

'Do you think it could be him?'

'Yeah, there's a good chance it could be. Trouble is, his settings prevent me messaging him. But maybe you could tell the police. See if they can get hold of him, somehow.'

'Yes, yes, of course. I'll call them now.'

'And once I'm at the hospital, I'll be in touch.'

'Thanks, Roxanne.'

The phone went dead and Roxanne flopped back on the bed, eyes wide as she stared up at the ceiling, her head pounding. But she knew she couldn't waste a second.

She tried calling the hospital – but they couldn't tell her any more than Sally already had – so she dragged on her snowsuit and left the room. She would catch the next train to Narvik. She needed to be there for her friend.

On the platform, she stomped her feet to keep warm. She didn't have long to wait before the train roared into the station, shrieking to a stop. She and half a dozen others climbed on board, and she moved along the almost empty carriage, and sat down next to the window.

The train moved away, passing stationary trains and scattered, isolated buildings on its way into the whiteness of the countryside. The sky was a light, hazy grey, with hints of blue, and a pale sun lit the clouds. As the train gathered speed, and rattled on its way, the rows and rows of leafless trees moving past became hypnotic.

A coal train rumbled by, as they continued along the track and curved their way into a tunnel. Everything felt so slow, bashing against the urgency she felt inside.

In Norway, the stunning fjords lying beneath snow-tipped mountains looked like a scene from Narnia. The views of the mountains could have been drawn with charcoals, strokes of black on white. Roxanne imagined Isla taking photographs, aiming for her dream to publish her book and write more articles. She gulped back more tears. She'd cried more over the last few hours than she had ever before. She had to get her act together. She was no use to her friend, or anyone else, if she fell apart.

She pulled out her phone, and texted Jack.

*Hi, Jack. Hope you got Sally's message. I'm heading for Narvik. Call me, please. Roxanne X*

The view opened up further with such splendour. How could anyone in their right mind take their own life when there was so much beauty in the world? But then who was she to judge her friend? Perhaps Isla had never really been in her right mind after Carl Jeffery.

Eventually, the train pulled into Narvik Station, brakes squealing, and Roxanne got up from her seat and hurried down the carriage, her adrenaline racing. The doors sprang open, and she disembarked onto the snowy platform, quickly spotting a taxi. She raced towards it and climbed into the back seat.

As the driver headed through streets buzzing with shoppers, all wrapped up against the cold and hurrying along snow-covered pavements, Roxanne tried to imagine, once more, Isla – the Isla she'd known for so many years – falling for a stranger, without giving Jack a second's thought. Isla taking her own life. It still seemed so out of character. So far removed from the friend she thought she knew.

'Women in the headwind,' the driver said, breaking into her thoughts, his pale blue eyes fleetingly meeting hers in the rear-view mirror. They'd reached Kongensgate, and he'd braked to almost a stop behind a queue of traffic.

'Sorry?'

'Over there.'

Roxanne turned to where he was nodding, to see a snow-covered statue of two women struggling in a windstorm. It made her heart break.

*It could be me and Isla.*

Roxanne imagined that she was the woman at the front leading, grabbing Isla's hand and holding on tight, battling onwards – hoping her friend would survive the storms, and always be there by her side. But Isla was behind, the wind dragging her back, her hand above her head, as a gust got the better of her.

A tear escaped and rolled down Roxanne's cheek, and despite dashing it away and taking a deep breath, a feeling of helplessness consumed her.

'You OK?' the driver asked.

She sniffed. 'Yes, yes. Thanks.' But she was far from it.

# Chapter 38

## Isla

**Sunday, 13 November**

Floating between asleep and awake, Isla could see Millie and her parents racing along a beach by the sea, young and carefree, the sun beaming down on them, making them appear haloed. She was there too, blonde hair in a high ponytail swinging to and fro. She was wearing shorts and a T-shirt with the Spice Girls on the front, and star-shaped sunglasses, and snatching glances over her shoulder, her little legs giving it everything as she darted across the golden sand. Giggling.

Her family were letting her win.

*Mum?*

They dissipated, like dandelion clocks floating on the air, up into a cloudless sky and beyond. Gone. Leaving Isla suspended in real time, unable to open her eyes, a pain in her arm, as if a giant dragonfly had stung her, over and over – her limbs left lifeless, heavy.

*Hello.*

The sensation in her neck and throat was intolerable. She'd only felt it once before. The day Carl Jeffery tightened a rope around her neck, intending to string her up. Why could she feel it now? Was it real?

*Hello.*

But she knew there was nobody there in the simmering orange behind her eyelids.

She'd dipped in and out several times now, attempting to grab on to what was real and what was not, only to drift back into what felt like a fantasy – a dystopian world where she knew people, but didn't know herself.

A door opened with a creak and soft footfalls approached.

*Where am I?*

*What's happened?*

Thoughts scrambled and tangled, as whoever it was moved to her side. She felt moisture on her dry lips – soothing.

'Isla, can you hear me?' The voice, a whisper, was barely audible. She couldn't even make out if it was male or female.

A brief memory of travelling through darkness on a chairlift, liquid greens zigzagging the night sky, came and went.

A cold hand touched her arm. She flinched inside, but knew she didn't move.

The voice continued, fading further, words muffled. Isla was losing the connection. Drifting deeper into her thoughts.

*Is any of this real?*

### Six years ago

Carl tightened the rope, his eyes wild. A hint of a smile twisting his lips.

Darkness called to Isla, as consciousness drained from her body.

*I should have known.*

Bronwyn had told her he'd acted weird when she tried to leave. Said she thought someone was watching her. He'd killed her, hadn't he? Pieces slotted into place. 'Bronwyn was abused by her father,' he'd said. 'A happy childhood brought up by two mums,' she'd said.

221

Why hadn't Isla taken it in? Seen him for who he was? The need for comfort after Bronwyn's death had blinkered her. She'd been a fool.

He slackened the rope and she gasped, tears creeping from the corners of her eyes like tiny bubbles of pain. 'Please,' she tried to say, but words wouldn't form.

'Are you crying because you wish you'd tried harder, Isla? I mean we could have been so good together.' He screwed up his face and moved so he was inches from her face. 'But you're all the same, aren't you?' he said, breath hot on her skin. 'Bronwyn. Clare. Sophie. Mother. Too full of your own importance, doing exactly what you want without a care for anyone.'

She went to try and talk again, but her throat closed in pain. 'I . . .' was all she could say.

'The police contacted me again about Bronwyn's death.' He moved back slightly and smirked, hands clenching the rope. 'They have doubts about me. I may have to take off.' He stroked her cheek with the rough rope. His once handsome face contorted, ugly – evil pumping through his veins. 'After I've dealt with you, of course.'

Something inside her, as she lay under the weight of him, gathered momentum. And, like a defeated army that somehow finds strength for one last battle, she lifted her hand, grabbed his testicles and twisted.

Shock and pain radiated across his face. Yelling, he fell backwards, letting go of the rope to grab himself between his legs and cracking his head on the wall.

Isla scrambled to her feet, the rope still wound around her neck. She stumbled into the kitchen, her eyes flicking over the worktop, and grabbed a knife.

He was behind her in moments, and she turned to see his face purple with rage, spittle forming at the corners of his mouth.

'Fucking bitch!' he yelled, dripping with sweat as he grabbed the rope and dragged her painfully towards him like the evil owner of a disobedient dog. 'You deserve what's coming to you.'

He cried out when she plunged in the knife. His scream told

of immense agony as she tugged the blade free from his flesh. He gripped his stomach, blood seeping through his fingers, his stare frozen.

With his free hand he grabbed her wrist and twisted. 'Bitch,' he spat.

Her body shook as she plunged the knife into him again. His drop to the floor was heavy, his cry ear-splitting.

'For Bronwyn,' she whispered, through the ache in her throat, as the knife tumbled from her hand and bounced three times across the wooden floorboards.

# Chapter 39

## Roxanne

Roxanne tugged off her snowsuit and raced towards the hospital lifts.

As she waited with nurses, doctors and a pale man with a drip, determination took hold. If this was Isla, and she prayed it was, they had another chance to put her broken pieces back together. Roxanne could be Isla's glue. With Sally and Gary and Millie, and maybe even Jack if she could convince him, they could work with Isla, make everything right again.

A lift descended, and the doors whooshed open. Inside, huddled at the back next to the man with the drip, she pressed the button for the high-dependency ward.

Once there, she hurried towards the doors and pushed the intercom. 'Hi, do you speak English?' she said into the metal grid.

'Yes. Can I help?'

'I'm Roxanne Furaha, a friend of Isla Johnson. I understand she is here.'

A few moments later a nurse appeared, smiling as she opened the door. She gestured for Roxanne to enter. 'Your friend is unconscious,' she said, as Roxanne followed her onto the ward. 'But there are signs that she is making progress.' She screwed up her forehead. 'Is your friend English?'

'She is, yes.'

'Does she speak Norwegian?'

Roxanne shook her head. 'I don't think so. Why?'

'It's just that her mutterings seem to be in Norwegian. But that's not unusual, as she may have heard someone speak Norwegian just before her accident.' She pointed to a side room. 'Please go ahead, I'll be with you in a moment. And don't be too worried by her injuries. They will heal.'

Roxanne approached the room and tapped on the glass door, despite being aware there was nobody inside to invite her in. Isla wasn't going to sit up and wave, excited to see her.

She edged open the door and stood in the doorway. Everything blurred in front of her, as tears swam into her eyes, her determination from moments ago draining away.

The beeps of the monitor sounded loud in her ears, and she desperately wished she wasn't alone, that Isla's parents were there, or Jack, to absorb some of the shock. It was as though the fear that had hovered about her since she first read Isla's email had thickened and lowered quite suddenly, about to consume her.

'Isla,' she whispered, taking a step forward and brushing the tears from her eyes. 'It's me, lovely lady. What have you been up to?'

But as she approached she knew. The woman's face was swollen, bruised and grazed from her injuries, difficult to identify, perhaps, but this wasn't her friend.

She touched the woman's arm. 'Oh God, where are you, Isla?'

The woman's eyes flickered open, and closed again, and Roxanne dropped into the chair next to the bed. She would have to tell Sally. But then what?

Where was Isla?

Who was this poor woman?

225

Why had she got Isla's bag, her identity?

She pressed her palms into her eyes attempting to halt tears, before burying her head in her hands.

'Please don't worry, the signs are good.' It was the nurse entering the room, and Roxanne looked up, a shimmer of tears clouding her vision.

'No, you don't understand,' she said, rising. 'This isn't my friend. This isn't Isla.'

'But she has identification.'

'But it isn't her,' Roxanne said again, a lump rising in her throat. 'You think I wouldn't recognise my own friend?' She paused. 'Can I see her bag?'

'Yes, yes, of course. It's in the safe,' the nurse said, leaving the room.

Roxanne stood over the bed, studying the woman's swollen eyes, the bruises as black as storm clouds on her forehead. 'Did you snatch Isla's bag?' she whispered.

There was no response.

The nurse was back, unzipping Isla's canvas bag. She placed it carefully on a side table, glancing at the door as though she wasn't sure she should be allowing Roxanne to look inside.

But Roxanne wasted no time in pulling out Isla's passport, and leafing through a notebook with jottings about Kiruna. There were pens, and her purse, which she opened to find a handful of pound coins, and a wad of Swedish kronas. 'Oh God,' Roxanne said. A wallet-sized photo of Isla with Andy outside the café, stared up at her through the transparent plastic of the purse.

She threw everything back into the bag and zipped it closed, handing it to the nurse and glancing over her shoulder at the woman in the bed. 'She must have stolen it,' she said.

'Perhaps, but we need to let the police decide that,' the nurse said, leaving the room with the bag.

Roxanne looked again at the woman. Had she snatched Isla's bag? Had Isla chased after her? Was that how it had happened? Had Isla chased the woman into the road, and was now hiding? But then how did that fit with her threatening to take her own life?

226

Roxanne pulled out her phone and began texting Sally. She was about to press send when the phone rang. It was Jack.

'Thank God,' she said. 'Are you OK?'

'I've just picked up Sally's message. I can't seem to get hold of her. Is there any news from Narvik? Are you there?' His voice was wispy and breathless.

'I'm in Narvik now. It isn't Isla.'

'Thank God.'

'Really? At least we'd have been sure she was alive. Where are you?' Her voice was rising in volume. 'Where have you been?'

'I stayed in a hotel near the airport overnight. I just shut down, you know, thinking – drinking too much.'

'You're an arsehole.' Roxanne regretted the words as soon as they left her lips. 'Sorry, I didn't mean that.'

He didn't reply for some moments. 'I'm at Camp Arctic. Can you come back?'

'Why?'

'Something's not right here.'

'You can say that again.'

'I just know Isla's here somewhere. Call me crazy. I can't explain it.' There was a crack in his voice, and Roxanne felt a pang of sadness. 'It's hell, Roxanne. I should probably fuck off. But something keeps calling me back.'

Roxanne looked at the woman in the bed once more. Her vitals beeped, and lights zigzagged across the screen by her bed. She was still and lifeless, eyes closed. *I'm no use here.*

'On my way,' she said, ending the call and leaving the room.

# Chapter 40

## Isla

Isla forced her eyes open.

A bolt of nausea rushed through her body, her head thumping as she leant over the edge of the bed and heaved.

She flopped back onto the pillow – random, incoherent memories dancing about her mind, kicking against her skull, painful as they intruded. Julian in his car: '*You were such a spunky young thing.*' Blood dripping – post-box red – from her hand onto her mum's dining table. Sara crying, holding Isla close: '*My dad died.*' Had that really happened?

She searched her wrist for her rubber band, desperate to put an end to the extreme anxiety and confusion. It wasn't there.

Her sore, dry eyes latched on to a window draped with blue and white checked curtains. Outside, from a white sky, snow tumbled – each flake unique. She'd read that somewhere: no two are exactly the same. Yes, she'd read that somewhere.

*Where am I?*

Her fear increased as she attempted to swallow and almost gagged.

She hauled herself up, limbs heavy, and propped her body against the wall. She was wearing pink, silk pyjamas. She never wore pink pyjamas – she never wore pink.

She spotted her mobile on the bedside table and, with a burst of adrenaline, she reached for it and fumbled, attempting to turn it on. It was dead. *I forgot my charger.*

Her eyes flicked over the room. No personal touches, just wood-clad walls, a print of the Northern Lights, a pine wardrobe and dresser, her clothes neatly folded on a chair.

She rose from the bed and staggered towards the window. Outside, footprints in the snow led to and fro. There were tyre tracks some distance away, but no car. A shed, a pile of wood, an axe and, beyond that, snow stretched endlessly under a milky sky.

*Where am I?*

She grabbed a blanket from the foot of the bed and draped it around her shoulders, before easing open the bedroom door.

From a small landing, doors led to a bathroom and another bedroom. She could see a double bed covered by a floral duvet. A window, open and letting in the cold, was draped by another set of blue checked curtains that flapped noisily in a light breeze.

'Hello,' she attempted, tugging the blanket around her and cautiously making her way down the stairs, but her mouth was so dry, and her throat ached. She could barely make herself heard.

She padded into a kitchen. Pine cupboards dominated the small room, and two wine glasses were upturned on the drainer.

*'Let's drown our sorrows.'*

She moved towards a door that led outside and tried the handle. It opened onto deep snow. She looked down at her bare feet, her flimsy pyjamas, and closed the door once more, knowing she wouldn't last five minutes in the freezing conditions.

She turned, a ball of screwed-up paper on the worktop catching her eye. She picked it up and flattened out the creases. The words swam before her eyes, as she tried to focus.

*My darling Isla,*
*I've been awake all night thinking – tormenting myself for coming.*
*I thought this was the right thing to do, as I missed you – I*

*really did miss you. But this morning, I found a text from my wife. She's having our baby, and I realised I'd made a terrible mistake coming here. I can't leave her. I thought I could, but I can't. I'm so sorry.*

*I love you, Isla, but I'm returning to Canada. I'll be changing my phone number, so you can't contact me – not because I don't want to hear your voice, but because it's easier this way. I'm sorry for the pain I've caused you. The mess I've made of both our lives.*

*Forgive me, Andy*

A woozy sensation had taken hold, as if she was drunk on a bobbing boat in the middle of a choppy ocean. Nauseous once more, she staggered towards the sink, falling against it and retching, but nothing came up.

The light in her head was fading, as though someone was blowing out candles. And, losing her battle with consciousness, she slipped down the worktop, landing in a heap on the quarry-tiled floor.

Everything went black once more.

# Chapter 41

## Roxanne

Roxanne sat in the waiting room at Narvik Station – a yellow, two-storey building close to the railway line – her phone open on the Internet in front of her, struggling to find ways to help Isla. Everything she came up with seemed futile or pointless.

Apart from Andy, it was the reunion that played on her mind the most. The odd way only Sara had turned up, and Trevor's strange comment on Isla's Facebook update.

Trancelike, she searched for Veronica's website. There was a contact address and, without thinking too much, she emailed her.

From: ROXANNE Furaha roxannefuraha@littleboxmail.com
To: VERONICA Beesley veronicabeesley@yomail.com

*Hi Veronica*
*You may not remember me, but we went to university together.*
*Isla Johnson mentioned that you almost met up for a uni reunion*
*the other night with Ben Martin, Sara Pembroke and Trevor*
*Cooper. Just wondered if she's been in touch with you at all,*

*especially in the last few days.*
*Cheers*
*Roxanne Furaha*

She felt, deep down, it was a waste of time. Surely she would have known if Isla had been in contact with Veronica. Roxanne and Isla shared everything. *Except they hadn't, had they?*

She signed into Facebook. Sara Pembroke had accepted her friend request, so she composed a message to her too.

*Hi Sara,*
*You may not remember me, but we went to university together. I understand you met with Isla a little while back at a reunion in Cambridge, organised by Trevor Cooper. The thing is, and this is really hard to say, it looks as if Isla may have attempted suicide. I know this is a total long shot, but I wondered if you thought there was anything strange about her when you met up, or did she mention a bloke called Andy? Or if you've heard from her in the last few days. I'm sorry if this all seems a bit odd, but I'm desperate.*
*Cheers in advance,*
*Roxanne*

She pressed send, before thrusting her head into her hands. What the hell was she doing telling Sara about Isla? Was she being disloyal?

*Fuck! Fuck! Fuck!*

The train roared into the station, bringing her out of her anger. She shoved her phone into her bag and rose. Determined to keep strong, she slapped away a tear rolling down her cheek, and strode from the waiting room and stepped on board.

An hour and a half later, she was back in Abisko, hurrying from the railway station, crisp newly fallen snow crunching under her boots, as she headed for Camp Arctic. She prayed Jack had found something out, and together they would find Isla.

Once there, she scanned reception for Jack's face among the guests, before dashing towards Alma.

'Have you seen Jack? The man I was with when I first arrived?' she asked, a little out of breath, as she fussed over the dogs, who'd greeted her with wagging tails.

'He left a while ago,' Alma said, glancing up from her computer screen.

'Left? Did he say where he was going?'

Alma shrugged. 'Not to me, I just noticed him leave.' She paused and tilted her head. 'I understand you still haven't found your friend.' Another pause. 'The police have been here asking questions.'

'Really? Well, thank God they're taking it seriously.' Although the fact they were made it all the more worrying somehow. 'We thought we'd found her in Narvik,' she said. 'But it wasn't her.' The words took shape in her head, and the mystery surrounding her friend deepened to a darker level. Isla hadn't been seen for over thirty-six hours, and it was well over twenty-four hours since she'd sent the email. If she'd taken her life, wouldn't they have found her by now?

She turned away, pulled out her phone, and tried Jack's number, but it went straight to voicemail. *Where are you, Jack?*

Her stomach grumbled and a wave of nausea washed over her. She hadn't eaten for ages. She would be no use to Isla if she passed out, so she tugged off her snowsuit and hung it up, before heading into the restaurant where she ordered game soup.

'I wondered, have you seen my friend?' she asked the waitress before she could walk away, thrusting the photo of Isla and Andy in front of her.

'Yes, I saw her a few times,' the waitress said, studying the picture.

'What about him? Did you see him?'

She shook her head. 'No, she was always alone.'

The dark, hot soup smelt rich and comforting, and as Roxanne ate, her stomach made grateful gurgling noises. One-handed, she did a Google search for 'Ben Martin' and 'Publisher', and came up with nothing.

There was a text from Leo, who had drifted so far from her thoughts since she arrived that she wondered if she would ever meet up with him again. She'd probably be alone for ever – would prefer it that way. Was she afraid of commitment? Too selfish to share her life? Or was it more than that? Had what happened to Isla in Australia affected Roxanne more than she realised?

As she left the restaurant her phone rang. It was Sally.

'Roxanne, where are you?' Her voice was tense.

'In Abisko.'

'Well, we're at the hospital, and it's not Isla.'

'Yes, I know.'

'You know?'

'Yes, didn't you get my message?'

'Message?'

'I sent you a text.' Roxanne thought back to how the call from Jack had come through just as she was about to send it. Had she pressed send? Had her mind been so full that she'd forgotten to press send? 'I was at the hospital, but I'm back at Camp Arctic,' she said, moving on as swiftly as she could, guilt engulfing her. 'I'm trying to find Isla.' It sounded weak. How could what she was doing – eating soup, for Christ's sake – be classed as searching? She put down her spoon, no longer hungry.

After a silence, Sally gave a little cough, and said, 'She's awake – the woman they thought was Isla – she's awake.' She paused, and Roxanne knew she was crying. 'The police spoke to her. She's a student, apparently, and admits she was pretty out of it last night. But she remembers someone pushing her in front of the car and insists she has no idea why she has Isla's bag.'

'Jesus. That's pretty weird stuff,' Roxanne said. 'Do you think she's telling the truth? Maybe she's covering her back.'

'I don't know.' Sally's voice was cracking under the stress and exhaustion. 'We're going to talk with the police now, and we've hired a car, so maybe we'll head to Abisko if we get no joy here. And, Roxanne.' There was a pause. 'If you hear anything – anything at all – call me. Please.'

'Yes, yes, I will. Of course.'

'Oh, and one more thing, the police have spoken to Andy Fisher.'

'And?'

'He admits meeting Isla in Canada, but he insists they didn't have a relationship. He was there with his wife and a whole group of them befriended her.'

'And they believe him?'

'He's nearly seventy, Roxanne. I can't see how it can be the same man Isla talked about.'

'No, no, you're right. It can't be.'

'I'll talk to you soon, love,' Sally said, before ending the call.

Roxanne left her half-eaten soup and returned to her room. She sat on the bed cross-legged, and tried Jack's number twice more, with no luck. What else could she do? Her eyes drifted to the window. It was still snowing, flakes tumbling from the sky, clinging to the glass. And although it was warm inside, it was as though she was out there in the cold.

# Chapter 42

## Isla

A car door banged, startling Isla awake. Unsure how long she'd been lying on the kitchen floor, she hauled herself to her feet with the aid of the worktop and looked out of the window. It was dark now, but an outside light lit the area – whoever it was had turned off the engine, and was sitting in the car, head down – no more than a silhouette.

Memories of thinking she saw Carl Jeffery in England swooped into her head. Was he out there now? Had he escaped and trapped her miles from anywhere so he could finish what he'd started six years ago? Or had he sent someone to do the job for him?

Panic surged through her body. She fumbled for a light switch and flicked it on, illuminating the kitchen. Her eyes skittered over the worktop, and she opened drawers and cupboards, searching for something to protect herself with, finding nothing but a dinner knife.

She staggered from the kitchen. A small hallway led to a front door, and another door opened into a lounge. She stepped into the room and froze, the light from the kitchen behind her streaming in. Hanging from the ceiling beam was a noose.

'No!' she cried, stepping backwards, and falling to her knees. She dropped the knife and buried her head in her hands.

Moments later there was a sound of a key in the door.

Isla crawled into the room and, with the aid of the sofa, she dragged herself to her feet again, a sense of doom washing over her. She hadn't got the strength to fight – not this time.

'Oh my God, you poor sausage.' It was Sara. She flicked on the lounge light, and leapt towards Isla, pulling her into a hug, the soft fur of her hood brushing against Isla's cheek. 'I didn't think you would wake up while I was gone.' She looked up at the noose. 'I should have taken that down. I'm so sorry. You really don't need reminding.'

'Reminding?' Isla's voice was thin and wispy, as Sara helped her onto the sofa, rubbing her arm affectionately. 'Why are you here? Why am I here?'

'You don't remember?'

Isla searched her mind. '*My father died.*'

'I just thank God I was here for you last night, that's all,' Sara said, leaving the room, and reappearing moments later with a glass of water. 'Drink up,' she said, handing it to Isla. 'You must be thirsty after sleeping off all that booze.'

Isla sipped the drink, the pain intolerable as she swallowed, her eyes on Sara, watching, spellbound, as she climbed onto the coffee table and took down the noose.

'I don't remember,' Isla said.

'No, well, that would be the alcohol, I expect.' Sara smiled.

Isla certainly had a headache, a feeling of nausea. She touched her neck, ran her fingers down her windpipe.

'I'm sure that will hurt for a while.' Sara threw the rope behind the sofa and it landed with a thud. She took off her coat, to reveal jeans and a cream cashmere jumper, and her eyes slid to a fire barely flickering in the grate, and then up to a mirror above.

Isla put down the glass, rose, and looked at her reflection. The bruises, deep reds and blues, on her neck, just as they'd been after Carl Jeffery.

Sara moved behind her. 'We look so alike, don't you think?'

she said, stroking Isla's hair. 'Do you remember us meeting up on Saturday morning?'

Isla shook her head, as she sat back down. Everything around her felt surreal.

'You were coming out of Camp Arctic.' Sara sat down next to her and took Isla's hand. It felt oddly comforting. 'I came there to find you. I knew where you were staying from your Facebook.' She paused, her eyes shimmering.

'Where are we?'

'Abisko in Sweden. You don't remember?'

Isla shook her head as a memory of sitting in departures at Stansted came and went. She could remember things before that, but her recent memories were almost non-existent.

'You said you didn't mind me coming over, especially when I told you my father died.'

'*My father died.*'

Isla vaguely recalled meeting Sara, but it was exactly that, an elusive memory she couldn't pin down. Tears gathered behind her eyes. 'I should probably get back to Camp Arctic,' she said, although the place wouldn't come to mind. Alcohol had never affected her this way. Yes, she liked a few wines, but she'd never got so intoxicated she'd forgotten things.

'I've just been out,' Sara said. 'There's been a deep snowfall. I'll take you back as soon as the roads are cleared.'

Isla rubbed her head. 'Could I use your phone? Call Jack?'

Sara smiled, and squeezed Isla's hand. 'Oh dear, you really don't remember anything, do you?'

Isla shrugged, reaching into her head and coming up with nothing.

'When we met up yesterday, you were in a dreadful state,' Sara said. 'The irony was, I'd come here to ask you for support, but you needed me more than I needed you. You were so down, Isla.'

'I . . .' she began, but the words died in her mouth.

'I suggested you came here to my lodge for a bit. I'm renting the place.' She looked about her. 'We spent the day together.' She paused.

'You told me about Andy.'

Isla remembered the note in the kitchen. It felt as though she'd entered another dimension. She was there, sitting next to Sara, but this was all happening to someone else. Was she dreaming? Her head began to swim again.

'We drank a fair bit,' Sara continued, and a memory of being handed a glass of wine, a flicker of knocking it back and the liquid warming her throat, an image of the two of them in deep conversation, '*My father died*,' came and went.

'We drowned our sorrows,' Sara added. 'You've been through so much lately.' A pause. 'Carl Jeffery,' she said, tilting her head. 'You told me how you'd seen him everywhere.'

'Did I?' Isla looked down at her pyjamas, ran her fingers over the silk, as everything continued to blur and distort.

'I changed you into those last night after you passed out.' Sara touched Isla's arm – Isla flinched, it was sore – before tucking a straying tendril of hair behind Isla's ear. 'I wanted you to be comfortable.' Sara rose and moved across the room, perching on the edge of the armchair.

Isla struggled to stay awake, her fingers searching her wrist for her rubber band. If she could only ping it, she might stay awake. But she knew it wasn't there.

'It was later that I found you.' Sara, now a hazy blur, tilted her head towards the ceiling. 'If I hadn't been here, Isla . . . well, I can't even say the words.'

Isla fought to stay awake, biting down hard on her lip, the pain returning her to the moment. Sara came back into focus once more, her blue eyes steel-like, as she stared at Isla.

'Oh dear, sweetie,' she said with a smile. 'I thought I was about to lose you.'

Isla shifted and began to shiver.

'The fire's gone out,' Sara said, leaning forward and touching Isla's hand. 'You're freezing. It's as though the cold has crawled under your skin and fallen asleep.' She gave a little giggle and jumped to her feet.

'I'll get into something more comfortable and chop some wood for the fire.' She smiled again as she left the room.

Her footfalls were light on the stairs. And it wasn't long before she was heading back down again. 'Won't be long,' she called, leaving the house.

Isla rose and staggered into the kitchen, her limbs heavy, as though wading through tar. Through the window, the outside light had illuminated the area. Sara picked up the axe and began chopping wood. Snow was falling thick and heavy now, a curtain of white.

Isla held on to the worktop to steady herself, desperate to piece things together, when a figure appeared in the distance, heading towards the house. She narrowed her eyes and peered more closely. Whoever it was, was battling against the snowstorm, with the aid of walking sticks.

Isla's eyes drifted to Sara who seemed oblivious to the person approaching. She ran her fingers over her naked wrist. Was Sara safe? Was she safe? Oh God, was she being foolish? Over-reacting? After all, it could be anyone out there. She'd got herself in such a state back in England over what was probably nothing. Maybe Jack was right. Maybe once she was back home, she should see a GP, get on some medication.

She tried the back door several times but it was locked. She leaned over the sink and banging on the glass. 'Sara,' she called, as the figure got closer, but Sara still seemed oblivious.

She remembered the window in the bedroom was open and made her way up the stairs. She would call out to Sara – warn her that someone was approaching. But it seemed to take for ever to reach the top step.

Finally, she stumbled into the bedroom, but the window was closed and locked. And outside all was quiet. There was no sign of Sara or the figure through the veil of snow.

Woozy, heart racing, Isla dropped onto the edge of the bed. She needed to find a key to the window, or better still, something to protect herself with. She threw open the bedside drawer, before looking in the wardrobe, but they were both empty.

240

A holdall and a rucksack were wedged into the corner. She reached for the rucksack and unzipped it. Inside she found a dark bobbed wig, a make-up bag and a yellow Nokia.

She would call Jack. But then she'd never memorised his number. She began to cry stupid tears. *Stop panicking, stop panicking.*

She could call the police.

And say what?

'*A friend's locked me in.*'

'*A friend?*'

'*She's outside, and someone's heading towards the house.*'

'*Someone? What house?*'

'*It could be Carl Jeffery. You have to listen. He tried to kill me.*'

'*When?*'

'*Six years ago.*'

'*Where are you?*'

'*I've no fucking idea.*'

And they would put her on hold. They would put her on fucking hold. And she would yell down the phone that they had to fucking listen, because she was trapped. Locked inside a house. 'Listen to me, you fucking morons,' she would scream, but nobody would hear her. Nobody would hear her.

Hands shaking, she switched on the phone, and within moments it sprang to life. The old phone didn't have a password, and several text messages came through, as though the phone had been turned off for a while. One stood out. It was from her. She opened it and read it.

*I don't know why you're being like this, Trevor. I never meant to hurt you. You have to understand I'm deeply in love with someone else.*

It was Trevor's phone. What the hell was Trevor's phone doing there?

She fumbled, hand shaking, trying to recall the number for the Swedish emergency services. But even if she could have remembered it, she couldn't keep her limbs from shaking, and she wasn't used to the Nokia format. Frustration and panic injected her heart with adrenaline, making it thump, as tears rolled down her face. Something was very wrong. This wasn't her imagination. She wasn't over-reacting. Something was very wrong.

She heard footsteps heading up the stairs and jumped, dropping the phone.

Behind her, the door opened.

# Chapter 43

## Roxanne

Roxanne's phone pinged, startling her out of her helpless trance.

From: VERONICA Beesley veronicabeesley@yomail.com
To: ROXANNE Furaha roxannefuraha@littleboxmail.com

*OMG, you're a blast from the past. Roxanne Furaha – long time! Are you still trying to save the world, getting pissed and shagging your way through half of the UK?*

*In answer to your question, nope, Isla hasn't been in touch.*

*BTW I don't know anything about any reunion. Maybe the message didn't get through to me. And I'm amazed Ben agreed to meet up, as he's living in Hollywood now. Last I heard he's got a small part in the next Bond film. I always knew he'd be an actor one day. He blagged his way into my bed enough times.*

*Listen, sorry this is a bit short, hon, gotta dash. Alfie Christie is here – remember him from uni? Cute with muscles to die for? He's my cockapoo walker, and he's about to take Maudie and*

*Freda for their trundle around Hyde Park. Plus, I've got a fashion
show to prepare! TOODLES!*
*MWAH MWAH MWAH*
*Veronica*

Roxanne absorbed the words. How could Veronica know nothing
about the reunion? Was Ben a publisher *and* an actor? Was that even
possible? Her head pounded. Had Isla lied about the reunion? Had
she been meeting Andy all along? She pummelled her temples with
her fingers. But Isla must have been at the reunion. Roxanne had
seen the photograph on Facebook of her and Sara.

Roxanne headed from her room, a dire need for something alco-
holic from the bar washing over her. She would contact Sally, and
Jack if he would only pick up. She dived along the corridor, bumping
into Alex coming out of his room.

'Sorry,' she said. 'I wasn't looking where I was going.'

'No, worries.' He closed his door. 'Doesn't get any warmer, does
it?' he added with a laugh. 'Makes the UK feel like the Sahara.'

Trying to hide her angst, Roxanne hurried onwards.

'Oh, hang on,' he said, trotting after her, the smell of his expensive
aftershave wafting over her. 'It's about your friend.'

Roxanne stopped, and turned. 'Isla?'

He nodded, by her side now. 'We got chatting with a woman
earlier, and I told her how you were looking for Isla. And she thinks
she saw her at the sky station on Friday.'

Roxanne's hopes rose. 'Who is she? Can I talk to her?'

He shook his head. 'She left for home, but she definitely thinks
she saw a blonde woman get off the chairlift and meet someone.'

'Was it a man?' She thought of the photograph of Isla with Andy,
her head whirring with confusion.

Alex nodded. 'She overheard him mention somewhere called God
Dag Lodge. It's a few miles out, apparently.' He shrugged. 'They got
in a car.'

'But you didn't notice the car.'

244

He shook his head. 'I didn't notice anything much. We were knackered, and the cold air and a couple of bevvies . . . well, you know.' He opened the door, allowing her to go through.

'Well, thanks,' Roxanne said, heading past him and not looking back.

A taxi stood outside, dropping off visitors. Roxanne knew she needed to move fast, so she stepped out into the darkness, raced across the snow and jumped into the back seat.

'God Dag Lodge, please,' she told the driver, as she keyed 112 into her phone.

\* \* \*

At her destination, Roxanne climbed out of the taxi, plunging her booted feet into the deep snow, which cracked under the pressure. She flicked on her phone torch and shone it around the area. The lodge itself was in darkness.

'Can you wait for me, please?' she asked the driver, who nodded.

As she stepped out across the snow, sirens rang out in the near distance. The police wouldn't be long now. Isla must be here somewhere. She had to be.

But, as she took in the silence, she began to wonder if she was wrong. Had she put two and two together and made eight? Had she been so desperate to find Isla that she'd hoped to find treasure where none had been buried?

Snow had stopped falling for now, but the air was freezing as she walked towards the lodge, and a mist formed before her lips as she stumbled. Everything was far too quiet, and any hopes she'd had were drifting away.

Her phone pinged, and she stopped and quickly read a text from Sally telling her they would soon be in Abisko. There was an email from Sara too. She would read it later.

With gloved hands, she banged on the door, and tried the handle several times, but it was locked. She peered through the window, to

245

see no sign of life. There was a notice on the glass saying the place was available for holiday rental. She punched the contact number into her phone.

'Hello, I'm at God Dag Lodge. I wondered if anyone is staying here at the moment.'

'Yes, until today. It's available from tomorrow if you are interested.'

'Could you tell me who is renting it out at the moment?'

'That is confidential, I'm afraid.'

'But it's very important,' Roxanne said her voice rising.

'Sorry. Would you be interested in hiring the lodge?'

'I'll get back to you.' She ended the call, and strode around the lodge, but there was nothing to see.

She was almost at a loss when the police arrived, and even more so when they searched the area and confirmed what Roxanne already knew: that nobody was there.

And that's when Roxanne broke down, sobbing into her hands. A stream of tears she couldn't control.

'Please be assured we're taking Isla's disappearance seriously,' a young police officer said, her Scandinavian accent warm, her tone comforting, as she rested her hand on Roxanne's arm. 'We'll talk to the owners, and make sure she hasn't been here.'

The officer was about to get into her car, when headlights illuminated the area and, with a skid across the ice, a car came to a halt.

A man was driving, and a wide-eyed woman was in the passenger seat. Two young children in bobble hats sat in the back. They all climbed out, the man and woman looking concerned as they approached, the children picking up snow and throwing it at each other.

'Can I help?' the man said, banging his gloved hands together. 'We're renting the place.'

\* \* \*

'The police have gone now, Sally,' Roxanne said later, her phone pinned to her ear as she headed down the hill in the back of the

246

taxi. 'Isla had never been there. A family have been renting it out for over a week, and they haven't seen her.'

'What will the police do now?'

'They'll search the area. They seem to be taking it seriously. But there's nothing suspicious up there.'

'What made you think she was there?'

Roxanne sighed. 'Somebody overheard the name of the lodge – and they thought it was Isla.' It suddenly seemed far too vague, and she began to doubt whether it had even been Isla. 'We will find her.'

'I keep clinging to that thought.' Sally paused for a moment. 'We've had so many lovely messages of support from family and friends. Millie's put an update on Facebook. Not about Isla's email, of course, but the fact we're searching for her. "Has anyone seen her?" That kind of thing.' She was talking too fast, almost manic. 'It's had lots of shares. And Abigail's tweeted about it. I didn't even know she had a Twitter account. It helps to know people are supporting us.'

'Yes, I'm sure.'

'We had a charming email from Sara Pembroke. She said you told her what had happened.'

'Yes, sorry, I shouldn't have . . .'

'No, don't worry. She sounded lovely. Said she and Isla are good friends, and she wants to help. I suggested she does what she can on social media. That's all anyone can do.'

Roxanne felt suddenly agitated. Sara and Isla weren't good friends, were they? 'Listen, I'll leave you in peace, and talk to you later.'

'OK, we should be there soon.'

Roxanne ended the call and looked out of the taxi window. It was snowing again, stunning to the eye, yet so dangerous if you get on the wrong side of it.

A tear rolled down her cheek.

*Where are you, Isla?*

Back at Camp Arctic, Roxanne hammered on Alex's door. 'I need to talk to you. Are you in there?' she called, pushing her face against the door.

Finally, the door flung open. It was Maddie, her dark hair damp and tied into a messy bun, a flimsy robe almost covering her body. 'What the hell do you want?'

'Alex sent me on a wild-goose chase,' she said. 'I need to talk to him.'

He appeared behind Maddie, wearing red silk boxers, his chest toned and tanned. 'What's up?' he said, sipping dark spirit from a tumbler.

'This woman you spoke to.' Her face tingled as the heat of the lodge hit her, her snowsuit far too warm. She unzipped it and wiggled it from her shoulders. 'What did she look like?'

'Jesus, here we go again,' Maddie said, flinging her arms in the air, eyes rolling. 'We're trying to enjoy our honeymoon, but you keep turning up, giving us the third degree like some out-of-work Sherlock wannabe.'

Years ago, Roxanne might have decked Maddie, but now she bit down on her anger. 'You know what it's about. I can't find my friend.'

'Well, maybe you should get yourself one of those little beepers you can attach to keys.' It was clear by her slight slur, she'd been drinking, and it suddenly hit Roxanne how young Maddie was. 'Very careless, losing a friend,' she went on, 'you should be more . . .'

'Maddie, please,' Alex cut in. 'Have a heart.'

'Yeah, well it's so fucking cold here, my heart's frozen,' she said. 'Why couldn't we have gone to Barbados, like I suggested?'

'What did the woman look like?' Roxanne was breathless, her eyes on Alex. 'Her hair colour? What was she wearing?'

'Dark hair,' Alex began. 'And when we saw her she was wearing a bright blue snow jacket with a mountain scene on the back. I remember because it was unusual.'

'Age?'

'About thirty.'

'Did she approach you?' Roxanne asked.

'Yes,' Alex said.

'And you told her about Isla.'

248

'Yes, I think so. I can't remember exactly how the conversation went.'

'So did you see the woman at the sky station on Friday?'

'No . . . no I don't think so,' said Alex, a slight irritation in his voice. Maddie moved in, took his arm and began tapping her fingertips up and down his chest. 'Listen, we really need to get on.'

'You know, I'm beginning to think this woman used you both to send me to the wrong place,' Roxanne said.

'Great, well that's sorted, then,' Maddie said. 'Now bugger off and leave us in peace.' And with that, she slammed the door.

Roxanne clenched her fist and raised it to knock once more. But she knew there was nothing more they could tell her.

As she headed back to her room, she pulled out her phone. She needed to update the police.

# Chapter 44

## Isla

'I feel such a fool,' Isla said, as Sara handed her her snowsuit.

She'd screamed. Worked herself up to such a point. She hadn't even known who was opening the bedroom door. How stupid was that? But then as Sara had pointed out, Isla wasn't herself at all, her nerves in shreds.

Sara had rushed to hold her close, soothed her. *'There, there, sweetie.'* Told her she would take her back to Camp Arctic. She could manage the roads from Resan Slutar Lodge, if it meant Isla would be happier – feel safe – be OK. It would be silly for her to stay with her at the lodge in the state she was in. She would help her pack her case, and take her to the airport, where she could catch the next flight back to England – be with her loving family.

'Wash your face, and get dressed,' Sara had said in a motherly tone, and Isla had done just that. Sprinkled her face with ice-cold water, trying to force herself fully awake. But still she'd felt odd, unstable – those wretched memories hiding somewhere inside her head.

Sara had been sitting on the bed when she'd returned to the bedroom.

'I found Trevor Cooper's phone,' Isla had said. And together they'd searched for it, Sara pulling back the duvet, looking under the bed.

'Are you sure?' Sara had said eventually. 'I can't think of a single reason why it would be here. Maybe you imagined it.'

'Maybe,' Isla had said, resigned to the fact that something was wrong with the workings of her mind.

'You're not well,' Sara had gone on, handing her a tissue. 'Let's get you back to Camp Arctic, and perhaps call a doctor before you travel home. We need to get you well so you can enjoy life, Isla. You're a long time dead, as my mother used to say.'

And now, as Isla stepped into her snowsuit and zipped it up, things were so very wrong. She'd attempted to take her own life. Sara was right, and Jack too. She needed help. She needed to go home.

Sara grabbed her snow jacket – blue with a mountain scene on the back and sleeves – and tugged it on. She held out her arm to Isla, and Isla latched on to her gratefully, like an elderly woman. As they left the house, Sara steadied her, taking part of her weight, as she led her towards the car, aided by the strong beam of her phone torch.

Once on the road – Sara concentrating on driving through the inky darkness – Isla spoke, her voice small: 'I thought I saw someone.' She almost wanted to bite back her words. It would only compound what Sara must be thinking. That she was losing her mind. There had been nobody at the lodge. Sara would have mentioned it.

'When?' Sara said, braking as she hit a slippery spot and skidding slightly.

'Earlier. Back there.' Isla glanced over her shoulder, unease crawling down her back. 'I think it was my imagination.'

'Yes, I'm sure it was. I didn't see anyone.' She effortlessly came out of the skid and carried on along the road. 'I wonder if your hallucinations are due to the trauma you went through in Australia.' She paused, glancing briefly at Isla and then back to the road ahead.

'But that was a long time ago. Why now?'

'Perhaps something triggered it. The appeal, perhaps?'

251

'You know about that?'

'Or it could have been something small. But then I'm far from qualified to analyse you.'

'Where are we?' Isla asked, as Sara pulled off the road near snow-covered trees, and turned off the engine. She left the lights on.

'Oh, Isla.' She leant into the side well of the car and pulled out a needle. 'You are so pathetically stupid.' Brightness had left her voice. Her perpetual smile vanished. It was as though someone had flicked a switch in her head. 'I've played you like a triangle. It was that simple. But then I knew it would be.'

Before Isla could react, Sara plunged the needle into Isla's hand and pressed down hard on the syringe. The pain was intolerable, and further weakness of her limbs was almost instant.

'It's a trial anaesthetic I've been working on at Tomlins Pharmaceuticals. It causes short-term amnesia and leaves you unconscious for absolutely hours. In fact, I injected you after we'd had a few wines on Friday. You slept until Sunday. I hadn't expected that.'

Recollections of meeting Sara at the bottom of the chairlift pushed their way in. The way Sara had cried, '*My dad died.*' The way she'd begged her to come back with her. '*I need a friend.*'

Isla knew now she had gone with her on Friday, drank wine, comforted her.

Sara smiled at the tears filling Isla's eyes. 'It will take a little while for the drug to fully get into your bloodstream,' she said.

'You won't get away with it,' Isla managed, squeezing her hand in an attempt to ease the pain, trying to understand why Sara seemed to hate her so much. 'They'll find the drug in my blood.'

Sara thought for a moment. 'Why would they do an autopsy, Isla? Why would they suspect anything, when you've announced your suicide?'

'I don't understand.'

'Anyway, it's virtually undetectable.' She seemed so sure, so pleased with herself.

Isla's head swam with confusion. 'But why?'

'You really don't know what you've done, do you?' Sara gave an enormous sigh and looked at her watch. 'I'm not sure I've got time to explain. I really need to string you up.'

With what was left of her energy, Isla grabbed the handle of the door. It opened and she fell out onto the snow, and began crawling away. It was a pathetic action. Sara was beside her in seconds, dragging her back, and opening the boot. She grabbed a rope and looped it around Isla's neck twice, before jerking it hard. Isla cried out in agony.

'When I was at university with you, Isla,' Sara said, her voice harsh and breathless as she dropped down on the ground beside her, 'Trevor and I became friends. You had no idea how much I loved him. Why would you? I barely registered on your spectrum. He only had eyes for you, of course.'

Isla's head pounded as she began to sob.

'I went through years of agonising plastic surgery so I could look like you – the woman who broke his heart. Two years ago, I got a job where he was working at Tomlins, and things moved fast. We went out. He said he needed me – wanted me.' She paused. 'He looked at me in that way he'd always looked at you.'

'Please stop.' Isla let out another wail, as tears streamed down her cheeks and dripped off her chin as though trying to escape.

'We moved in together. Everything was perfect. And then he saw you on the train.'

'It was nothing.'

'Nothing? Nothing! He came home and told me how awful things were for you, that there was an appeal and you didn't want to know the outcome, and then he told me he'd never stopped loving you. He left me, Isla. He left me because of you.' Her voice was manic and disjointed. 'I knew about what happened to you. Everyone knew. So it didn't take long to find you on the Internet. It was easy tormenting you, once I started researching, especially once I got a copy of the biography Carl Jeffery's sister wrote.' She smiled. 'Have you read it?'

Isla shook her head feebly.

'There's so much about you in there. You should probably sue. No wait, you can't, you'll be dead.'

'We just talked on the train, that's all.'

'And exchanged numbers.'

'But I love Jack.'

Sara got to her feet and pulled Isla along the ground. Isla struggled to crawl behind her, as she ploughed through the snow towards a clump of trees. 'Even though you broke his heart into teeny tiny pieces, he kept on loving you. Who'd have thought it?'

Fear thudded painfully, as snow soaked through Isla's snowsuit, the cold seeping into her bones.

'Well, you can imagine how I felt.' Sara stopped and looked up at a thick, snow-covered branch, the car headlights lighting the area. 'I stole his phone the night you met him on the train, so he couldn't contact you. I even sent a few messages to you pretending to be him, just to unnerve you. You were so easy to wind up – like one of those toys where you turn the key and let go, and they manically whiz all over the place bashing into things.'

She laughed again. 'I admit I went a bit crazy with my fake Facebook message from Trevor. I'd had a few wines. I should have known you would block the profile, and I wouldn't be able to see you any more. And I needed to see your every move, Isla. Fortunately, for me, no harm was done, as you added me around the same time. Anyway all of it was just passing time, waiting for the moment I could remove you. Eliminate you. Paint over you.' She yanked Isla to her feet with a single jerk. 'He will never love me if you're in the picture.'

'Has it always been you?' Isla whispered, everything hitting her so painfully, as the pieces fell into place.

'Of course. I enjoyed stalking you. I even used Trevor's sports car that day at Millie's party. He left it in the garage when he took off. And I called the tapas bar too, so you'd walk home alone, but you ran too fast across the park. I didn't have time to reveal myself. Did you like the flyer – and what about the butterfly? The bloke in your apartment upstairs happily let me in when I said I was there to bring you a gift.'

Isla shuddered, her eyes on the tree, fear thudding in her chest. She'd never felt so helpless. Not since the day Carl Jeffery attacked her.

'I think hanging is quite apt in the circumstances,' she said. 'Carl Jeffery hanged his victims, didn't he?' She paused and stared deep into Isla's face, long and hard. 'Did you know that a year ago, my father killed himself?'

'But you said he'd just died. You talked about him. Texted him.'

'No, I didn't. He'd been dead a long time when we met in Wetherspoon's.' She paused. 'I had no idea he was suicidal. Apparently he couldn't live without my mother. His note didn't even mention me. Do you know how painful it is to lose someone you love like that? To accept that they didn't care about you enough to even mention your name in their final goodbye?'

She paused, and her face stretched into a cold smile. 'Your family will feel that pain. They'll think you didn't care about any of them at the very end, that the only person who meant anything to you was Andy. Just like my father only cared about my mother. Just like he never cared about me.' There was nothing behind her eyes as she slung the free end of the rope over the branch with a chilling thud. Had Sara put Isla's head in that noose back at the house, almost killed her? How did she expect to get away with any of it?

Tears kept coming. But they would stop. They would stop soon.

'Why didn't you kill me the first chance you had? Why pretend to be my friend?'

'Oh, Isla, where would be the fun in that?' She tugged hard on the rope, levering Isla off her feet. The pain in her windpipe was intolerable. And, as Isla rose up, clawing at the rope, desperately trying to loosen it, her legs moving like a child doing doggie paddle, the life she was clinging to began to fade.

'Sara!' Someone approached – Isla knew the voice. Was it in her head? Was he really there?

The figure was a blur, black and misshapen in the light.
And as consciousness left her, she thought she saw his face.
*Jack.*

# Chapter 45

## Roxanne

Roxanne sat by the window in reception, waiting for Sally and Gary, fumbling open Sara's email on her phone.

> *Hi Roxanne,*
> *Of course I remember you. Lovely to hear from you, although the circumstances are totally awful – you and Isla were inseparable at university, if I remember rightly.*
> *I'm shocked and truly upset to hear about Isla. She seemed great when I saw her, and we've exchanged a few emails since then and met up in Hitchin. She did mention Andy at the reunion. In fact, she wouldn't stop talking about him. I didn't mind, it was nice to see her so in love.*
> *If there's anything I can do, please just shout. Keep me updated.*
> *Love Sara x*

It didn't make sense. Had Isla confided in Sara about Andy, and not her?

Her thoughts whirred as she opened up old emails from Isla, trawling through their daft exchanges, trying to find something Isla said that would give a clue to her state of mind – her whereabouts. But there was nothing.

It was as she closed the final email that – like a bullet from a gun, about to blast everything she'd seen and heard up until that moment into a thousand pieces – it hit her.

She fired off a message to Sally asking her to forward Isla's final email. And waited.

She'd never fully understood why Isla hadn't mentioned Gary or Millie in her email to Sally. She'd idolised her dad and sister, and even if it was over between her and Jack, surely she would have said sorry for the pain she'd caused him. Isla was a good person. *Wasn't she?*

Roxanne dragged her fingers through her hair, growing agitated and impatient, when the email pinged into her inbox.

To: SALLY Johnson sallyjohnson@windlemail.com
From: ISLA Johnson islajohnson@windlemail.com

*Dear Mum*
*I'm sorry I can't go on living.*
  *I fell in love for the first time in my life in Canada, but I was let down so painfully. Andy is my everything. Without him, I can't go on.*
  *I've been writing a blog since August – www.travellinggirlblog. com. It began as my travel blog, but later it was where I privately wrote my thoughts. I've sent you an invitation to read it, in the hope that when you do, it will help you to understand what I've been through and why this has to be goodbye.*
*Isla xx*

'Oh, my God,' Roxanne whispered, her thoughts confirmed. The email couldn't have been from Isla. Isla's email address was *islajohnson@windlemail.com*. The email Sally had received had come from *islajohnson@windlemail.com*. There was no 'j' in the address. No 'j' for Jane.

Doubt crept in. Maybe Isla had another email address, a secret one. But then she wouldn't have contacted her mum with it, would she? And Isla had only ever used one email address in all the time Roxanne had known her.

Roxanne rubbed her face, her heart knocking against her ribs. She was suddenly certain Isla never sent it. And it was the email that had directed them to the blog. If Isla hadn't written the email, she hadn't written the blog posts either.

Isla had never been suicidal.

Before she could register her thoughts, the door opened and Sally, Gary and Millie fell through, a sense of exhaustion wafting from them. They looked so pale – so cold.

Roxanne shot up and, after a shower of hugs, Millie headed off to find their rooms, and Sally and Gary settled on one of the sofas, fingers entwined, her head resting on his shoulder. But Sally wasn't sleeping. Her eyes were wide open, as though she daren't close them for fear of missing a single clue that would lead them to their daughter.

Roxanne looked down at Gary and tried for a smile.

*How are you doing?* she wanted to say. But she didn't have to ask. His skin was pallid, his eyes bloodshot. He was thinner too, if that was possible, his face unshaven. She knew exactly how he felt – she felt it too.

'All right, love?' he said, dragging his head up, his voice quivery and quiet, as though someone had turned down the volume.

Roxanne perched on the edge of an armchair opposite them.

'I don't think Isla sent the email,' she said, and began desperately trying to explain. They looked confused, tired, helpless. She could almost hear their unvoiced fears, as they avoided her stare, their eyes shimmering. *If she didn't write it, who did? If she didn't write it, someone's taken our daughter.*

Roxanne needed to say something, anything that would help. But what could she say? *We will find her. Everything will be all right. Don't worry.* Her throat seemed to swell. Did she even believe that any more? Empty words filling empty spaces. She headed away to call the police.

'Don't you see?' she said down the phone. 'If Isla didn't write the email, she must be in danger.' But they seemed to struggle to understand the relevance. 'Something's not right,' she insisted, voice rising. 'You must do something.'

'We're doing everything we can, Miss Furaha. But we have little to go on. Your friend sent an email saying she was going to take her own life. We don't . . .'

'But that's what I'm saying. She didn't send it.' *You fucking moron.*

'Calm down, we are doing all we can.' A pause. 'We've organised a search, and I'll send two officers to Camp Arctic now.'

When she returned, Sally was in floods of tears. 'I keep thinking about her when she was a little girl,' she was saying. 'Seeing her with a high ponytail and a tinsel halo, the day she played an angel at infant school.' She let out a sob. 'She was so excited to be allowed to be barefoot on stage.'

Roxanne reached over and squeezed her hand.

'Gary wanted a son, didn't you, Gary?' Sally continued, as though she was doing a documentary on her daughter. *This is your life, Isla Johnson.*

He nodded, eyes shimmering.

'He even bought a football. But, once she was in the world, it hadn't mattered, had it, Gary?'

He shook his head again. A determined shake, as though he didn't want his head filled with memories he couldn't handle.

'She wound you around her little finger from the moment she could smile.' Her voice broke off and she pushed her head into her hands.

Hearing footfalls on the wooden floorboards behind her, Roxanne turned to see Millie approaching. She handed Sally a key.

'Mum said you've seen the police, Roxanne,' Millie said.

She nodded. 'They're going to search the area and send over officers.'

'Good.' Millie's eyes looked red and sore. Her hair scooped into a messy ponytail. 'Can I get anyone some coffee?'

'No thanks, love,' Gary said.

'Loganberry juice?' Millie went on, as though determined to fill the air with words.

*Would it be wrong to ask for gin? A double – no triple, maybe even a quadruple gin, no ice, no mixer, just mind-numbing, thought-squashing, intoxicating, gin?*

'I'm fine,' Roxanne said. *Fine? What a stupid, stupid word. Nobody here's fine.*

'I've finally heard from Julian,' Millie said. There was a sharpness in her tone. 'He said he'll put a message on his model railway forum about Isla.'

*And that will help, how?*

'That's kind of him,' Sally said, pulling a tissue from her bag and mopping her eyes.

Millie picked up the jug of juice and began pouring. She filled the glass so it splashed over the edges like a waterfall. She didn't seem to notice, just picked it up and sipped it. 'Julian's an arse,' she said almost to herself, taking the glass from her lips and tapping her chin with it three times. 'When this is over, and we find Isla – because we will, I know we will – I'm going to tell him that. I'm going to tell him he's a fucking, fucking arse, and I want a divorce.'

The quiet that followed, broken only by Alma tapping on her computer keyboard, and the dogs' heavy breathing, seemed to go and on, as though they were travelling in an endless dark tunnel, with no bright light at the end.

'Excuse me!'

Roxanne looked up to see a woman of around forty with a mop of wild blonde hair. Next to her was the boy Roxanne had spoken to the night before.

'Apologise,' the woman snapped at the boy.

'Sorry,' he mumbled, head down.

Roxanne rose to her feet and gestured for the woman to move

away from Sally and Gary. And they headed into the dark, empty restaurant.

'I found my son with a wad of money,' the woman continued. 'The thing is, he lied to you.'

'Lied?' Roxanne's eyes slid across to the boy.

'Someone paid him to tell you he'd seen the woman you've been looking for. They said he was to tell you he'd seen her with the man in a photo. I'm so ashamed, and so sorry.'

'So he didn't see her?' Roxanne continued to glare at the boy. 'You didn't see Isla with the man in the photo?'

'No,' the boy said, head still down, as he scuffed his boots along the wooden floor.

'Oh my God, you little shit,' Roxanne spat. 'Why would you do that?'

'Now calm down,' the woman said curtly. 'There's really no call for foul language. He's said he's sorry.'

'Oh, so that makes it all right, does it? You misled me. She could be dead because of you.' Roxanne's deepest fears were out there now – they were real.

'I was paid a thousand kronas,' the boy said, with a shrug. 'Who wouldn't lie?'

'Who the hell gave you this money?'

'A woman,' he said. 'She was old-ish, about thirty.'

'You bloody idiot,' Roxanne said, stepping closer, and the boy cowered.

'Enough,' the woman said, adding something in Swedish and, grabbing the boy's arm, she hurried him away.

Roxanne pulled out her phone and called the police again, relaying to them what the boy had told her, insisting, once more, that something was very wrong.

'Two of our officers will be with you shortly, Miss Furaha, and please be assured we have police searching the area.'

She ended the call and, after several deep breaths, returned to reception.

'Has anyone heard from Jack?' she said, deciding not to mention what the boy had said. For now, at least, she wouldn't worry them further. There was nothing they could do.

Sally shook her head.

Time seemed to slow even more, crawling along like an injured animal. This was all too much. Roxanne felt so helpless. Should she go out in the snow and hunt for her friend? But where would she start?

'I think I'll call it a night,' Millie said.

'Of course – try to get some sleep, love.' Sally dropped a shredded tissue onto the table in front of her. 'We can start afresh in the morning.'

'No, no, we can't just give up,' Roxanne said, her eyes darting over their helpless faces. 'There must be something more we can do. There has to be.' But the truth was, there was nothing. She'd failed. Isla was in danger, and she'd failed her.

Suddenly the door swung open, and they all looked towards it.

'Jack!' Roxanne cried, as he stumbled in, Isla wrapped in a blanket in his arms. He laid her on one of the sofas, as everyone rushed towards them.

'Call an ambulance,' he yelled over to Alma, his teeth chattering, dried blood on his forehead. 'Call an ambulance. Now!'

# Chapter 46

## Isla

Isla opened her eyes.

A monitor beeped, and there was a muffled distant chatter of faceless people. She was in a bed on a hospital side ward, attached to a drip that pumped clear liquid into her veins. Her head ached. Her body ached. Everything ached.

Jack was on a chair next to her, head slumped to one side, sleeping.

As though sensing her stare, he stirred and opened his eyes. He looked so pale. 'Isla,' he said, leaning forward and taking hold of her hand.

Her mouth was dry, and that familiar feeling of nausea oozed through her body. 'What happened?' she said, her voice croaky.

He gripped her hand, his bloodshot eyes filling with tears. 'Sara tried to kill you.'

A snip of memory squeezed through. *They'll think you didn't care about them at the very end. Just like my father never cared about me.*

Panic bubbled up inside her, and her eyes shot to the door. 'Where is she?'

He looked down and closed his eyes. 'She's dead, Isla.'

'Dead?'

He nodded. 'Hanged herself.'

She leant over and grabbed a cardboard tray from the cabinet, and retched. Jack edged forward and pulled back her hair.

'Your mum and dad are here,' he said, as she lowered her head back onto the pillow. 'And Millie and Roxanne. They've just gone to get something to eat.'

'You saved me, didn't you?' she whispered.

'I just got to you in time, thank God.'

'Tell me what happened, Jack?' she said, wanting desperately to fill in the gaps. 'From the beginning.'

'OK.' He took a deep breath. 'I came back to Camp Arctic, realising I'd made an awful mistake leaving. That's when I saw her.'

'Sara?'

He nodded. 'Even though she was wearing a wig, I knew it was her. I was going to approach her, ask her what she was doing there, but she left quite suddenly – got in a car and drove away.

'I followed in my hire car, keeping my distance, and saw her pull into the drive of Resan Slutar Lodge about three miles out. I parked up and carried on on foot.

'She was outside chopping wood. She saw me. Struck me with a bloody great piece of wood, like a woman possessed.

'I woke later, lying behind a shed. She'd covered me with snow – left me for dead, I reckon.'

'Oh my God, Jack.'

He touched his head. It had been patched up with stiches.

'I was freezing. Thought I was going to die of hypothermia.'

'Your worst nightmare.'

'I know. I hate the fucking cold.' A hint of a smile crossed his lips, but it vanished as quickly as it came. 'I could barely walk, but managed to climb into the back of her car. I crawled under a pile of blankets. Figured if I kept warm, I could do something. But I must have passed out again, as I came round when she'd parked up with you.

'I got out of the car, adrenaline keeping me going, I guess. I saw what she was doing to you, heard what she was saying. She was one

265

cruel bitch,' he said, his eyes darting with anger, as though he was back there. 'I've never known evil like it.'

'I have,' Isla whispered, squeezing his hand.

'Isla!' She looked up to see her mum and dad rushing through the door towards her. 'Everything is going to be OK, lovely girl,' her dad said, as they hugged her so close.

'Is it?' Isla said, but nobody seemed to hear.

# Chapter 47

## Isla

*Six weeks later*

'Hey, remember when we made lasagne for the first time at uni?' Roxanne said.

Isla could hear her friend talking, could even make out the words, but she wasn't computing.

'How to burn pasta in one easy lesson,' Roxanne went on, with a forced laugh. 'And scorchio mince.'

But Isla was trancelike. Thoughts of Sara consumed her, as they had since she got back from Sweden. The efforts the woman had gone to to ruin her life had been so extreme, it made her sick to think about it. Fake Facebook profiles, a blog pretending to be Isla, and the setting up of the reunion only scratched the surface of what she'd done. Truth was, Sara hadn't even met Ben or Veronica.

Isla had tried so hard to piece it all together. Had Sara chosen the name Andy for her phantom lover, after seeing Isla's Canadian holiday acquaintance on Facebook? Had she found Isla's mum's email address when Sally left her settings open? Isla knew she may never know.

'Earth to Isla, come in, Isla,' Roxanne said, waving her hand in front of her friend's face.

Isla covered her mouth, trying not to cry. 'Sorry,' she said through her fingers. 'I'm really not myself.'

'No, no of course you're not, lovely lady.' She paused. 'Isla, you do believe me that I never slept with Trevor Cooper, don't you?'

'Oh God, Roxanne, of course I do. You don't have to keep asking. She just made that up to put a wedge between us. And she could never do that.'

But Sara had at the time. She'd planted the doubt, and Isla had sucked it up. And she'd fooled Roxanne and her parents too, led them away from Abisko, by pushing a woman in front of a car in Narvik and planting Isla's bag on her.

'Do you want to go home?' Roxanne asked, looking deep into Isla's eyes.

Isla nodded and laid down her fork on the bed of chicken and crisp lettuce leaves she hadn't touched. 'I'm really not hungry, anyway.'

'You should eat.'

'I do eat.' It came out as a snap. 'Sorry, sorry . . . I know you're just being kind . . . I'm so sorry . . .'

'You've got nothing to be sorry for.' Roxanne placed her hand over Isla's. 'I just thought if we came out for a meal it might help, but it's clearly not working.'

Isla shook her head. She knew Roxanne wanted to talk. Bring out the pain and swaddle it in so much love that it would suffocate and die. But it was going to take a lot more than that.

'How did she get the photograph into my room at Abisko?' Isla whispered. Every little bit of what happened moving around her head like the living dead. 'How did Sara get it in there?'

'Probably when the room was being cleaned – housekeepers take little notice of who stays in which room. If Sara popped in when your room was being cleaned, and left the photo, a cleaner wouldn't have batted an eyelid.'

'Maybe.' Isla ran her fingers over the rubber band on her wrist.

Her skin was pink and raw, and a scab had formed where she'd drawn blood a few weeks back. Tears itched behind her eyes. *It's way too soon.* This was going to take a long time to get over – if she ever could.

Roxanne tilted her head, eyes shimmering – the pitying look. Isla had seen it so many times since Abisko, since she'd appeared on the front cover of newspapers two days on the trot. People had looked at her the way they'd looked at her six years before.

There had been a media storm after Sweden, just as there had been after Australia. Flashing cameras blurring her and her family's vision as they left the hospital, and later in the UK as they left the airport. Journalists talking on phones; a woman with silky blonde hair, and a rainbow-coloured blouse, from a news channel; a man wearing a blue and white checked blazer she recognised from the TV.

'Hey, Isla! Why do you think this has happened to you twice?' one had called, as her parents rushed her to the car.

'Can you tell us more about Andy?'

'Are you sleeping with Trevor Cooper?'

'Is there a connection with Carl Jeffery, Isla? Or are you just unlucky?'

'Why do you think Sara killed herself?'

'Any chance of a link to the blog?'

'Do you think killers are drawn to you, Isla?'

Snappy, clever headlines followed Sweden. Photos of Isla and Jack filled pages. There were pictures of Sara too, at university and more recent ones. Her metamorphosis, they seemed to think, was a story in itself.

There were images of Trevor Cooper too, poor innocent Trevor, whose only guilt seemed to be loving Isla, and the photograph of Isla and the red-headed man sitting outside a café found its way on to the front page. He was Steven Russell, a maths teacher from Stevenage, a father of equally red-headed twins. He'd just happened to sit down at Isla's table on a busy market day, when she was writing in Hitchin. It wasn't taken in Canada. Sara had simply snapped them from a distance and cropped out landmarks, and based the fictitious Andy on the man.

Isla felt for Steven Russell, an innocent victim hounded by the press on his way to work, and when out shopping with his wife and children. But then surely Isla was an innocent victim too.

But now Isla's story was yesterday's news. The media had moved on to new disasters and tragedies, and she was left with darting memories of that awful night in the cold.

'I'll take you home,' Roxanne said, raising her hand to catch the waiter's attention. She wasn't herself either – not really – a faded image of Isla's crazy, fun-loving friend. It had sucked the life from everyone. They were empty shells on a deserted beach, pecked dry by seagulls.

* * *

Back at her apartment, Isla didn't turn on the light. The darkness held an odd kind of relief now; she could hide among the shadows, unnoticed. And the fact she couldn't open the windows, because of the noisy traffic, felt oddly comforting.

She sat down on the sofa, and Luna jumped onto her lap and curled up. As she stroked her fur, the cat's purr soothed, and Isla's eyelids dropped closed. As soon as she drifted into the kind of limbo before sleep took hold, the memories came, haunting, jumbled and frightening. Sara's mocking face was always so clear, as though it was in the room with her.

Sometimes Isla would startle awake in the early hours, and thrash about, hot and sweating, certain she could hear Sara's voice, cold and cruel. Other times she felt trapped in her night terrors with no means of escape.

'Isla, I'm here,' Jack would always say, pulling her close. Holding her until the sun rose.

The piercing sound of her mobile's ringtone woke her, and she leant over and flicked on the side lamp. She rubbed her eyes. It was probably Jack, telling her he was on his way home from his father's.

She picked up her phone, letting out a gasp as she registered the caller, the phone slipping through her shaking fingers and clattering to the floor.

She picked up her phone, letting out a sigh as she rejected the caller, the phone slipping through her shaking hand and clattering to the floor.

# Chapter 48

Isla's phone vibrated across the floor, continuing to blare out its ringtone, Trevor's name on the screen like a danger sign.

She reached for it, her mind whirring. Why was he calling? Could he fill in some of the torturous missing pieces that kept her awake at night?

Before she could think too much, she pressed answer.

'Isla? Isla, is that you?' His voice was as soft as ever, his Scottish accent stronger than she remembered. 'Can we talk? Please.'

'What do you want?' She couldn't hide the angst in her voice, the slight croak of sleep.

'They gave me my phone back, and I knew I had your number. I just wanted to call, talk to you. Explain. I feel I owe you that much.'

'You owe me nothing, Trevor. You weren't to know.' A sharp pain dug her forehead, a swelling in her throat and scalding tears settled behind her eyes. She was regretting picking up already. She didn't need this. 'There's nothing to say.'

'I just want you to know how sorry I am. For you to understand.'

'It's not your fault.' She ran her fingers through Luna's fur, trying to find comfort in the smooth softness, but finding none. 'You didn't know what she would do.'

There was a pause – a long pause – and a bubble of fear rose in Isla's chest. Surely he hadn't known.

'No, I didn't know. But I feel . . . I don't know . . . in some small way responsible.'

'Responsible?' Isla's heartbeat quickened. She glanced at the door. Jack would be home soon.

'Can I try to explain? Tell you how it happened?'

It was as though he needed to offload. Ease his conscience?

'Will you listen, Isla? Please?'

'OK,' she said, her voice so quiet. Maybe it would help in some small way to know. *Perhaps.*

He drew in a breath. 'I met Sara again a while back.' It was as though he was about to tell his life story. 'She got a job at Tomlins, and we just sort of clicked. We always got on well at uni, but when I met her again it was different . . .' He sucked in a sigh. 'I really liked her. She was funny, beautiful . . . she reminded me of you.'

'Don't, Trevor.'

'No. Sorry, I didn't mean that.'

'Just get on with it,' she said, dashing a tear from her cheek.

'We had so much in common. Although, looking back, I suppose even at the start there was something not quite right under the surface. A desperate need to be loved, a fear I would let her down. I suppose I'd been a bit like that myself once.'

'Where are you going with this, Trevor?' Isla said, uncomfortable that he was still jabbing at their past.

'All was good between us, until her father killed himself. That day changed her. It was as though a switch flicked in her head. She'd thought when her mother died that he would turn to her, but he never did. And then he took his own life. His loss sent her reeling. But the worst part was he never even mentioned her in his note. Only that he couldn't live without her mother.'

Isla's mind travelled back to that awful night. This wasn't new news. *'They'll think you didn't care about them at the very end. Just like my father never cared about me.'*

'I tried picking up the pieces, suggested she should see a counsellor or something,' Trevor was saying. 'But her pain changed her.

273

She became obsessive, checking my mobile, insisting I was having an affair. She confronted women in shops and restaurants just for looking at me. She told me she would rather die than lose me. I stopped loving her, Isla, but I'd kind of accepted the way things were. Some sort of Stockholm syndrome, maybe . . .'

'No, you didn't love your captor, Trevor.' Isla tried to hide the desperation in her voice. 'You were just weak.'

'OK, yeah, I asked for that. I was pathetic. Even now I can't explain why I stayed. But the moment I saw you on the train, everything changed.'

Isla felt sick. This was too much to take in. 'So you told an unstable woman that you loved me?'

'No . . . no it wasn't like that. The irony here is I don't even love you, Isla.' She heard him swallow hard.

'You lied . . .?'

'No, no . . . well, not exactly, I loved talking to you. That brief time we spent together was the most normal interaction I'd had with a woman in over a year. It was great seeing you, and I realised how messed up my relationship with Sara was. Being with you made me see I had to find the balls to leave her.'

'So you told her you loved me to get away from her?' Anger bubbled. *All of this – all of this, and you didn't even love me.*

'It wasn't like that. I got pretty pissed after seeing you, knocking back wine as I waited for her to come home. Before she'd taken off her coat, I told her I'd seen you on the train and we'd swapped numbers. I told her what you'd been through, that I still loved you.' He paused for a moment. 'She began sobbing, clinging to me. Begging me to stay. Threatening to take her own life. I told her you were with someone, and I knew I couldn't be with you, but I couldn't be with her either, knowing I loved you. It just came out, my words taking on a drunken life of their own, and it didn't matter if they were true or not; it was my escape, my bid for freedom. I was desperate, Isla. But you have to believe me, I'm so, so sorry.'

'Stop saying sorry.' Isla battled her tears. Every painful, dreadful moment she'd been through was because Sara had thought Trevor loved her, yet he never had. 'You knew Sara was unstable, but you sent her after me,' she said, wishing her voice sounded stronger.

'I didn't know, Isla. She was messed up, yes, and, yeah, our relationship was pretty toxic, but I never dreamt . . .' He let out a sigh. 'You see things on documentaries, on TV and films – read novels – but you never expect anyone you know to be that damaged. That deranged. I just wanted out. I didn't know she would come after you – you have to believe me.'

'Well, newsflash, Trevor, she did.' Her voice trailed off. Helpless. With trembling fingers, she ended the call before he could say any more.

At first, she was silent, her body numb, cheeks cold with tears, her brain trying to process everything. But the pain rose like a volcano erupting. She covered her mouth, as a twisted, hysterical laugh escaped her lips, and Luna jumped from her lap, glaring back with frightened eyes as she raced from the room. Isla knew she sounded quite mad. Perhaps she was. Perhaps this time she really was going crazy. Perhaps this time they would put her in a cushioned cell where she would scream and scream and scream until she lost the will to scream any more. Perhaps she and Sara were more alike than she realised.

She pinged her rubber band. Crying out as it stung her wrist, blood trickling from the shattered scab. Was she finally broken?

She turned her phone over in her hands. She would call Jack. Tell him about Trevor. But then she couldn't keep putting him through it. He would be happier without her. She'd known that for a long time now.

She put down her phone, and, with a yank, tugged free her engagement ring and placed it into the palm of her hand, the light from the lamp glancing off the diamond. She couldn't let Jack see her go crazy.

He hadn't talked about their engagement since they'd returned from Sweden. Perhaps not wanting to put her under any more pressure, or maybe the thought of being with her for ever wasn't what he wanted any more. She couldn't blame him. She wasn't the woman he fell in love with.

She clenched her fingers around the ring, nails digging in her flesh, as tears rolled down her face. She'd put Jack through hell when he proposed. Not committing – confusing him – a whirlpool of mixed emotions swimming in her head that she hadn't been able to control.

But the doubts hadn't been about Jack. A cliché really – it's not you, it's me. *It's me. It's still me. It has always been me.*

She'd wanted to tell him the moment she'd feared for her sanity, the day she got back from Canada and someone – *Sara* – had followed her. She'd wanted to tell him from the second she'd thought Carl Jeffery could be free that she was scared she would become the person she'd been after the attack.

'I'm not good enough for you, Jack,' she'd wanted to say. '*If* I'm losing my mind, you need to go – leave – get out of my life – not walk me down the aisle.' He was far too good for her – he deserved better.

But she'd stayed silent. Something had stopped her from pushing him away. Her intense love for him had always won through, battling against the darkness – the thought of losing him too much to bear.

Now, she placed the ring on the table, and pulled the cuffs of her cardigan over her hands and dried her cheeks.

They'd been so happy at first. She'd never dreamed she would get over Carl Jeffery, but when Jack appeared in her life, he'd made that happen. He'd saved her.

She stared at the ring for some moments. Could Jack save her again? Was there any way back?

She knew the old Isla was inside her somewhere. She could feel her sometimes. A small bright spark would flicker and dance in the darkness, and she would try to coax her out, want to swing her round, tell her everything would be OK. But it was always fleeting. Old Isla would disappear almost before she arrived, leaving a heavy sadness that would drag her back under.

'It's over, Jack,' she rehearsed, a fragile whisper into the silence. Words she didn't want to say, but knew she had to.

Her eyes grew heavy once more. They were almost closed, when the front door opened.

'Jack,' she said, as he approached, overwhelmed with love and relief at the sight of him.

'Are you OK?' He leant over and touched her face, concern in his eyes. Lately, her cheeks were always puffy, eyes swollen. She was a mess. 'Did you go out with Roxanne?'

She nodded. 'Yeah, yeah I did. How was your dad?'

'Good, yeah.' He dropped down next to her and kissed her softly on the lips. 'We're getting on pretty well. He'd love to meet you.' He paused. 'When you're ready.'

A silence hung between them for a short while, before he stood up once more. 'I could murder a glass of wine. Fancy one?'

'Yes,' she said, picking up the ring and pushing it into her pocket as he walked away. She would talk to him. Tell him he would be better off without her. *Soon.*

He opened the fridge and grabbed a bottle, and two glasses from the cupboard, before heading back to the sofa. He filled the glasses and handed Isla one.

They sat in silence once more, snippets of Trevor's phone call darting around her head. Sara had threatened Trevor with suicide if he didn't stay with her. Had she always been close to the edge herself? Was that why she took her own life the night she attacked Isla?

'Why do you think Sara killed herself?' she said, running her finger around the rim of her glass. 'Do you think she knew Trevor would never love her, once he found out what she'd done?'

Jack shrugged, not meeting her eye.

'Maybe it hit her what she'd become.' She paused, looking at his profile. 'Jack?'

He was silent for a beat too long, before shrugging once more and saying, 'Sara was evil, Isla.'

'Her parents messed her up. Trevor walked out.'

'It's no excuse.' He bit down hard on his lip. 'Lots of parents mess their kids up, and some go a bit AWOL. But Sara didn't just lose the plot, Isla. She was evil. Calculating. The lengths she went to to hurt you were beyond cruel.' He tensed his fingers around the stem of his glass. 'She got exactly what she deserved.' He turned and they linked eyes. Isla blinked away a mental image of Sara swinging from the noose. Memories of Jack's anger when he talked about Carl Jeffery flashed into her mind. *If I could get hold of that bastard, I'd rip his head off, and fuck the consequences.*

'Everything is going to be OK,' he said, putting his arm around her shoulders and pulling her to him. 'She's better off dead.'

His words over the last six weeks, like everyone else's, had held little comfort. But now something shifted.

'You killed her,' she whispered into his chest. It wasn't a question, and she wasn't even sure he'd heard her, but suddenly it didn't matter. All Jack's actions since they'd met had proved how much he loved her and always would.

She waited until he'd leant over to refill their glasses and slipped her ring back on.

# Epilogue

## *Isla's Journey*

### by

## Isla J Green

## **Introduction**

I began *Isla's Journey* three years ago when I first met my husband, Jack. At that time, it was a private travel journal, a mixture of memories and photographs of places I had visited.

Jack told me once that I should put my work together as a book. I'd laughed, embarrassed, but have never forgotten the faith he had in me – the faith he still has in me.

More recently, it was suggested I could weave my extraordinary life's events into the book. I agreed, and admit it's been therapeutic writing it. A good way to purge the demons.

People sometimes ask me how I'm doing. They'll even come right out and say things like, 'How do you cope with the fact two people wanted to kill you?' or 'How will you ever fully get over it?'

I wonder myself at times. There are dark days – and I accept that there always will be – where I watch people, strangers, wondering what they are thinking. Wondering what they are capable of.

But I have my family, and my amazing friend, Roxanne. And I have Jack, and our baby daughter with her green eyes and a smile just like her dad's. Being a photographer, I liken these wonderful people in my life to the brightness control on a dark picture.

So I tell the people who ask that I'm mainly doing OK, all things considered, thank you very much for asking.

This book is *my* version of events that led me to where I am today. This is *Isla's Journey* . . . so far.

## Chapter 1

*I arrived at the University of Warwick twelve years ago, a naive yet happy eighteen-year-old. It was a bright but cold autumn morning, and it was to be the beginning of the rest of my life . . .*

Dear Reader,

We hope you enjoyed reading this book. If you did, we'd be so appreciative if you left a review. It really helps us and the author to bring more books like this to you.

Here at HQ Digital we are dedicated to publishing fiction that will keep you turning the pages into the early hours. Don't want to miss a thing? To find out more about our books, promotions, discover exclusive content and enter competitions you can keep in touch in the following ways:

JOIN OUR COMMUNITY:

Sign up to our new email newsletter: http://hyperurl.co/hqnews-letter

Read our new blog www.hqstories.co.uk

🐦 : https://twitter.com/HQDigitalUK

📘 : www.facebook.com/HQStories

BUDDING WRITER?

We're also looking for authors to join the HQ Digital family! Please submit your manuscript to:
HQDigital@harpercollins.co.uk

Thanks for reading, from the HQ Digital team

# Keep reading . . .

**If you enjoyed *Her Last Lie*, then why not try another gripping thriller from HQ Digital?**